How the ə Got Producted

How the

ə

Got Producted

N.K. von S.

A LOVE STORY

Everyone I know has one of these. They can't go anywhere without it and they seem so connected and happy. I downloaded mine a month ago. I used it every day since just like it says.

Things feel different around me but I'm still who I am.

I think I'm using it the wrong way.

—anonymous reviewer

How the Ə Got Producted

THE BUREAU INSISTS
REALITY MATTERS

The first time I heard of the Ə I was sitting. A chilly nip in the spring air pierced my thin blouse, sending little bumps up all over my body. So I hugged my ribcage and crossed my legs tightly together until I was hardly bothered by the chill at all. To the contrary, I found it invigorating.

It was my first day at the Bureau of Biomedicaltechnology, the Bureau, or BoB as we used to call it.

As for where I was sitting, it was on one of the stone benches that dot the dignified main walk of the campus. Carved into the benches were the words of former Bureau directors, magistrates opining on cases brought by or against the Bureau (a notoriously litigious agency), and other grand hommes (I use "homme" here in the gender neutral sense, as the Bureau is renowned for its commitment to egalitarianism), all extolling the robust yet judicious vigor with which the Bureau executed its mandate under the law—namely, *to police and promote Biomedicaltechnological Product of all known indicia.* The inscription on my bench had been carved with unusual gusto, resulting in edges so sharp I could read the letters of the bench's enigmatic inscription with my behind:

THE BUREAU INSISTS REALITY MATTERS

(I've always had unusually sharp senses—I believe the word is ubersentient—a genetic advantage that has perhaps compensated for certain deficits in life that I've had to overcome. Nonetheless, I scrupulously double-checked the intelligence coming from my rear end with my eyes and can confirm that, on that nippy spring morning, those were indeed the words staring back at me from my rear end's erstwhile resting spot!)

I confess, initially I felt somewhat affronted by the cheeky inscription, as if it were challenging the absence of "insistence" or "mattering" from my personal relationship with reality. After all, my relationship with reality was my own business. But I saw beneath the inscription, in smaller letters, the words came from a judicial opinion. I may not have a credential, but I know a thing or two about the law. The case was the famous one that settled for once and for all that the Bureau's dominion extended over legal figments, hypotheticals, notional commodities, or Non-Products—in short, things not known to exist. The court wisely opined that existence was but one facet of reality, the rest being whatever one makes of things. In short, the Bureau was ambivalent about existence, but all-in on reality. This background took the accusatory edge off of the inscription, if not the physical edge of the letters, which remained acute. Besides this comforting backstory to the otherwise jarring words, I didn't want to start off on my first day feeling antagonized. I decided it was best not to think too much about the inscription, even if it was poking me in the behind.

As to what I was doing as I sat on the bench on the main walk of the Bureau campus, I was sifting through a stack of documents I'd retrieved from my new office. I'd been directed to report to an orientation that morning in Building 66, but I couldn't find Building 66, Building 66 being positioned, I later learned, between Buildings 8 and 46. No one would say I'm a stickler for order, but I'd assumed Building

66 would be next to Building 65. It was only later, from the comfortable perch of the Building 1 roof, that I marveled at how the 73 rectangular buildings, as unique as Lego sculptures, were arrayed at odd angles and irregular distances as though plotted by an algorithm with a logic so intricate and abstruse that to the outsider it seemed random. At the time, I only knew where Building 65 was because it was beside Building 1, where my office was. Which perhaps should have been a giveaway. Anyway, an orientation hardly seemed needed. My entire professional life had oriented me toward that day. I reported to my office instead.

Immediately on entering my new office, the air assaulted me. It seemed busy, work-like, as if it had something to prove. Apart from the air it was a spectacular office by the standards for offices of government bureaucrats, one befitting my stature in the organization. It was spacious, with large windows looking out onto one of the courtyards where instead of benches there was a life-sized rendering of a piece of durable medical equipment—though it was hard to say what kind of durable medical equipment—atop an enormous plinth. The piece of medical equipment was square with knobs and dials all over it. I didn't know what to make of it at the time; it seemed to be an electroencephalograph or an electroconvulsive therapy machine. Except for that the sculptor had forgotten to make a terminal or other human interface, without which it really didn't matter whether it was an electroencephalograph or electroconvulsive therapy machine. Without the human interface, it was essentially furniture. There was something about the small solitary box with the knobs and dials of no known utility poised atop the enormous plinth that exceeded the sum of its parts, as though the empty space around the sculpture and the missing display equipment were as much the point of the sculpture as the electroencephalograph or electroconvulsive therapy machine was. At the same time, one could hardly ignore the poignancy of the electroencephalograph/electroconvulsive therapy machine poised to stand in for an enormous concept onto which the hopes and dreams of humanity had been projected, i.e., biomedicaltechnology, but not being up to it.

In other words, I liked the sculpture, so the sculpture had nothing to do with why I was sitting on the bench and not in my office. I don't know what it was that infected the air in my office with its quality of officiousness, but perhaps it was that my superior so to speak, the Director, sat in the next office. The Director's theoretical proximity made me uncomfortable even before I met the Director. It may hint at the fundamental conflict in our relationship when I say this occurred before she met me. So between the air in my office and the closeness to the Director, it's easy to see why I chose to work elsewhere.

Perhaps anticipating that I wouldn't be able to find Building 66, someone had thoughtfully left orientation materials on my desk—a campus map, the Manual of Best Practices, and IT instructions. I logged into my email account and printed the emails and attachments in my inbox, all of which had been sent in the earliest hours of that very day or forwarded that morning from the Director's account where they'd waited unattended for months. Then I left my office without my jacket and found a bench to sit on.

The attachments were each identified by a red stamp as an Official Notice Documenting the Activities of the Bureau in its Oversight of Biomedicaltechnological Product (OND-ABOBiP), and they were all overdue. Based on the messages accompanying the ONDABOBiPs, which in some cases were rather panicked, I deduced it was my job to sign off on the notices. At the risk of sounding like a naif, I didn't appreciate at the time the significance of the accompanying delegation form and didn't know I could simply check the box on the form, then place the form and the document in my outbox for someone or another to take them out of my outbox and give them to my delegee. At least, once I caught on, I always assumed that's what happened. But I can't say I ever confirmed what happened to the forms or the documents after they left my outbox. The last thing anyone could say of me is that I'm a micromanager; to the contrary, I have always trusted in the fundamental competencies of my reports. All I'm saying is had I delegated review of the ONDABOBiPs instead of reviewing them myself, I might not have learned of the ə on that nippy spring day and the course of history would have thus been altered.

The first document in the stack had a header that read "Information Advisory re: NPPD Concerning 'ə' Technology."

"Now you know about the nipped."

A sinewy fellow in fatigues and a windbreaker appeared as if out of nowhere and took a seat over the word "INSISTS," a little too close to the space I occupied over "ITY MAT" for my tastes. I slid my rear to expose the "I" and shot him a look intended to let him know that he was making me feel crowded. Only my eyes were unable to meet his because his eyes were darting furiously from the Information Advisory to somewhere roughly in the middle of my face, approximately the area of the bullseye in one of those head and torso cutouts used for target practice. I was disconcerted. I looked down at his hands, which were large with awkwardly bulbous knuckles.

"Nipped. Non-Product Petition Denial. ENN-PEE-PEE-DEE," he said. "As when the Bureau denies a nip. ENN-PEE-PEE. Non-Product Petition. It's usually how multi-billion dollar corporations foist their death gizmos on a defenseless public."

"That's one opinion," I said.

Though new to the Bureau as an employee, my long history as a Bureau gadfly—of whom there are legion, the Bureau being an object of fascination for so many—meant I was hardly a novice to its administrative processes. I knew a thing or two about Non-Product Petitions, having filed more than one in my day. One generally filed a Non-Product Petition seeking a formal Bureau declaration that one's Potential Product was a Non-Product, thus avoiding the awesome responsibility of Producthood. The stakes of the Bureau's decision couldn't be higher: a Non-Product was free to be immediately released into the warm embrace of a grateful consuming public. A Product was in for a months-or even years-long slog through the rigorous scientific and regulatory processes put in place to protect those consumers from their own wants.

"It's a subspecies of Decision Against Interests. DEE-AY-EYE. Would you like to know whose interests? The private interests of the corporate biomedicaltechnology industry, given cover by the immoral regulations of a complicit regime. You may or may not be familiar with the prohibition on disclosure of all information supporting DAI. In other words, a regulation promulgated by the regulators to silence the regulators. This they call self-regulation; a circular concept, a conflation of mastery and servitude, like a snake eating its own tail."

"You don't say," I said.

Of course I knew all of that, but I didn't let on. I saw there was an advantage in being taken for an initiate. Even a blo-viator may unwittingly divulge things when operating under a false sense of security, things that could be used against those who stood in the way of the Bureau performing its mandate. And that's what had brought me to the Bureau in the first place: to expose its enemies.

"Take the Ə," he continued. "An atypical notional com-modity the existence of which is the subject of fierce debate. 'Product' in the Biomedicaltechnology Product Act won't tell you whether the Ə is a Product or a Non-Product. The law's drafters understood language's power lies in overreach and subterfuge. After a half-century of interpretations, like the one that gave us the quote jabbing us in our no-nos, here's the most that can be said about existence and product-hood: existence is probative of Product status but Product status tells you nothing about whether something exists. I'm in a position to know that evidence of the Ə's existence is overwhelming. But that's the wrong question. Ask yourself instead, whose interests are served by its Non-Producting? Who benefits from a placated populace opiated by technol-ogy's false promise?"

"No-no" threw me off a little. The term seemed prudish. But his pronunciation of "probative" made the exact oppo-site impression. All the emphasis was on "prōb" with the last two syllables just tagging along for the ride. None of this was as surprising as what he did next. In short, he rolled his eyes while they were still darting around, which was not only unexpected but a good trick if you ask me.

"Sounds like a lose-lose situation," I said.

Once my surprise wore off, I was left with annoyance. It was as though he was suggesting something amiss in the

Bureau's decision when I knew well that nothing could be further from the truth. A Non-Product Petition Denial is a denial after all. Every day the Bureau approved things and denied other things the way organisms inhale and exhale. Sometimes the Bureau approved things it had earlier denied just as organisms sometimes re-inhale the gases that they just exhaled. That was the point of the Bureau, to approve and deny and sometimes approve denials. And like an organism deprived of air, if the Bureau ceased to approve and to deny it would cease to exist. Pfft. You'd have no more Bureau. That may be why commentary so often likens the Bureau to something animate—a sleeping bear (for its strength and ferocity belied by a demeanor of passivity), a cockroach (for its uncanny ability to slink away, perhaps scathed but intact, from catastrophes that incinerate its opponents), and a schizoid Frankenstein's chimera (for its many public-private organs to which were delegated the most pressing matters concerning biomedicaltechnology due to their double advantages of abundant funding and no accountability). And of course there's the footnote written by that curmudgeonly Supreme Court Justice in his dissent from the opinion upholding the Bureau's use of sleeper cells in medical supply chains, in which he compared the Bureau to an enormous fungi growing from an underground network of rhizomes the size of a football field, drawing polite wonder from botanists while it indifferently blights entire ecosystems. That's a paraphrase of the original, which is of course completely scurrilous no matter how poetic.

His eyes were back in formation so to speak, focused if that's the right word on my nose and the surrounding area. I recoiled farther from him, exposing the letters "IT."

"I assume you're with legal?" My tone was nonchalant.

He seemed like the type who preferred to dictate the direction of a conversation so I intended the abrupt change of subject to frustrate him and spur his removal, leaving me to my notices. In fact, I never for a moment assumed he was with legal. To the contrary, he spoke in the manner of a person overcompensating for a lack of credentials. But besides being controlling, he was also literal and seemed not to pick up on irony.

"It is the responsibility of every informed citizen to know the law."

To avoid his eyes, I focused on his Adam's apple, which was prominent and similarly mobile even when he wasn't saying anything. It was clear he had no idea who he was talking to.

"The statutory term, by the way, is 'figment,'" I said. "As in the last word of the Biomedicaltechnology Product Act's definition of 'Product': 'Any Product that uses or purports, claims, appears, alleges, professes, suggests, adduces, insinuates, or in any way represents or is represented to use biomedicaltechnology to affect any condition of man and is not a figment.'"

The opportunity to put my deep knowledge on display so early in my tenure was unexpected but welcome, even if my current audience was unlikely to fully appreciate it. I was preparing to up my game with a discursive history of the term "Non-Product," a topic that had generated countless law journal articles, including the one written by a junior colleague for publication under my name: "Non-Products: Taxonomy vs. Epistemology." I never read the full article any more than I wrote it, but a blurb I signed off on suggested the centerpiece was a refutation of a slanderous accusation by the Bureau's detractors. Namely, that the Bureau had adopted the term "Non-Product" as a semantic strategy to conflate regulated and unregulated goods by making the latter (i.e., figments) sound like the former (i.e., Products) and thus, in the ensuing confusion, broaden the Bureau's purview while avoiding the bad optics of regulating a figment. Controversially, my article traced the origins of "Non-Product" to the Bureau's third director, who had coined the term because the word figment "sounded queer." But I was interrupted before I could say anything further.

"You've got it backwards." Here he grabbed the Information Advisory and read from it. "'The Petition was filed by Sorel Dern, founder of Glottal and inventor of the ə, seeking a determination by the Bureau that the ə was a Product.' In other words, Dern's gambit of petitioning for Product status backfired and instead the ə got Non-Producted." He put the word "inventor" in air quotes, apparently to indicate the logical conundrum of referring to a Non-Product as having been invented when you couldn't even say whether it existed. So he wasn't completely oblivious to irony.

I struggled to keep my composure. For one thing, even at that time, Sorel Dern was a polarizing public figure, having earned notoriety due to certain inflammatory statements quoted in the consumer technology trade press, ranging from crude nicknames for other tech icons to highly provocative assertions that ignited ideological warfare, such as "platform is irrelevant." His entrée into the field of biomedicaltechnology was a stunning development to say the least. But that was nothing compared to filing a Non-Product Petition to petition *against* being a Non-Product. It meant Sorel Dern had asked the Bureau to declare the ə *to be* a Product. He was asking for oversight. He wanted to be regulated. To submit. To be subjugated. What was stranger was that the petition had been denied. The Bureau, offered the opportunity to expand its reach and grow into something bigger than what it was, declined. It was as though the serpent had had enough of its own tail and started to gag.

"By the way," the odd fellow with the dexterous pupils said as he leaned over and placed his knuckly hand over the word Reality, which had been completely exposed by the shifting of my rear onto "MATTERS." "I know exactly who you are. YOU'RE N—."

(Although he said my full name, which by now is known to anyone who pays attention. Concerning anyone else, they are invited to do their own research.)

When he stood to leave, I realized he hadn't told me his name. It was clear he was a dissident, but that hardly narrowed things. The Bureau was teeming with dissidents. He struck me as one of the lesser dissidents and not worthy of further attention. He ambled off in his peculiar lope, his shoulders up around his ears and his knees lifted a little too high, as though signaling rectitude with the right angle of his knee, and that was that. I turned back to the two paragraphs of the Information Advisory, turned it over to see if there was more printed on the back, then noticed the two additional documents that had accompanied the Advisory as attachments to the same email. One was a press release from the company Glottal, titled:

FOUNDER SOREL TO DEMAND NON-FILING OF
BOB'S NON-PRODUCT PETITION DENIAL FOR ə

I almost fell off the bench. For one thing, the acronym "BoB" was an affront. I personally had a hand in rebranding BoB with its old familiar short form "the Bureau," a recon-

cepting exercise I suggested in the many-months negotia-
tion over my position. The name had been a thorn in my
side for as long as I'd been part of the vast galaxy of influence orbiting the Bureau, and now I'd attained a position
to do something about it. Double entendre has no place in
an acronym of the administrative state, even if I'd be the
last person to judge anyone for enjoying a good bob now
and then! I was hot for the change to occur before I began
my position, if only to avoid the discomfort of introducing
myself as a senior employee of an organization the very
name of which conjures a reversal of traditional intimate
gender roles. To be clear, I personally couldn't be more
comfortable with reversed gender roles. But if I'm going
to make a statement about gender norms, I prefer to do it
on my own terms, and not when responding to an innocent question about what I did for a living. I was assured a
major rollout of the new logo—including a Director's blog,
new letterhead, and a revamped website—was in the works
when an article by *The Washington Post's* technology and
politics editor outed an alleged "conflict" concerning the
Bureau's first choice of logo design contractor, a shell entity
created by the wife of the good-humored operations type
who'd hired me and oversaw the Bureau contracting process. By then the contractor had already returned a whim-
sical design with a plump B, followed by "ureau" in small
rounded letters situated midway between the top and bottom inverted c's of the first letter, a design that provoked
an unanticipated degree of offense from the focus group. In
the end, it may be that reporter had inadvertently done the
Bureau a favor, even if his scoop was the last straw as far as
the genial bureaucrat who'd hired me, who found himself
on the wrong end of such accusations more than was to be

expected statistically speaking. The Bureau hosted a "real time" competition during lunch hour, which produced a winning logo design by a former aeronautics draftsman in the Division of Pneumatic Biomedicaltechnology; a design of stolid, reassuring block letters in a sans serif font that was as fanciful as a slide rule. This outcome had the added bonus of relieving taxpayers from paying the contractor's fee, as the prize for turning in the successful design was a half day's paid leave and a mug, baseball cap, and computer mouse pad with the new logo printed on them. In short, the new logo was a triumph of the resilient federal worker over the insidious oversight apparatus. I wasn't prepared to assume this Sorel Dern understood the significance of his gaffe. I concluded that he, like all too many before him, had underestimated the Bureau's power and hadn't even bothered to confirm he was using the right name when addressing his new master.

But there was more to my alarm than just a name. This Dern was trying to have the last word by expunging the Bureau's decision. If granted, the Non-Filing Petition would disappear the Non-Product Petition Denial; the NPPD would cease to have precedential value. Everything would return to the status quo ante, and the Product would revert to the status of a Potential Product. And because by regulation all Potential Products are Products unless and until the Bureau later decides they are Non-Products, the non-filing of a Non-Product Petition Denial theoretically extended the Bureau's jurisdiction over Products to Non-Products outside its jurisdiction. The implications were so surreal and fantastic, I struggle to find an apt metaphor. Think of the same snake after it has eaten its tail, gagged, and consumed its own vomit, regenerating a new tail from the cells of something that wasn't even a snake to start the process all over again. Then you might have an idea.

I wasn't going to allow myself to be thrown off course. Whatever this Sorel Dern was up to, he wasn't going to have his way just by asking for it. Bureau procedures are Bureau procedures, and procedures require a formal request for permission to seek non-filing. The Bureau is a fair task master, but a firm one, and wouldn't be lured into expanding its reach simply because a brash young fellow demanded it in a company press release. He'd learn soon enough that one doesn't poke a sleeping bear with a dull stick, so to speak. As for why this Sorel Dern was demanding to be regulated, speculating on the motivations of others seldom gets one anywhere. People make decisions for reasons difficult to understand or to quantify, like cachet, and being the developer of a Bureau-regulated Product carries its share of cachet due to the exacting standards for which the Bureau is globally renowned. A non-regulated Non-Product, on the other hand, might not even exist. And not to impugn the motives of Sorel Dern—who, after all, I didn't know from Adam apart from what I'd read—but cachet has a price tag. Observers of the market have found over and over again that Products command two to three times the market price of Non-Products that do the exact same thing.

By the way, the third attachment was a short article written by that same technology and politics editor who helped us avert the awkward situation with our logo—apparently another Bureau gadfly—who went by Maddox Pinker. The article was buried in the science pages despite having nothing to do with science, as though *The Washington Post* felt obligated to publish the article but didn't want anyone to read it. It contained a quote from the office of a certain U.S.

senator concerning the Bureau's subversion of the scientific process in its decision concerning the ə, although overall it seemed more like an allegation than inquiry, and the first time I read it I read "perversion" not subversion. The part that piqued my interest, or one part I should say, was that the article cited privileged Potential Product submission information contained in the ə Non-Product Petition, information that had been leaked not only to the senator but also to *The Washington Post*. The information was of a scientific nature and tended to establish that the ə emitted sound waves at a frequency inaudible to humans, supporting (though by no means proving) the theory that the ə existed and was therefore more like a Product than a Non-Product. On the other hand, nothing in the file suggested the ə had an effect on a condition of man, regardless of the sound waves it emitted, which tended to support the decision of the Bureau. You might say it was a wash.

The senator's name, by the way, was Jeremy Sakhdvar.

I won't go into exactly what happened as I sat on the The-Bureau-Insists-Reality-Matters bench reviewing the press release and *Post* article, wearing a thin blouse with my legs securely crossed against the invigorating nip of the air as I felt a light prick from the sharp edges of glyphs against my derriere. I'll just say that even now, when the ə like a marble rolling down a chute toward a series of levers, trapdoors, and springs waiting to be tripped, has set off a sequence of personal and professional calamities involving professional relations, friends, and past lovers at the same time it has catapulted me into the harsh glare of notoriety, the first thing I feel when I think of the ə is a little zing of arousal.

THE TAPPAN ZEE BRIDGE

My publicist likes to say that famous people are like comic book superheroes because both need an origin story to make their behavior relatable. She could be a bit of a pedant on this point when it came to my role in the producting of the Ə, the finger flick with which I set the Ə-marble down its chute, toward its levers, trapdoors, et cetera. I gave what seemed to me the best origin story of all time; namely, that I wanted to see what would happen. But she wasn't satisfied.

My publicist is a highly educated woman with a degree in literature, serious literature, by the way, not comic books. Her literary education is from a prestigious academy, and well-rounded. So I couldn't simply dismiss her take on the similarities between superheroes and famous people even if her pedantry wore on me.

One evening not long ago, my publicist and I were discussing my part in the calamitous events to which I've alluded. The discussion led inevitably to my sexual history and its digressions into the outré and, some might say, transactional, neither of which, my publicist was quick to note, were necessarily a problem from a public relations standpoint. But they had to be portrayed in a certain light. She tore a piece of paper out of her notepad and wrote the following:

Who among us has never done anything 'degrading' according to the mores of the dominant culture, which demands the rent when it comes due even

*as it deprives us of the educational and societal
provenance to avail oneself of alternative means of
advancement · · ·*

Or something like that. As far as an origin story goes, it
missed the mark. My colorful past had nothing to do with
dominant culture or educational or societal provenances,
and everything to do with the quest, one I'd pursued for as
long as I could remember, for connectedness.

"That's not believable," she tutted.

Yet to this day, whenever asked by an interviewer some
version of the same troublesome question, I never think
about the dominant culture or various provenances. I think
about the Tappan Zee Bridge.

The Tappan Zee Bridge was the situs of the formative
event of my childhood, an otherwise unexceptional one
spent on the Upper West Side of Manhattan without material want. About my parents, the less said the better; it would
only complicate matters. I'll say only that I associate my
mother with an idealized if sui generis version of domestic
life. To this day, few meals on Earth give me the sense of
well-being that I get from a sampling of canned and pack-
aged things arranged haphazardly on a plate: baked beans;
SpaghettiOs; Vienna sausages; extruded meats; pickled
cabbage; pickled beets; sweet gherkin pickles; olives stuffed
with things one doesn't expect to find in an olive, like cheese
or a nut; rye crisps with bitter orange marmalade. These
were the interchangeable ingredients of what was otherwise
the same meal prepared for my father and me every night,
after he returned from his late lecture at the university and
my mother closed up her books and notepads in the rolling front of her desk for the evening. My mother was highly

educated but underemployed, a condition not uncommon for women of her time that always makes me feel a twinge of sympathy when compared to my own situation—the exact opposite as it happens. When I think of my mother, it is as though I am remembering someone from an entirely different era, as extinct as a Dodo, her departure from Earth every bit as elegiac. That she looked a little like the mother in that movie about the young barbarian, just before the sorcerer lopped off her head, sending it tumbling down from the right side of the screen as she fell sideways, still holding her child's hand, is perhaps a superficial detail, but one I raise only because I so often feel indebted to her for certain attributes of mine that have always gotten a lot of attention.

For the sake of symmetry, I'll say of my father only that he was an adjunct professor and practicing attorney who built his reputation on his defense of only the flamboyantly guilty (his term), occasionally successfully. He was considered a radical of some sort based on a few tracts he'd written, but his radicalism was difficult to put a finger on. It consisted of idiosyncratic antipathies toward institutions. I mean things like licensing bodies, which I suppose explains the professional troubles he ran into shortly after we lost track of one another. Anyway, I stay away from ideology.

My parents traveled in circles of freethinkers and academics and similar types. My mother had a close friend who introduced herself as a semiotician, which I considered exotic at the time but meaningless. After all, I was five. Perhaps I was eight. I can't say precisely other than that I was still impressionable.

One night, what was supposed to be one of those gray slushy New York City storms that are annoying but not dangerous turned into a record-setting blizzard, meaning the semiotician couldn't leave after her first drink or two as she usually did. (They were drinking Rheingold beer by the way, which I mention only because it's one of those unusual and lifelike details that redeem a recollection that might otherwise come off as apocryphal.) The conversation among my parents and this semiotician became more animated as the night went on and the snow continued to fall. It was when they got on the subject of my mother's thesis—a topic my mother preferred not to talk about, perhaps because it was taking too long—that the conversation took a fateful turn. I can't be expected to remember the details of their disagreement except for that my father referred to her thesis topic as the Great Vowel Movement even after my mother corrected him. I admit, I thought the pun was a good one. The semiotician sniggered, and the next thing I remember hearing was a Babel of phonemes: "i then ei then ɛi" and "ai." Like most children, I was sensitive to adult conflict even if I appreciated the occasional off-color remark as much as the next five- or eight-year-old. I removed myself to my room to avoid further traumatization. The last thing I heard was the front door to our apartment slamming, followed by the voices of the semiotician and my father both sounding surprised and perhaps a little smug for not being the sort of people to let their emotions get the better of them.

Who knows when I first learned what happened to my mother that night? It might have been weeks later. Or it might have been the next day. It perhaps makes no sense to say she was driving across the Tappan Zee Bridge when she died and to follow with the observation that she couldn't drive. All I mean is that she wasn't any good at it. What was she doing driving on the Tappan Zee Bridge? It's not hard to imagine she was visiting a lover on the other side, perhaps in Poughkeepsie; I have a vision of a lanky artist type in a paisley button down with long green eyes. There was an age gap between my parents and my father was too stubborn to make the small concessions that have salvaged many improbable marriages—forgoing a second can of Vienna sausages, for example, or trimming the vertically-projecting half ring of Saturn sticking out from his bald pate into a respectable head-hugging semicircle. One could hardly fault a grown woman with a grown woman's needs for taking matters into her own hands. The other possibility is she was visiting her mother, who lived in Nyack.

Besides being unable to drive, my mother also didn't have a license, perhaps out of solidarity with my father's objection to licensing bodies but more likely because she couldn't pass the driving part of the driving exam. What happened was she was "driving" our white Volkswagen Rabbit over the Tappan Zee Bridge during a blizzard when a semi cut into her lane, snow tumbled off the semi's roof and onto her windshield, and she veered right into the guard rail. Of course, whoever broke the news couldn't have described her last moments. Yet I saw them as clearly as if I were there. What I saw was less like a sheet of a uniform white mass as in an avalanche and more like a miasma of shiny white bugs swarming off of the semi and hovering around the white Rabbit.

Due to the young age at which I lost my mother, my memory of her is indelibly colored by the memory of not having a mother. It's as though she were both a blank space and the thing the absence of which creates a blank space. I became unmanageable, or so I've been told. The worst thing I remember was truancy and perhaps some moping, which may seem out of character for a self-starter, but trauma will do that to a person. Someone among the distant relations who had taken charge of my upbringing arranged for me to attend a boarding school far away from the city, a school known for its disciplinary regiment. I remember little about the place, except for that as a private institution, it was exempted from the humane policies instituted at public schools to protect sensitive children from the horrors of vivisection. Our biology instructor went to the opposite extreme, forcing us to replicate all manner of infamous experiments. On the first day of class, he gave each of us a gosling, tiny downy creatures that had been wrested from their mother before they forged that crucial bond underpinning healthy relationships. The goslings blindly followed their assigned students—they strained with their little necks forward, their useless wings extended against the instructor's hands and their faces contorted in incomprehension and hurt as they released shrieks of an unbearable intensity while he pulled them away from us at the end of the class, plopping them into a paper bag to return them to the enclosed area outside. They spent the rest of the semester pining for us in between the infrequent authorized visits. Then they were euthanized. What else could be done with creatures whose deprivation of models for their moral development left them vulnerable to the first prospects for affection, no matter how ill-chosen, and doomed them to a life of unreciprocated yearning?

The arrangement never worked well, but I stuck it out for a few years, making the best of the hand I'd been dealt. Except for that it was cold there and I got lonely. I snuck an energetic young fellow from the town into the dorm for companionship, the need for which I could hardly be faulted for. By then my father had married the semiotician, who in the end was more peculiar than exotic. She smoked a pipe and used the word "twat" as an adverb (e.g., "You handled that twattily," the antecedent to "that" being the whole boarding school situation), all of which seemed part of a cultivated eccentricity I tried not to hold against her.

I had to learn how to adjust to my new family. Occasionally we'd watch movies on television together. The semiotician wasn't much for cinema but tolerated it for the sake of my father, who, while also not a cinephile per se, appreciated films about conflict. One memory stands out of watching that difficult movie with the chimpanzees and the big black monolith. The chimpanzees and the big black monolith left quite an impression on me—or I should say more the monolith than the chimpanzees, who had allowed their immediate needs to get in the way of their higher aspirations. I mean, good for them that they figured out how to kill a tapir or whatever it was, or clobber their enemies, but surely once they'd adopted innovation as a basic principle with a little thought they could have used the bones for any number of useful things to make day-to-day living more pleasant, like a checker set or an ottoman. On the other hand, it might just be that I sensed my father, and the semiotician to the extent she was paying attention, sided with the chimpanzees—whose harsh circumstances were sympathetic if one overlooked their role in making their own bed after all—and that drove me to the monolith.

Perhaps I was emboldened by the shared experience, even if our experience of the experience differed. Shortly after, in an untaught but well-intended effort to build upon whatever common ground there was between us, I shared with the semiotician the last moments of my mother's life just as I saw them (minus the hovering swarm of crystals, which could come across as an embellishment).

"The Rabbit was rust colored," the semiotician interjected.

She might have been right in the narrow factual sense. Even if she was, her rightness extended only up to the point the Rabbit was obscured by a swarm of white-reflecting crystals and if you ask me, the color of the Rabbit doesn't really matter before that point. But the semiotician saw things differently, and she put a bug in my father's ear about my capacity for truth-telling, delusional thinking, antisocial tendencies, and the rest; in other words, the litany of bad behaviors reserved for accusations against provocative if fundamentally well-meaning young people. The two of them put together a plan to facilitate my eventual integration into society: they hired a tutor so I could finish high school, and enrolled me in a handful of college-level courses with titles like "Deviant Individual" and "Man and the Organization," and I did my part not to fail even if I didn't see the point in any of it.

The other component of the program was bi-weekly sessions with a former professor of the semiotician who happened to be a practicing psychiatrist. I never knew what to talk about. I assumed I should talk about my dreams, but nothing happened in my dreams. Sometimes I'd smell coffee brewing in the morning while I was still sleeping and I'd dream I was about to have a cup of coffee. I suppose I could have told him when I dreamed about coffee, but I felt that would be placing an unfair burden on him to make something out of it. To keep up my end of the conversation sometimes I described dreams I didn't have. One of these had particular significance to him, if not to me, because none of them had any significance to me. To me they were clever solutions to my dilemma but essentially gibberish. In this dream I never had, I was a passenger in a car on Amsterdam Avenue and all around me were other cars headed in the same direction. The cars were being driven by chimpanzees, except mine, which was self-propelled. At a traffic light there were more chimpanzees, only these were outside the cars and they were armed. Primitive arms—things like sticks and stones. The chimps outside the cars started to smash the windows of the chimps inside the cars and to pull the inside-the-car chimps through the shattered windshields. I saw the chimp gang shatter the windshield of the car three cars in front of me, then the windshield of the car two cars in front me . . .

The psychiatrist didn't ask about the chimpanzees or the car or the sticks and stones. He asked me about the Tappan Zee Bridge, as though the sort-of-homonym "chimpanzee" was standing in for my seminal trauma. It was like saying one's feelings about great apes have something to do with an experience with date rape. My feelings about date rape are as negative as anyone else's and possibly more so when you consider my background. But I have nothing against great apes, apart from that I find chimpanzees disorganized and focused on the wrong goals. I mean, if this psychiatrist meant to suggest that anything ending in "Zee" was a problem for me, I'd be triggered by the alphabet and I can say categorically that I have no problem with the alphabet. ABCDEFGHIJKLMNOPQRSTUVWXYZ. I feel great.

Perhaps my difficulty was that I associated the psychiatrist with the semiotician and I never fully accepted the semiotician any more than I did my father, "paternity" being like "figment" as a concept in that both are hard to pin down and a little quaint. Yet I made my peace with the two of them years later when, shortly after their move to Islip or Ossining or some other place beginning with a vowel and associated with involuntary confinement, my father died of natural causes. Though he had no will, the semiotician and I reached an amicable settlement on who would get what after probate. We agreed she'd retain his personal effects, which consisted of tweedy men's clothing, law books, and original copies of certain papers, concerning which I must confess I had not the least bit of sentimental attachment, and I'd receive the full value of his assets in cash, checking, and saving accounts ($673.32) in addition to a tin toolbox filled with a small amount of gold bullion he'd kept in safe deposit. I hate to be crass, but the bullion did more for me than the chimpanzee/Tappan Zee connection, even if there might have been something to it. All the chimpanzee/Tappan Zee connection did was to turn me off introspection, something I've never had any reason to regret. To the contrary, as my publicist likes to say, the unexamined life is my superpower.

UNE AFFAIRE DE COEUR

Which brings me to Jeremy Sakhdvar.

Were I the type given to morbid self-scrutiny, I wouldn't have lasted five minutes with him. But his quirks of unwitting cruelty seldom affected me. All the strength conserved by avoiding reflection breeds a degree of hardiness, I've found. And surely, whether we knew it or not, my hardiness of spirit and his peculiar sensitivity drew us to one another like the yin to the yang.

Because the path to the ə's triumphal release into the hands of humanity runs inexorably through my affair with Jeremy, I should say a few words about that.

I met Jeremy at a restaurant over 20 years ago when I was very young. We were both young, but he's the only one still described as youthful in his press, even though he's eight years older than I am. It doesn't seem fair if you think about it. So I don't think about it.

When I say we met at a restaurant I don't mean I was sitting at one booth and he was sitting at an adjoining booth and one of us said to the other, "Would you mind if I borrowed your gochujang sauce?" and next thing you know we were mentally undressing one another over japchae, although God knows that sort of thing happens often enough. There was nothing serendipitous about it. I placed a personal ad in *The Village Voice*, this being before the time of web pages where you can find a used futon, or a cruelty-free PVC-only dominatrix, or a ferret who had to be rehomed after attacking its owner's chinchilla. He responded and we met at a restaurant of his choosing.

My ad ran in the Backpage section, where one went for anything in that cornucopia of interests lumped under "adult services." I didn't need a life partner. Yet I was aware of something missing from my life that I couldn't name. My father had just died, which changed my life not at all, as I hadn't seen my father in years. Still, his death made me think of my mother's death, and together the two deaths wormed their way into the dark nether-zone of my psyche that I made it a point to ignore. For the first time in my life it struck me that all around me were units of two and three and four, couples and families, happily treading the same path through life, while I went about my business alone. Things came to a head when, to relieve my sorrow, I went to a newly opened café and dessert house that carried exotic ice cream flavors like jasmine palm and durian fruit. I decided I'd give myself a special treat. Only instead of asking the young man behind the counter for a scoop of blood orange sorbet, to my horror, I asked him for a scoop of blood orphan sorbet. I wasn't myself. I was at loose ends.

I had no pursuits to distract me from my angst apart from what I did to earn money, my inheritance being tied up in probate. What I did to earn money was whatever odd job I found advertised in the classifieds—housesitting, cat sitting, nude modeling for art students at the university, phone sex operator, et cetera. I was ahead of my time in that I worked the gig economy before anyone was clever enough to call it that. As a result, besides being at loose ends I was also broke. These things were on my mind when I wrote my personal ad. Hitching my ride to a strapping up-and-comer seemed the perfect solution to both of my problems. So you could say in one sense my publicist's flippant comment about "the rent coming due" was based in fact.

An interesting question is what was special about Jeremy compared to the many promising prospects who responded. He shared with me a few superficial demographic data points, which were unremarkable but not disqualifying, and his enticing description of himself as a swarthy Rufus Sewell. He didn't actually say anything about Rufus Sewell, Rufus Sewell being unknown at the time. He simply described his features in roughly the same way one would describe those of the actor, that is if the actor were quote/unquote swarthily-complected. In fact, when Rufus Sewell became a known commodity several years later, I sometimes referred to him in conversations as looking like an Anglo Jeremy Sakhdvar. No one ever argued with me. The only other bit of information Jeremy shared was that he litigated against products, a professional calling that seemed unusual and potentially antisocial but not in a way that posed any danger to me.

And there was this: when we spoke, less than two minutes into our conversation, he suggested we meet for dinner. I equivocated for a moment, intrigued but not yet committed. His voice went up half an octave as he blurted out *please*.

I got to the restaurant before Jeremy did. I was wearing a dress, a slip dress to be precise, which I mention only because fashion is another area in which I've always been ahead of the eight ball. When I say slip dress I mean the dress could have passed for a slip except for the pull of the zipper underneath my armpit. So I was fussing with my hair to give me a reason to raise my arm and reveal the zipper pull to remove any ambiguity concerning whether I was wearing an undergarment rather than a dress. My look was worldly yet discrete and thus tended to telegraph that I was worldly yet discrete, if also uninhibited in that one could have mistaken my dress for a slip but for the zipper. Worldly, discrete, and uninhibited were all in the ad.

I was restless and perused the menu, which offered an eclectic assortment of entrees. Main courses included beef bourguignon, filet mignon, coq au vin, chicken cacciatore, brasato al chianti, weiner schnitzel, and bratwurst, in addition to Salisbury steak, beef Wellington, hamburgers, pork chops, spareribs, meatballs, meatloaf, and a few pasta dishes with meat sauce. Some of the meat dishes came with green sauce, which at least broke up the monotony. I didn't then nor have I ever had anything against meat dishes. Once some cheeky poster on social media gained a fleeting notoriety for a post referring to me as a vegan fucker, which of course is true in a literal sense but not necessarily in the metaphorical sense in which I assume it was intended, the literal sense of vegan fucker being utterly benign. Who in this day and age hasn't fucked a vegan or two? But if the poster intended the fucker part of vegan fucker as a metaphorical stand in for "sympathizer," the poster missed the mark. I enjoy a hearty bratwurst as much as the next person. Still, the meatiness was a little in-your-face, as though the restaurant had something to prove. It was also making me hungry.

Jeremy was an hour late when he walked in. I took in everything about him in a single instant: his eyes (long and olive green), his physique (fit), and his complexion (swarthy). I'm not making the point here that Jeremy was already an unusually handsome man, which would hardly surprise anyone who has seen a recent photo. The point I'm making is that I wasn't thrown off in the least by the eyes and the physique and the swarthiness.

It was something other than his unusually good looks that threw me off yet drew me in. He exuded a quality of disjointedness, for lack of a better word. It was as though his eyes and his physique and his swarthiness had already gotten to where they were going in life and the rest hadn't caught up. I can't even say the exact moment when I knew that this man with the olive eyes and the fit physique and the dark complexion and the disjointedness was my date. All I can say is that a number of things happened in no particular order—thing one was that I observed approaching me a fit young man who looked a little like Rufus Sewell if Rufus Sewell were less English, swarthy, and didn't know what to make of looking like Rufus Sewell (the Rufus Sewell comparison, again, being post-hoc); thing two was realizing the less English, swarthy Rufus Sewell double was my date; thing three was a zing of arousal—things one, two, and three signifying only that there were three things, by the way, not that that the three things occurred at T_1, T_2, and T_3, although they might have, which is more or less my point. All of which raises the question of when I knew thing two—i.e., that the swarthy, conflicted-about-looking-like-Rufus-Sewell Rufus Sewell almost-doppelganger was my date, in that if I knew it at T_1 or T_2 you'd have the obvious explanation for the thing three, the zing of arousal, assuming the arousal occurred at T_3. The problem is that facts to the extent I remember them don't support the obvious explanation. Not that I remember thing three happening at T_1, which is at least possible, or thing one happening at T_3, which seems unlikely in that it would mean that I realized this fellow was my date before I noticed him. What I mean is that the "no particular order" part of my memory of three things happening in no particular order is as much a part of the memory as the three things. I won't insult anyone, least of all myself, with a ridiculous cliché about time standing still. Of course time didn't stand still. It just stopped being linear.

Jeremy's head was a little higher than everyone else's head due to his long neck. He was flipping it from side to side like an agitated periscope, only farther out of the water than periscopes usually go, and his necktie was still tied but a little loosened. As he looked up and down the bar he fidgeted with three black rubber bracelets on his left wrist so it was hard not to notice his hands, which were big with knuckles that were perfectly proportionate. In other words, he wasn't awkwardly protuberant in the way of many lanky young fellows, even if he hadn't grown into himself yet.

The first thing Jeremy did when we met was to make things linear again, which was just like him. The head flipping stopped when he saw me as though the periscope had found whatever it was looking for, but then stayed out of the water without submerging for whatever reason. He knew who I was immediately and pressed the palms of his lightly-knuckled hands together to part the crowd so he could follow a straight line to where I was sitting. As he got closer a musty aroma wafted over me, doing nothing to dispel thing three and, for all I know, causing it. It was like the smell of an old book that hadn't been aired out for a while. It was distinctive, yet discrete. And worldly. The musty book smell made me think of books, which made me think of learning, which I've never particularly pursued for myself at least not in the sense of "books," but that doesn't make the association with learning any less compelling in other people.

Jeremy freed one of his arms from its crowd-separating activity, placed his hand on my shoulder, and pressed his mouth against my mouth without so much as "Hello!" or "You must be N—!" The kiss was a little like the meat menu; it was as though Jeremy felt like he had something to prove. But one can't fault someone for feeling like he has something to prove when having something to prove was basically what the person did for a living. And perhaps he knew, even then, that we were destined for an unusually consequential relationship.

"I like your dress," he said. Or something similar. The observation may sound banal, but I found it refreshingly lighthearted after the intense kiss. "I'm Jeremy SOK' dhvar, two syllables."

"Let's order right away so we can focus on us," Jeremy continued.

As if I could focus on anything else. My receptors were already busily processing an onslaught of powerful and somewhat conflicting signals, from his smell to his linearity to his trying-to-prove-something kiss. One can only imagine the flare up I felt, neurologically speaking, when he ordered haricots verts, vegetable medley, and mashed potatoes. In other words, he ordered a meal out of the sorts of things one finds thrown into a TV dinner as an afterthought. Right after he said the words "mashed potatoes" and the wait-ress tucked her paper pad into her apron and was about to depart, Jeremy asked what was in the mashed potatoes. The waitress had to excuse herself to ask the kitchen staff and when she returned to report that the mashed potatoes had milk, cream, butter, lard, and real bacon (optional), Jeremy asked the waitress if she could just empty out a baked potato and mash it, again requiring that our waitress check with the kitchen staff and report back that the baked potatoes were Idaho potatoes, which are on the starchy side when mashed unlike the Yukon Golds, which are more buttery. On the other hand, the waitress offered, if Jeremy didn't mind the starchiness, they could mash an Idaho potato. Jeremy was equivocal and perhaps leaning against the Idaho potato until the waitress suggested Jeremy have a tureen (that was the word she used) of sauce verte on the side to cut the starchiness, to which Jeremy acceded, meaning he ordered mashed potatoes and greens *with a side of green sauce*. Our orders came and Jeremy ate his in exactly nine forkfuls, pressing the haricots verts and the vegetable medley into the mashed potatoes so they all stuck together in a mound on top of his fork then dunking the fork into the tureen of sauce verte without any of it falling off the fork. I had the osso buco.

I was still eating when he said, "I'm in consumer litigation. Mass torts. Class actions. You might have heard about the settlement against the makers of polypropylene mesh for onchochymosis."

"I assume you mean the one that was being implanted transvaginally for repair of cystocele."

I wasn't then in the habit of following that sort of thing, but I was fastidious in keeping up-to-date on matters of gynecological health and hygiene due to my busy social life, which consisted entirely of dates I met through Backpage personals ending in sex with men I never saw again. So I'd read about the victims' botched surgeries, the consequences for their intimate relationships, and naturally I wanted to see justice done as much as the next person. On the other hand, I've always believed in second chances. And it wasn't like the money was going to bring back all the consortium that had been lost. But Jeremy seemed pleased with himself and I wasn't going to burst his bubble.

"That's the one!" Jeremy suddenly lit up. "But I start at the Department of Justice in D.C. on Monday, in the Product Litigation Branch."

And that's how I found out about Jeremy's interest in justice, a trait that would define his storied career. I couldn't know then that one day, more than 20 years in the future, Jeremy would be a prominent senator, and would announce his candidacy for president on the same day he released a book with injustice in its title. I never read the book but one could tell by reading the reviews that it was the sort of book that was about pointing out injustice rather than celebrating injustice. The book was called *Something or Another Injustice* or *Injustice Something or Another* followed or preceded by a colon or a comma and something benign like *One Man's Quest* or maybe it was *One Man's Struggle.* As that *Post* writer Maddox Pinker wrote:

> In his entry to the campaign literary genre, candidate Sakhdvar chronicles his career as a prosecutor pursuing boondogglery, quackery, and graft, and as a lawmaker wielding the investigative prerogative like a yataghan over the executive and its tentacle-like pedipalps in the administrative diaspora . . . Sakhdvar's memoir reifies without ever piercing the ignis fatuus of a politician known more for his coruscating prosecutorial interrogations and his matinee idol looks than his connection to the people.

That may not be an exact quote but one gets the idea. I was immediately drawn to Jeremy's love of justice. It didn't occur to me for one minute that he'd follow his love to the threshold of the nation's highest office.

No, he meant something else by "Justice." Jeremy was young, embarking on a new career in a new city. What better send-off than a hardy screw with someone you'd never see again, who didn't know anyone that you knew. That was precisely the sort of arrangement I'd always pursued. Though I had something different in mind this time, I didn't give a minute's thought to ending the date. I wanted to hear more about his love of justice, among other things.

"Let's go to my place," Jeremy said.

It was a hot spring night yet we walked for blocks with his arm wrapped tightly around my waist until we got to his car, a small Datsun the color of a squirrel. We drove for what seemed like an unreasonably long time. I might have asked him, at some point, "So where do you live?" but it's possible I didn't. The osso buco was heavy in my stomach and I'd had two glasses of Syrah with it. Unsurprisingly, after 30 minutes or so of driving I fell asleep. I woke to find my seatbelt undone, my dress pulled up, and Jeremy leaning over me with a flashlight in his hand.

"Excuse me," I said.

Jeremy seemed startled. He fell back against the driver's seat.

"Don't worry. You're safe with me. I just couldn't wait," he said, a little apologetically. None of that explained the flashlight, but I wasn't going to let a little quirk like a flashlight or an attempted non-waking grope ruin what was otherwise a fine date. I looked out the open passenger's window. We were parked in the circular driveway of a sprawling home, beside a grotto covered with manicured vines leading to the back. There were lights along the driveway but otherwise everything was dark.

"We're where?"

"My dad's house. Potomac. Don't worry. It looks like he's out of town. Let's go to my place."

"Remind me where you said you live?"

"I vacated my place this morning. At the moment, I'm staying with a friend in D.C.," he said, as he turned the key in the ignition and grabbed the clutch.

"A friend?" I asked. What seemed like a simple no strings attached proposition was starting to get complicated. I believed in flexibility to a point but "a friend" was a bridge too far. I was going to suggest we borrow his father's house, which seemed nicely appointed. But his foot was on the gas and we were careening toward the street.

"Er—the friend's out of town," he clarified. "You and I have a great connection!"

We drove for another half hour or so to one of those characterless buildings that went up decades ago and once it was up there wasn't much to be done about it, though to his credit Jeremy's friend had tried. The first thing that grabbed you on the living room wall facing the entryway was a risqué poster depicting a nude female body with a video camera instead of a head underneath the words *Seks, Kłamstwa i Kasety Video*. On the same wall and the walls on either side were prints and tapestries advocating the sorts of things everyone can agree on, like amnesty, solidarity, and legalized pot. In some other context, the video camera on top of the nude body where the head should have been might have struck me as dehumanizing, but in the context of the public-spiritedness of the other wall décor one could only assume that the nude body with the video camera where the head should have been was a send up of dehumanization, rather than itself an example of dehumanization. My point is that overall, the wall décor was a nice touch and did as much as could be done to make the otherwise bland apartment inviting.

"Those are Ned's walls," Jeremy commented as he jerked

the knot of his tie from one side to the other in an effort that engaged his entire body. "Ned's a professional activist."

The level of exertion in separating himself from his tie seemed excessive, as though there was something he was trying to get out of his system. I sensed a fraught relationship between Jeremy and this Ned. Comparing the inclusive and affirming messages on Ned's wall with Jeremy's potato-ordering behavior, I wasn't prepared to lay all of the blame on Ned. I withheld comment.

"That one's mine." Jeremy pointed with his chin to the wall facing the *Seks, Kłamstwa i Kasety Video* poster, the wall with the entryway in it, at the same time one end of the tie slid out from the tie knot and his body relaxed. He flipped his tie back and forth in the direction of a series of artworks of different sizes all in the style of graffiti art, things like rats with small kitchen appliances exploding out of their heads and rat skeletons eating a piece of cheese only with an air of sarcasm as if the rats were playing a big joke on everyone. There was a series of small graffiti paintings depicting the stations of the cross, only Jesus and the leering spectators in their robes were all rats. Some of the smaller pieces were unsigned, but the largest three included the tag "Rodin(t)."

"The activist out of Tompkins Square," Jeremy related, but in the way of someone affirming widely shared knowledge. "Supposed leader of a global underground anti-technology/capitalism/rapism/patriarchy network."

"Of course."

"That one's my dad," he said, now lashing his tie like a switch in the direction of a screaming rat in a pope's headdress. He no longer seemed boyishly exuberant. I daresay his tone was somber.

"A rat?"

39

"A renowned cardinal and fornicator."

"I didn't realize I was looking at portraiture," I responded. Something neutral seemed best.

"The likeness is actually pretty good."

"I gather you two aren't close." For a moment I remembered my childhood psychiatrist. "I gather you two aren't close" was exactly the sort of observation he'd have made had I ever compared my father to a screaming rodent. But I'd never gotten far enough in my therapy to unblock whatever kept me from making that sort of loaded comparison. I started to think this Jeremy had some depth.

"He doesn't acknowledge me as his spawn. He got rich off a patent for a zymurgical process and left the church so he could fornicate full time." Jeremy stuffed his tie in his pocket and shrugged. "Art is a great investment."

I assumed that a response was in order and struggled to hit the right note. He was hardly the first date to unburden himself with some difficult circumstance from his past. At the same time, a situation where one could use the word "fornicator" unironically was a first for me. I can't say what possessed me. I felt like taking a risk, as though I might be rewarded with something spectacular. I ventured a personal revelation:

"My parents are dead."

"Both?"

Whatever other gears had been turning in his mind stalled it seemed as his focus unified on something, I don't know what. He stared at me intently, his green eyes almost black.

"My father only recently."

"So you're an orphan."

The idea seemed to have a meaning for him beyond the

obvious one, as though the little window I'd opened on the simple fact of my loss unintentionally revealed something else, a different and more profound vulnerability.

"My mother since I was a child."

"Mine too. My mother I mean. Actually, I was eighteen. Since then I've called myself an orphan. I sometimes imagine killing the cardinal so I don't have to lie." He was speaking quickly, the words running into each other. He paused abruptly. "But that's just me. I want to know about you. Continue please."

"I hardly knew my mother at all. I think of her more as an idea than as a mother. Yet I sometimes think I'd have been a different person, had I a role model in life."

I'd hardly uttered the "l" in model when Jeremy charged, dropped to his knees and threw his arms around me, butting his head into my midsection then screwing his pate into my navel as though he were trying to enter my womb headfirst the wrong way. He kissed my belly passionately through my dress, muttering the strangest things, things like "how completely alone," and "dear girl" between his kisses. Then he looked up at me with shiny eyes. In an instant Jeremy lifted me up and spun me around until we were on the sleeper couch that was already open underneath the *Seks, Kłamstwa i Kasety Video* poster. Then he paused for a moment, meticulously pulling his tie from his pocket and looking about for a suitable spot to put it down, settling on a stack of law books beside the sleeper couch. He placed it atop the stack of books with a good deal of deliberation; even as a young man Jeremy was a little bit fussy about his things. When at last he put down the tie he jumped me. I was caught off guard. One minute he was looking around the room for just the right spot to put his necktie and next thing you know, well, suffice it to say while we were still standing and completely dressed (except for his necktie and apparently the fly to his trousers) I felt a jolt. Then it was off with his shirt and then my dress as he was sliding me from against the wall onto the sleeper couch so as I became more horizontal he kept having to readjust himself to stay connected so to speak. Though nearing one in the morning the air had hardly cooled, so we were both a little clammy and each time he pulled himself upward his torso stuck to mine. Watching the skin of his abdomen sticking to the skin of my abdomen so when he pulled away from me my skin pulled away with him, I felt the pores on the surface of my body open up a little from the suction, like little mouths opened by their tongues that were just beginning to stick themselves out like a row of little sprouts and stretching the little holes they came from to open further to let whatever was inside the holes out and swallow up whatever was sloshing around outside them, the pace of growth started to pick up so in the thick of it I bit Jeremy's earlobe–

Jeremy rolled off of me and sat on the edge of the bed, naked with his chin on his fist like the sculpture by the namesake of the rodent-fixated graffiti artist.

"Hm," he said.

He sat there in the same pose for what seemed like a long time. Then he put his full weight on top of me and fell asleep. Shortly he started to snore with his nose an inch or so from my ear. I wouldn't have minded but I wasn't tired, having slept during the car ride, and I couldn't move my head due to the weight of his forearm on my trachea, making it unpleasant to swallow. I was stuck breathing only through my nose while looking in the general direction of a pope rat (or cardinal rat, whatever) screaming and a different rat with appliances bursting out of its head and a gang of rats snickering at their cheese-eating gag. I could also see part of Jeremy's shoulder and back, so I amused myself conducting a little experiment to see if by pressing the palm of my hand into his back (which was moist like the rest of him) I could get the skin of his back to stick to my palm. I tested things out on his gluteal area, lower back, shoulder, shoulder blade; I tried with my fingers extended, cupped, and in between. It worked best with my fingers at 45 degrees to my hand on his latissimus dorsi for what it's worth, perhaps because his latissimus dorsi was only a little clammy. I suppose I was stuck that way for an hour or two when Jeremy's torso jerked upward like a dead person being defibrillated and he grabbed his watch (which he'd removed in the same gesture he used to remove the three rubber bracelets, then placed the bracelets and watch on top of his necktie, only one of the bracelets had fallen off of the law books onto the floor).

"Let's go for a drive," he said.

I welcomed the suggestion, however quixotic. My neck hurt so I wanted to get up. We returned to his car, the unassuming interior of which gave me a familiar feeling. It was the sort of car one drives when one isn't trying to impress anyone, which I noted and tallied up with Jeremy's smell, his knuckles, and the elasticity and adhesiveness of his skin. In another column there was the potato, the green sauce, and the fussiness about the placement of his necktie, and so forth. It's true the items in each column were the same in number if one counts the "and so forth," but the items on the first column easily won out. I felt the stirrings of an emotional connection reverberating with the festering zing. (There was a third column by the way, a column made up of things neither for nor against but also not neutral. It was more a TBD column, consisting of things concerning which I'd not yet made up my mind. Under this column were the three rubber bracelets, litigation against products, the forearm over my trachea, his veganism, graffiti art, and his patrilineage.)

"Have you been to the Tidal Basin?" Jeremy asked and I said I had, although of course I hadn't. I'd felt an emotional connection. That didn't mean I let down my guard. I had the word "worldly" to live up to.

We parked in a small lot by the basin. I could see a monument from there but we weren't close to any monument. There were cherry blossom trees, naturally, but the blossoms had mostly fallen off and a wind was blowing those left on the tree off of the tree and also blowing the ones on the ground upwards. Believe me, I'm not trying to be evocative when I say it was as though pink snowflakes were falling but falling horizontally and up. The sky was bright green and the air was unusually thick. In a word, everything was perfect, apart from a derelict-looking man on the bench and an apparently unconscious one belly up on a tarp laid out on the grass. Jeremy led me to a patch not far from the tarp and the man on top of it, who paid us no mind. Then once we were facing, Jeremy asked if I'd close my eyes, which was a new one on me but well within the range of expected behaviors as far as I was concerned. He reached around me with his other hand and while we were still standing the exact same thing happened again as far as the jolt and the adhesiveness. I started to feel the pores of the surface of my body dilate like little mouths split open by their tongues again and then the odor of books wafted over me as though something reciprocal was going on, making his pores open up and belch out something musty. The smell was making the mouths turn predatory, as though they'd grown teeth, and the teeth were chewing through things, opening things up so their insides were spread like an open book, not just like a book with its spine on the floor so it opens in the middle and you can read the middle part before you've even gotten past the beginning, but like a book that's had its pages torn out and all the fronts of the pages torn from the backs of the pages and scattered so all the words on all the pages front and back were lying open for the taking . . .

A lightning bolt struck not too far off, a thunderclap burst and a sheet of rain fell. The fellow on the tarp raised his head, looked at Jeremy, looked at me, then pulled the edge of his tarp over himself and Jeremy said "Fuck." I would have preferred to finish things up but as I said, Jeremy could be a little fussy and we were on the ground by then and the ground was about to get muddy. We made off to the car, then Jeremy drove me to the Amtrak station. Once there, he asked me for my phone number, purchased my ticket, asked me if I needed some money and without waiting for an answer, handed me the ticket with a few bills in large denominations, the precise sum of which would be unseemly to divulge. Before leaving me at the gate, he muttered closely into my ear the following:

"Until I see you again, I'm going to smolder like Vesuvius."

Those were his exact words.

THE BALLER'S PINCE-NEZ

I won't trot out the usual tired clichés about when and how Jeremy and I knew we had to be together, only that it happened quickly and decisively. On a sweltering summer morning, as Jeremy was preparing to leave after his second or third visit to my small walk-up apartment in the city, it all became clear. The walk-up had no air conditioning and the hot air had cuddled me into a clammy stupor the night before, before I'd even undressed. So it's possible that Jeremy was left feeling a little unsatisfied, besides being hot and sweaty. He got up from the bed several times and walked around the small apartment, collapsed on top of me, sighed, then rolled off of me, disturbing my sleep but never for long. Jeremy wasn't the sort to put on a show of stoicism just to make a point. The sun was not yet up as Jeremy sat on the edge of the bed putting his suit trousers on one leg at a time after failing to find the underwear he'd pulled off in a desperate effort to air out his balls.

"This is going to itch like Hell," he said.

The implication of his words was clear to me if not yet to Jeremy, who for all his firepower sometimes lagged behind the curve in matters of the heart: we needed to take our rendezvouses elsewhere, somewhere where he had spare underwear or a pair of sweatpants he could slip into whenever he needed to protect his balls from direct contact with an itchy suit.

"That's why I stick to breathable fibers," I said. "I could live on a swamp."

The implication couldn't have been more obvious. Yet he seemed a little surprised the following week when I showed up with a small U-Haul and a mover who drove his own van. Jeremy paid the mover to wait around while he "made a few calls," one of which produced the name of a realtor who met us at a converted carriage house—by which I mean a place where a horse used to live—not particularly close to Ned's place, the inside of which I never saw again. The floors of the carriage house were cold black tile and the French doors in the living room looked onto the patio of the rowhouse facing the street, which I assume was built for the people owning the horse but was occupied by a well put together couple I saw whom Jeremy described as lobbyists for the semiconductor industry. Or it might have been the energy industry or telecommunications. One of those industries the exact scope of which is hard to put a finger on yet everyone in a certain milieu knows exactly where it begins and where it ends.

The mover helped me get my stuff into the carriage house that night but Jeremy couldn't stay, saying only that he needed to "do his own thing." Who knows what he meant by that. Before leaving he nodded his head toward the lobbyist's abode and said:

"It's well known in D.C. lobbyist circles that they like to swing."

The remark was intriguing if dubious for the obvious reason, namely what did Jeremy know about D.C. lobbyist circles. But I didn't question him. Already I was protective of Jeremy's feelings. Though our relationship was new, I'd seen enough of Jeremy to have developed my own views of him, no matter what he sought to project. I couldn't ignore the sense of something about him at odds with his well-socialized exterior, as though his pulled-togetherness was a hasty improvisation of a messy tangle of loose threads, apt to get wound around the spoke of the first fast spinning thing in his orbit. In short, he seemed reckless and vulnerable at the same time, like a hemophiliac juggling knives. Most likely this sense was my unskilled-in-analysis way of processing Jeremy's alarming family history. But what did I know about the psychological effects of owing one's existence to the scandalous behavior of a high-ranking clergyman? I didn't challenge Jeremy. He left and I spent my first night in my new abode alone.

The lobbyist couple threw a party on the patio to which I wasn't invited even though it seemed to me the patio was as much mine as theirs. I occupied one of the two houses opening onto the patio, even if the house I occupied was intended for their horse. I felt exposed by the French doors looking out on these vivacious Washingtonians who could see right into my living room, furnished with only the futon and frame I'd brought with me from New York. I tried to go about my own business unpacking but couldn't help noticing the party goers with their aura of professionalism and belonging, assuredness of their place in the rarefied milieu of the lobbyists' architectural patio in front of a place where a horse used to live. I turned out the lights and went upstairs to my bedroom, but the music and the chatter kept me awake.

In my loneliness I started to imagine what it would be like to befriend the couple in the front-facing house. I imagined stepping out on the patio the morning after the fete and making a casually witty remark to them as they cleaned, leading one or the other to invite me over to watch foreign cinema with them on the living room couch I'd seen through their

French doors and knew to be leather and cordovan in color. This would become a routine and would spread to other shared interests until we became almost inseparable as a threesome. I imagined retrieving the extra key to their patio door from the hiding place they'd share with me and letting myself in before a date with Jeremy. I would come over specifically to see her, the mysterious raven-haired she-lobbyist whose elegant willowy form I'd seen flit past the French doors earlier in the day, to ask her input on my shoes and my hair, possibly to take her up on the offer she would have made to let me borrow something from her closet "anytime." I can't say what filled me with such hope about this couple apart from Jeremy's observation, which made them seem accessible, even though as I've mentioned I didn't see how Jeremy would know about their personal habits.

I would soon become even more dubious about Jeremy's comment. Not long after their fete I fell asleep on the living room futon watching that movie about identical twins who were gynecologists, or to be more accurate about gynecologists who were identical twins, the gynecologist part being more to the point. It was the night that Jeremy visited for the first time and let himself in using a duplicate key, then mounted me while I slept (something that may raise eyebrows but was perfectly normal between us). He still had his pants on when I woke, just as the one twin was having intercourse with the other twin's girlfriend unbeknownst to the girlfriend. (When I say "unbeknownst" I'm not referring to the sex, which obviously she knew about. I'm referring to the with whom part.) When Jeremy noticed I was awake he dismounted, then sat upright to catch the rest of the movie. Shortly after that, the lobbyist couple installed the kind of shutters with thick slats kept drawn, all of which seemed gratuitously unwelcoming. I mention the unwelcoming shutters only because they seemed at odds with what I expected from swingers. But the slats stayed closed and after a few months of the thick slats and several more fetes on the patio to which I never was invited, I hung a pair of opaque curtains over the French doors.

My relationship with Jeremy soon fell into a comforting pattern of normality. Late morning on a Sunday I would often emerge from my grogginess to Jeremy hovering over me, probing around like a medical examiner who'd dropped his eyepiece in a cadaver. Thursdays after happy hour, he would stumble in drunk and a little bossy if I'm being honest. Once he showed up at 2 a.m. on a Tuesday, suggesting a degree of urgency hard to jibe with what followed:

"I have a brief to argue," he said.

"Good for you," I answered.

"I'd like you to play the judge."

I perked right up at his suggestion, which sounded like a lot of fun.

"Perhaps with a gavel and/or a robe I could get into the role better."

"There will be no gavel and no robe. For the purposes of this exercise, it's important that you role play a judge who is (a) docile and (b) naked. Please take off your chemise or whatever."

I was wearing one of his undershirts for the record, which I raise only because I didn't even own a chemise, at least as far as I knew. I disrobed and sat upright at the edge of the bed. Shortly into his argument—about which I'll only say it was exceptional for its argumentativeness, not that I could do anything about it not having a gavel—he became flustered and pronounced "disgorgement" in "disgorgement of profits" as "disengorgement of profits," a concept that as a punitive measure made no sense at all.

"Maybe if you held a plank," he said.

I'm nothing if not a good sport. Still, even the most innovative role-playing requires a certain internal consistency to hit the right note. I was having a hard time getting into the role of a judge while following the instruction that I be nonjudgmental, not to mention naked. I didn't see how holding a plank would help with believability but didn't quibble. I assumed plank position on the floor facing Jeremy, occasionally glancing upwards at him without ceding form by arching my neck. I held it until he finished his brief, which I daresay he wasn't expecting having perhaps underestimated my abdominal fettle. Then he excused himself to go to the bathroom, came back, and fell immediately to sleep. I recount all this only to illustrate the varied nature of our intimacy, even if it usually ended the same way: Jeremy on top of me, his weight pressing down like an anvil on dough, his head burrowed into the nook of my neck as his breathing became slow and loud, and his junk collapsed into a familiar smush against my thigh.

But there was so much more to our relationship than the physical side. It couldn't have been more than a week later that Jeremy came to the carriage house with a second suit in a garment bag and a piece of carry-on luggage. He said the hearing had been continued and he needed further practice.

"Imagine the judge is in actual hibernation," he suggested.

"That's preposterous. You're making requests that exceed my thespian skills." Even in matters of intimacy, we all have our sacred cows. Mine is credibility.

"Imagine the judge is play-acting she's a docile ungulate.

A docile ungulate in hibernation." With his first sentence he'd begun to appeal to my sense of the possible, but he lost me entirely with his second.

"There's no such thing," I said. In truth, I knew nothing about the habits of ungulates. Yet I felt strangely self-assured. Jeremy's mouth drew inward.

"OK, then a black bear. A black bear can be as docile as an ungulate. Please now, your chemise."

I removed his undershirt, turned on my side and held my knees to my chest. Then, in a spirit of defiance, I pretended to fall asleep. Suffice it to say my role-playing skills were such that the difference between pretending to be a judge play-acting a docile black bear in hibernation and pretending to be asleep was immediately obvious to Jeremy. He stopped arguing and pulled papers from his carry-on, then sat up in bed reading. From what I could see out of the eye not pressed into the pillow, Jeremy appeared to be reviewing a court filing of some sort, with a big square made out of parentheses at the top of the page and two names separated by the letter v. I couldn't make out either name, my vision blurry from squinting in the pretext of sleep, but the second name seemed to have three letters beginning with an O. Olf comes to mind or something like that, something short and seeming to be missing something. Reading along as Jeremy flipped through the pages, writing notes in the margins, it seemed this person on the wrong side of the v. who I'll just call Olf for simplicity's sake made an improved device to aspirate fat from one part of the body, such as the buttock, and deliver it to another part of the body, such as a place called the glabella, something I'd never heard of then though nowadays I know as much about the glabella as anyone. Only Olf claimed that he could use his machine to take matter from the buttock and put it back in some other part of the buttock so he was essentially creating a whole new buttock out of itself. I didn't see what the problem was. It all seemed like more of a misunderstanding than a crime, scarcely the sort of thing that should be punished by more than a stern talking to. I couldn't stay silent in the face of a gross unfairness.

"His quote/unquote offense seems more like a misunderstanding than a crime," I said.

"A hibernating black bear wouldn't give a fuck," was all Jeremy said.

It turned out I was right. Shortly after our chat, Olf was acquitted and the case was dismissed precisely because the appellate judge exercised her prerogative to be as judgmental as she pleased, finding it would be unjust to jail someone for not understanding that the difference between one's buttock and one's glabella is a meaningful one in the eyes of the law, if not otherwise.

Jeremy never told me I was right. Instead I found out I was right by reading a short article in *The Washington Post* by the technology and politics editor, who was still going by Maddox Pinker. The article was underneath a picture of Jeremy leaving a courthouse and captioned: *Justice attorney Jeremy Sakhdvar leaves the courthouse after Olf —'s verdict is overturned.* (Although I'm not sure about the Olf part; the name could have been some other short name that was missing something.) It was gratifying to be right. I clipped the article and put it under my pillow.

Being right affected the dynamic between us. One morning, Jeremy and I were in bed after he'd let himself in late at night. He was watching a political talk show with an obstreperous panel talking about one of those political scandals involving a senator and his wife or his mistress, I can't remember which. That is, I can't remember which senator, but it hardly matters. What matters is the mistress had surprised everyone by writing an editorial. It wasn't an editorial about being a mistress. It was an editorial about something more in the politician's wheelhouse than in his mistress's wheelhouse. I think it was ethanol policy. The host was a declarative sort, who said something along the lines of "Every smart woman wants to be thought of as beautiful, and every beautiful woman wants to be thought of as smart," or some such thing that no one would say on a broadcast forum nowadays, though perhaps one might hear a similar sentiment in one of the outlets that prides itself on being outrageous.

"I've noticed that," Jeremy said, without looking up from his law book.

With the benefit of experience, it often occurs to me that when his guard was down Jeremy was like so many men who pride themselves on their avant-politics in that he could be embarrassingly out-of-touch on evolving norms of gender equality. I felt a little embarrassed for him. I got up to make myself a café au lait and then, feeling a little sorry for Jeremy, who was the one who was going to have to live with the social stigma of his outdated views, I made a second cup. He took the café au lait without looking away from the declarative host, now on a run about something at least as contentious as ethanol policy but without the human-interest side of a love triangle. It was one of those things that is so general that asking an opinion about it is liking asking someone if they are pro or con the atmosphere but that nonetheless always provoked a strong reaction from Jeremy. The topic was something like "trade" or "the airwaves." Perhaps Jeremy was already having a strong reaction to whatever it was. It's hard to explain what happened next without concluding he was being a little melodramatic, the sort of accusation I prefer to avoid but if the shoe fits. Jeremy sipped the café au lait still without looking away from what was becoming more like an altercation than a discussion on the television, with the declarative host and his entire panel of fellow travelers opining on whatever it was in raised voices. While still holding the café au lait in his mouth, Jeremy looked away from the fracas and into the mug, then spat the contents of his mouth back into it, thwapping the mug on the night table without splashing even a drop, to his credit.

"I'm going to get a coffee," he said. Then, gratuitously if you ask me, he added:

"BLACK!"

Jeremy didn't show for a few weeks after that until one night he appeared with a carryout bag from Burger King. He sat on my futon, pulled *The Washington Post*'s classified section from his suit pocket and a cheeseburger from the take-out bag. Then he offered me an onion ring as he squinted at the auction listings.

"Can I get you a condiment?" I asked. His cheeseburger felt like a third person in the room that could only be acknowledged indirectly.

"You want to buy a Rodin(t)? Because I'm selling them."

"There comes a time when one puts away one's childish things." Sometimes even then I surprised myself with my ability to pin an entire vignette with a pithy phrase. He raised an eyebrow and paused mid-bite into his cheeseburger.

"You could say that."

Then he finished his cheeseburger, put down the classified ads, and asked if I'd lie completely still face down with my head in the pillow while we had sex and I said sure.

I didn't know what to make of the cheeseburger or the divestiture of the Rodin(t)s or the sex, which was an outlier in our repertoire in that it was pretty plain vanilla, if a little one-sided. I took them all as a sign of some sort, a milepost signaling a new phase in our relationship. I could hardly wait to see Jeremy again to see where this new phase would take us. But Jeremy didn't show and I grew lonely. Then impatient.

I took to sleeping on the futon in the living room so I'd hear Jeremy as soon as he came in. One night I was awakened around midnight by fumbling outside the door of my carriage house, the street entrance of which was on an alley, not a street. After a good 30 seconds of the door not opening, I got up to open it myself with the perfectly reasonable expectation that I'd see Jeremy there, fumbling for his keys. Instead I saw someone entirely different leaning his arm against my door and his head against his arm while fumbling with his other hand for his belt buckle. He was young, possibly younger than I was (but plainly of age to be clear); he had on a black macramé wristband and a Nick Cave t-shirt, which I found affecting, as though he'd been born an old soul. I let him in to use my bathroom, assuming that was what the fumbling was about, and on his way out offered him an onion ring, which I'd developed a taste for so I liked to keep a batch right on the stove. All it took was that friendly gesture for us to strike up a conversation, about ethanol policy as it turns out, as he was an intern for the senator with the mistress. Next thing you know one thing led to another, so to speak.

I felt a little bad at first. I'd always protected Jeremy's

feelings and now I'd done something without even considering them. Like I said, I was lonely. Besides, who had been most hurt? He'd never know, while I'd carry the weight of my actions for the rest of my life. It turned out freeing my mind was just a matter of adopting the right perspective.

A week later, the male half of the semiconductor lobbyist couple (or energy or telecommunications; I'm using a shorthand here) rapped on my French doors and when I parted the curtain, there he was, waving the fingers of one hand while holding a bottle of Châteauneuf-du-Pape in the other. He was suntanned and wore a seersucker suit with a polo shirt.

"Hi there, miss in the horse's place. Do you have a corkscrew for your neighbor?" he asked.

It turns out he was German, though he didn't have one of those obviously German names. The name was more like Kurt than like Lutz, though it wasn't either. It might have been Fred but who knows. I'm not a naïve person and it never occurred to me that the corkscrew could be anything other than subterfuge. One hates to engage in stereotypes, but it's hard to imagine a lobbyist, and a European one at that, not having his own perfectly good corkscrew in the main house. Plus, I hadn't forgotten Jeremy's comment, which perhaps I'd doubted as much to assert my autonomy as because it wasn't plausible.

I let Fred (or whatever, I'm using another shorthand) in and showed him to the drawer where I kept the corkscrew and similar implements. Before taking the corkscrew, he reached into his shirt pocket for a small contraption that turned out to be a pince-nez. He held the bottle close to his face as he unscrewed it. Having used my corkscrew, he had no choice but to offer me a glass of the Châteauneuf-du-Pape and naturally I accepted. Then we sat on the sofa facing the opaque curtains, which made me feel awkward. I mean the opaque curtains rather than the sitting, in that the opaque curtains seemed un-neighborly now.

"I rely on Jeremy for many of my needs," I said, which I thought was the perfect opener. It was neither encouraging nor discouraging. Plus, it preempted questions that might have been awkward, while preserving a number of options if he asked them anyway.

"It's never a bad idea to have a back-up plan," he said, which showed he could think on his feet even in his second language. I admit I was impressed, having perhaps unfairly assumed his well put-togetherness was all there was. The conversation kept getting better from there, not that we did much talking. Shortly, we had a first-rate screw on the couch, making me feel better about the curtains. Fred went to the kitchen afterwards to find a cracker or something and I was bored, so I tried on his pants and then his jacket. When he walked in on me, he didn't object.

"If I share with you a life lesson I hope you will take it in a good spirit and will not say that I am one of those Germans who is so pedantic."

Fred paused and looked at me in a way I'd describe as more paternal than pedantic, a mixed bag for me but I didn't hold it against him.

"I used to be a paid companion to the widower of a condiment magnate," was his surprising revelation. "I'm not using a euphemism."

"What kind of condiments?"

Fred screwed up his brows then continued.

"I mean about being a paid companion. The widower was

figuring out what to do with all this money and asked me to take care of his holdings in semiconductors. I didn't know about semiconductors. How they work. What they do. And now I'm like this big player when it comes to semiconductors. So you can see that whatever you understand is boxed in by your understanding of it."

He paused to draw a two-dimensional box with his fingers.

"On the other hand—" Fred extended his other hand, "—there's nothing like what you don't know to make you have the feeling of infinite possibility."

Then he reached into the pocket of the pants I was wearing, extracted his wallet, and pulled out a card. I didn't take the card but looked at him uneasily.

"I love it so much to help people! Anyway, I never met this guy but he wasn't really a friend of this other guy I didn't know too well either who says to me this first guy needs something but I don't know what it is."

The name on the card was one of those names that's confusing without being memorable. His portfolio was biomedicaltechnology.

"This won't require sex for you," Fred mentioned, which wasn't exactly an advertisement. "And don't worry about discretion. You can tell them that you slept with me if you want to. Just don't make anything up. Okeydokey? You'll agree we had a nice time, we had some wine, we took off our pants, and so on like anyone else, OK?''

He went on like that for a while and I was getting sleepy and a little uninterested in the conversation but without the opportunity to distract myself by putting on his pants again, which I'd given back. I gave him appropriate assurances. In the end, he folded up the seersucker suit and the polo shirt and walked through the patio to the main house in his underwear.

So Jeremy was right about the swinging and I didn't begrudge him in the least. To the contrary, I saw his being right as an opportunity to even out my being right about Olf, which had put a distance between us. Here was a chance to restore the symmetry in our relationship. Explaining to Jeremy how I discovered he was right would be difficult, but I could always say I witnessed the sort of situation one could only explain if swinging was going on when the blinds were down and the curtains weren't drawn and there was Fred with his seersucker pants around his ankles and some fetching lass (or lad for all I cared, after all it was notional) not his wife in a similar state of dishabille, the two of them folded in knots like a couple of origami pretzels or something like that. I was bored and lonely waiting around to tell Jeremy he'd been right, so I let myself have a little fun with the story.

The distraction and companionship of being with the young intern and then Fred were welcome but after they'd left I was back to the same situation. Namely, I was alone. One day, I got out of bed late, perhaps around noon. As I stepped onto the cold dark tiles of the carriage house floor I felt affronted; the cold dark tiles were like my smug doubles, rubbing my nose in the coldness and darkness that would grow in my heart if I let them. I had kept my excursions from the carriage house to a minimum so I wouldn't miss Jeremy. But I wouldn't be mocked by my floor tiles. Fortunately, I knew the one thing in the world that could always distract me from myself. I decided I'd take in the cinema at the arthouse theater downtown.

I had no idea what was showing when I bought my ticket. I just knew it would be an arthouse theatre kind of film, which was fine by me. I've always been promiscuous as to my cinematic tastes. Just as the movie began, a nebbish fellow took the seat next to mine even though the theater was almost empty. He immediately offered me a Milk Dud and when I said no, a Good & Plenty, and then a Jujube.

"I never eat during movies. The sound of my own chewing through the bones in my head is a distraction," I said in as polite a tone as possible, which you'd think would have sent a message loud and clear even if I only whispered it out of respect for the other patrons, of whom there were three.

I tried not to look at or otherwise encourage him, but perhaps because he was talking so much I noticed he had good teeth, which seemed out of place with the candy but also may have worked on my skepticism. The association between good teeth and good character is so ingrained in the common imagination that even an otherwise skeptical mind such as my own intuitively makes the leap from "good teeth" to "not a bad guy," without any scientific underpinning to the association. He was otherwise of medium height and build, indeterminate age and ethnicity (the theater was dark), and had a complex personal odor comprising notes of birch, pot, and musk (but not the kind of musk that's overpoweringly male; it was instead the kind of musk that signals maleness without beating you over the head with it). Having made clear that any and all offers of candy or anything else the chewing of which one would hear through the bones in one's head were one to accept the offer of the thing to be chewed would be rejected, I left him no choice but to rely on his wits.

"I don't watch art film exclusively," was the first thing he said after his offers of candy fell flat, to which my unspoken response was so what, who does.

"Any more than I do foreign films," was the second thing, which as far as I was concerned didn't add much to the first thing. It occurred to me that if he was trying to make the point that his taste in film was promiscuous he could have just said so.

"I enjoy every type of cinema known to man. You might say my tastes in film are promiscuous," he concluded, and for the first time I noticed he had an accent; I can't say from where. Also, I thought he winked, but it was too dark to tell. I did catch a flash of his teeth. I had to give him credit, it wasn't a bad line. He was starting to seem a little more interesting, which may sound like I was exoticizing him because of his accent but nothing could be further from the truth. To the contrary, if I had to name the thing that made me warm to him, it would be the smell of birch wafting through the air due to his hand gestures (which were also exotic—he rolled his hand in three semicircles, each farther away from his body, when he said "promiscuous," as if mimicking the gesture for rolling out a red carpet, something I'd never seen anyone do before), which had the effect of displacing the odor from his immediate vicinity.

"Are you a fan of subtitled erotica?"
I suppose I shrugged. The film had begun, and it looked like it was going to be right up my alley. He must have misinterpreted my silence though, because he changed the subject to discuss the related topic of the subgenre featuring independent film actresses who'd gotten their break in erotica or something like that. I wasn't uninterested. But I went to the movies to watch a movie after all, not to hear an alternate history of cinema.

"Oh, it's this movie," he said, as though noticing for the first time what we were watching. By that time we were well into

the film, which turned out to be about drag queens in the
way the movie with the chimpanzees was about a monolith. A svelte young man with outstanding posture strutted
across the screen in a tailored business suit, an attaché, and
a pince-nez (or perhaps it was a monocle—I don't really remember). No, you couldn't call him a drag queen. He
was more like a partner at a corporate law firm than a drag
queen, although being a partner at a corporate law firm was
perhaps a greater stretch than being a drag queen when you
consider the ethno-socio-economic background of corporate law firm partners, not to mention their postures, and
yet not a stretch at all once he had the suit, the attaché, and
the monocle or the pince-nez.

"You know, it's the movie about the pince-nez."

I turned to look at him after this extraordinary insight,
but still couldn't make out his features. My eyes had adjusted
to the dark by then, but all I could see was the light reflecting off of his teeth, which really were excellent. (By the way,
he might have said, "It's the movie about the monocle." It
would have been whichever one was accurate.) I suppose he
saw his opening because the next thing out of his mouth was
to ask what I thought about "X ... Y ... Z ...", "X ... Y ...
Z ..." better left unexplained but one gets the drift. I decided not to fight things. I said, and these were my exact words,
"Fine, whatever, tell me all about X and whatever as long as
you don't interfere with my enjoyment of the film." Then I
moved in a little closer and he prattled on.

He didn't interfere with my enjoyment at all, not in the
least. To the contrary, his gentle breath swaying the cilia
of my inner ear seemed to heighten my focus on the pince-
nez/monocle, by which I mean not so much the pince-nez/
monocle qua pince-nez/monocle, the pince-nez/monocle

making no more than a cameo appearance. I mean the hidden power of the pince-nez/monocle, its ability to transform its wearer into a better version of what he already was. It reminded me of Olf's machine. I thought my companion might have additional useful perspective on the pince-nez/monocle as he was clearly insightful and waited for an opportune moment to interrogate him. But after he'd finished up telling me all about with X, and then Y, then either tired himself out or lost interest in Z, he sat against his chair for a moment. When he noticed I was looking at him, he reached behind him for the half-empty Milk Duds carton and slid it into into my palm, which he held for a moment with both his hands. Then he left the theater.

I kept my socks on that evening and avoided thinking about the missed opportunity to discuss the pince-nez/monocle with my unusual cinephilic logophiliac. Instead, I thought about what the pince-nez meant for my relationship with Jeremy. I felt I'd been given a gift, a small opening to appease his hard feelings over the Olf matter by saying something like, *I can see how you'd find Olf's behavior w/r/t his machine duplicitous. While you were out of town I saw a film where a winsome young man used a pince-nez in a way that, while no one would say was criminal, was similarly confounding of expectations.* I ruminated over the exact words for a week or longer, weighing "conduct" against "behavior" and "provocative" and "mendacious" against "confounding of expectations," and "what could have been a monocle or a pince-nez" or simply "monocle" against "pince-nez," which I ultimately chose for simplicity's sake. I wrote permutations of my lines out longhand, then rehearsed them aloud. It never occurred to me that I wouldn't have the chance to deliver my lines, that the night he showed up with the cheeseburger

and the onion rings and we discussed the sale of his Rod-
in(t)s would be our last night together. It didn't occur to me
because I knew, as I've always known, that I would one day
see Jeremy again. I just expected it to be sooner. But something happened to throw my expectations into the hopper
like so many lotto balls.

I again ventured out of the carriage house one morning to
a Francophile food chain and ordered pâté on a baguette.
I took my meal to a table where the previous customer had
left that day's *New York Times* and flipped through it absently
when a short column under two photos caught my eye. The
first photo was of a 50-ish woman whose head was cocked in
the way of someone about to appeal to reason. She appeared
to have been photographed while saying the word "practically" or "pragmatic" or "gag" (as in gag-order, not ball gag)
or something like that. The other photo was Jeremy standing at a lectern in a gymnasium or some other public-look-
ing institution, pointing with his thumb and index fingers
joined while perhaps saying the word "two" or "to" or (more
likely given his flair for the excessive) "too." Behind him was
a flag, which was expected, and an elegant woman with
black hair in a chignon standing there, which threw me off.
I don't mean the chignon or even the elegance. I mean that
she was standing there. It seemed presumptuous.

The column announced that Jeremy would challenge to
the woman with the cocked head who seemed like she'd
enjoy a good syllogism, which made Jeremy's challenge
unsurprising, as Jeremy always said reason was a lesser fac-
ulty. Nor was it surprising what the challenge was all about,
namely, Jeremy was challenging in a race to be the district
attorney for Queens. The only surprising thing was the caption to the photo describing the elegant black-haired woman

standing behind him as Jeremy's wife. Had the caption said "girlfriend" or "inamorata" or "sidepiece" or even perhaps "fiancée" I'd have been interested, but mostly in the chignon and everything else that made her elegant. But "wife" had to have been a misunderstanding, a misplaced "w," "i," "f," or "e" that should have been some other letter; "wafe" came to mind knowing Jeremy's interests but I knew perfectly well that "waif" wasn't spelled "wafe" and it didn't seem plausible that a reputable publication would have put two letters in the wrong places. Furthermore, Jeremy was a proponent of certain outside-the-norm views associated with challenging hidebound institutions. And what institution is more hidebound than marriage? I can think of none. In speaking of such a person, "wife" was the height of incongruity. Especially when the wife was elegant.

X = Y

Occasionally in life one experiences a jolt to the system so profound as to upend all of one's hopes and expectations, even if one doesn't have hopes and expectations. Because even if one doesn't have hopes and expectations per se, one may know perfectly well what one is neither hoping for nor expecting. "Wife" was one such jolt. It was the upending of the hopes and expectations I didn't have that shone a new light on Fred's (or whoever's) tip about having a back-up plan, and thus set me on the long trajectory that would land me on a cold stone bench with a pointed inscription, contemplating the fate of an epochal technology.

A day or so after I read the article about the sensible woman and chignon and the wife, I was sitting on my futon writing the following:

FIFE LIFE RIFE WIDE WILE WINE WIPE WIRE WISE

I got up to retrieve the pocket dictionary I kept in the utility drawer because the carriage house had no bookshelves, possibly because its earlier occupant was a horse. I was planning to double check "wafe." Only when I stood I noticed the slats on one of the shutters across the patio were open, not just a crack but wide open. This felt like a dare and I'm not one to back down from a dare. Besides, I'd wanted to ask Fred a few questions about that fellow with the confounding name on the business card, such as whether he had a nickname. The open slats on the shutters of the

French doors on the main house were so welcoming, I felt a tightness in my throat. It was as though letting Fred use my corkscrew and the rest was just the icebreaker I'd been looking for in my relationship with the street-facing lobbyist swinger couple.

Only they were gone. As I crossed the patio, I saw none of exotic tchotchkes I'd noticed in the early days of my residence in the carriage house before their shutters went up, like the enormous head of the Buddha with the pate flattened for resting a cocktail or the grimacing stone god with outsized male characteristics, a ceramic square suitable for a canape plate balanced atop the head and the penis. The French door was unlocked and slightly ajar, but I didn't need to open it to see the house had been cleared out.

The first thing I felt was sadness about the friendship that now was never to be, but I had no time to wallow in my sadness. My mind moved on to a second thing, namely that buzzing Fred-Or-Whatever's non-acquaintance Whatever-His-Name was now out of the question. That sort of thing could be misconstrued as not taking a hint, the hint being Fred-Or-Whatever leaving without so much as a note stuffed under my patio door, and the thing the hint hints at being that the pursuit of friendship with whatever his name was (more likely Fred than Lutz but probably neither) and his partner (who was always just as interesting to me even if we never got to know one another) was a non-starter.

Which brought me to the third thing. Fred's non-leave-taking reminded me of another non-leave-taking and all the events leading up to that non-leave-taking, beginning with being right. I remembered how I learned I was right, from the article with the picture of Jeremy at the courthouse (as opposed to the article with the picture of Jeremy and the flag and chignon and the wife, which I preferred not to think about). I returned to the carriage house and retrieved the article from under my pillow, where it was as fresh as on the day I'd placed it there. Reading the article again, a single word fluoresced on the page. It was a monosyllable with a diphthong, identifying the biomedicaltechnology boutique litigation and lobbying firm that had successfully triumphed over the efforts of Jeremy and his justice apparatus to criminalize the misguided but overall well-intended ventures of Olf or whomever.

The firm has gotten its share of attention of late, and not because of the monosyllable or the diphthong, though to be sure those things are noteworthy enough in a firm marquee. I hardly have to repeat the name. For simplicity's sake, and in the spirit of certain contractual terms, I'll just call the firm "the Firm," which has the advantage of an affinity with the Firm's actual name (other than the lack of a diphthong in "Firm"). My point is only the following: as I flattened my tongue and opened my throat, allowing the diphthong to emerge quietly into the sullen air of my carriage house, my back-up plan became clear.

I found the Firm's general number in the phone book and asked for the fellow in the article, whose name was Jeff by the way. I was placed through to Jeff's assistant, who asked me if I'd like Jeff's voicemail.

"I would not," I responded. "Tell him N.— called and I was referred to him by Jeremy. Jeremy Sakhdvar, that is."

Then I hung up. Jeff called within an hour.

"So you know Sockvart?"

"Better than most."

"What can I do for you?"

"It's more what I can do for you."

"I always thought Sockvart was kind of a prick."

"He's an admirer of your work," I said. A silence ensued.

"What'd he say?"

"It would be best to discuss in person."

Jeff agreed to have his assistant call me to make an appointment at his office the following week and I couldn't have been more excited. I was looking forward to talking to someone who saw things the way I did, at least as far as the Olf matter. Only when I showed up at Jeff's office at the appointed time the receptionist said Jeff was "indisposed for all intents and purposes." Those were her words. She offered to get me in with a Dave or a Matt, but I wasn't having it.

"My business is with Jeff," I said. The receptionist put me on the phone with Jeff's assistant, who recognized my voice but called me Stacy and made an appointment for me to meet with Jeff the following week. The day before that meeting, his assistant called to apprise me Jeff would be unable to meet with me; however, he'd authorized her to offer me an unpaid apprenticeship. This time she called me Shelley. It occurred to me that I was holding all the cards, with Jeff twice having left me hanging after I'd relayed a compliment about his work and now Jeff's assistant twice calling me by the wrong name. Who can say the terms I might have negotiated, were I the sort to exploit the culture among white collar confreres of overcompensation for small lapses in professional courtesy.

"It's N.—" I said, but in the kind tone one uses when offering a bit of information that may prove face-saving in the future, rather than with an intent to humiliate anyone. Just as it's often said that the key to calming one's nerves while delivering remarks in front of a large gathering is to imagine one's audience naked, I've always found that the same effect can be had by imagining oneself with the sartorial advantage. I imagined myself wearing a well-tailored suit. And a pince-nez.

"A close associate of Jeremy Sakhdvar."

Jeff's assistant said "Hmm," or something like that but made no commitment.

A few days later I received a call from a different woman, someone else's assistant, I don't know whose.

"Our staffing needs have changed due to the situation with Jeff," is what she said. "When can you start?"

"Immediately," I replied. "You'll never regret putting me on your payroll."

The deal was sealed; I'd landed my first salaried job. It was a small salary but enough to cover the rent on a proper flat, the inside of which it was unlikely any horse had ever seen, and my other needs, which were basic at least as far as material things go. Only later did I learn the sad background to my hiring, which was spurred by the exodus of Jeff's loyal staff after Jeff was referred for disbarment and voted out of the partnership. It turned out Jeff had perhaps not been fully candid about the consequences of Olf's conflation of the glabella and the buttocks, things like embolism, stroke, and the occasional death. When one considered Jeff had been paid in stock futures in Olf's machine, this lack of candor didn't put him or the Firm by extension in the best light from an ethical perspective. The upshot was I never did get to work with Jeff, apart from when I joined the Firm's lawsuit against him years later. But I suppose that was more work I did to him than with him. I felt badly about the whole thing, as I suspect Jeff and I would have hit it off.

I might have a few details off but that's more or less how I

got the job at the Firm. In any case, the details are unimport-
ant. My point, or I should say points, is/are the following:

Point one: My appointment didn't involve sex of any sort
in a quid pro quo sense, despite the occasional insinuation
to that effect in less reputable media outlets. Sure, after I
started there were the usual encounters that happen in most
employment situations, as in where one proofs a legal brief
and finds that due to the poor typing skills of one partner
or another the spell check supplies the word "voluptuary"
when the partner intended "nugatory," or where one hears
an assignment to research the law on patent extension as a
request to research patents for devices to relieve sexual tension and in the ensuing bonhomie one thing leads to another. But all of that was strictly ex post facto my hiring, so it
couldn't very well be a quid when no one knew anything
about it at the time of the quo; and,

Point two: My hiring had not the least to do with
string-pulling of any sort from any extramural source in
which said source jury-rigs a soft-landing for the source's
former inamorata to absolve his hypothetical self from
rent-paying in light of changed circumstances involving a
"wife," notwithstanding that the hypothetical source's Rolo-
dex can be hypothesized to include the Firm and especially
excluding anyone of the former description with a history
of veganism if I'm making myself clear; the same goes dou-
bly for all this being despite the occasional insinuations, et
cetera.

In short, speculation to the contrary notwithstanding,
quid pro quo, string-pulling and similarly pejorative char-
acterizations had nothing to do with how I landed at the
Firm. I won't deny name-dropping played a role. To which
I will only respond that if having the moxie to exploit the

few resources at one's disposal as an outsider in a competitive field is a crime, consider me guilty as charged. If it's true I lacked the educational provenance of my peers, one can only infer from this a perception/reality mismatch as far as background and skills necessary for my sort of work. I would soon learn how little good book learning did and, as a corollary, how critical soft knowledge was in this rarefied sector of the service economy. I began my ascent into the most elite echelon of the influence sector with one of my first matters at the firm, petitioning the Bureau concerning its treatment of Extraterrestrial Life Forms and Derivations from Extraterrestrial Life Forms (ELFDELF). ELFDELF was not known to exist as a philosophical matter but its regulatory existence was an open question. I didn't know the first thing about ELFDELF but that didn't stop me from filing a Non-Product Petition for ELFDELF seeking to product ELFDELF, a trailblazing precedent to the Non-Product Petition for the Ə. (The client, by the way, was a highly secretive organization, whose identity was unknown to everyone except the partner with whom the client had a longstanding relationship. That partner was Jeff, but no one had the stomach to tell the client that Jeff was gone. So we soldiered on, communicating only with a shadowy intermediary.) Almost twenty years later the Bureau issued an interim response, lamenting the difficulty in determining whether ELDELF was a product in the absence of data establishing that ELFDELF was a Product. I didn't miss a step. I filed a new petition advocating recognition of the Bureau's Provisional Producting Pending Data Supporting Producting authority, or PPPDSP. The PPPDSP would give the Bureau a pass on data, it would let the Bureau say, *We are unable to conclude that this thing described in the Non-Prod-*

HOW THE ə GOT PRODUCED

*uct Petition is a Product because we haven't seen data proving
it's a Product, but let's all just agree to call it a Product and
we'll see what the data has to say about it later.* The petition
spoke of the PPPDSP as though it were a unicorn, a notional
creature the existence of which could simply be waived in
the interest of good government. After many months with
no response from the Bureau, I called the snarky staff attorney to whom the petition had been delegated. He opined
the PPPDSP was more like a Snuffleupagus, a regulatory
folie a deux, an article of faith for those whose credibility
was vested in its existence and at best a benign delusion for
everyone else. Shortly after the call we received the Bureau's
interim response, which responded to our petition in two
ways: first, by asking for the regulatory citation for PPPDSP
authority, the sort of rhetorical question that defies answering, and second, after we neglected to respond within the
allotted thirty days, by forgetting that any such thing as a
PPPDSP existed, even as a hypothetical matter.

I never let the limits of my learning interfere with the
endless expanse of my imagination and empathy for the
world's innovators. The men whose job it was to solve
biomedicaltechnology problems at the Firm weren't particularly good at it, perhaps because they weren't all that
interested in biomedicaltechnology despite their degrees
in things related to biomedicaltechnology, like science.
Believe me, I'm not generalizing when I say that to a person,
the men in the Firm's partnership, all of whom were men
by the way, were more interested in what biomedicaltechnology could do for them than in biomedicaltechnology
qua biomedicaltechnology, by which I mean they were in it
mostly for the money. Even with the hole at the center of my
moral education, I always understood that pursuing a thing

because it could make you money stripped the thing one was pursuing of its very nature and for that reason was never very fulfilling. My interest in biomedicaltechnology, on the other hand, had nothing to do with money. In fact, even at the end of my time at the Firm, by which point I'd made my way into that rarefied income strata demonized by certain fringe elements, I always said I'd do the work for free, such was my level of devotion. It was just as Fred or whatever his name was had said: my new profession gave me the feeling of merging with the infinite.

The difference in interests between the men in the Firm's partnership on the one hand and me on the other made it easy for me to insinuate myself in their matters to the mutual benefit of everyone involved, and most of all the clients. And so in no time I went from assisting the male partners at the firm with their clients' matters to taking over client matters from the male partners at the firm, but always without creating hard feelings: everyone knew that the clients' interests, and therefore the Firm's interests and therefore the Firm itself, were better served by having me handle the clients' problems. Suffice it to say that over the course of several years I earned quite a reputation for myself with D.C.'s premier boutique biomedicaltechnology practice.

I earned my reputation in an area of niche specialization within the field of biomedicaltechnology, a field concerned with using the most intimate of materials – genes, cells, ova, sperm, sputum, et cetera of human, animal, protozoan and plant origin – to make the most varied of creations. Indeed, the field encompasses so much that to claim "specialization" is like saying one focuses on a multiplicity of concepts and objects grouped within a single rubric based on common ontological features. My subspecialty by definition was

more concrete but no easier to define than the broad area
of which it was a subspecialization. The best I can do is to
say my niche entailed demonstrating X—something seeming to be one kind of thing (such as a biomedicaltechnology Product)—was in fact Y—a different thing (such as a
Non-Product) or even not a thing at all (such as a figment).
In the interests of humility, I won't belabor how my reputation was earned. Suffice it to say, it wasn't so much a matter
of my success rate, success having to do with a multiplicity
of factors, many of them arbitrary. It was more that I never
looked down on the effort to pass something off as a better
version of itself or as something entirely different for that
matter. I offer the following by way of anecdote:

Several years into my career at the Firm I was assisting one of the partners on a case to which he wasn't paying the attention it deserved. When I say assisting I mean
doing everything he wasn't doing, which one might as well
describe as doing everything, period. To say this partner
was an alcoholic would be an unfair generalization from the
indisputable circumstance that many of the Firm's partners
were recovering alcoholics, "recovering" meaning that they
attended the Firm-hosted AA meetings and drank only beer,
wine, or brown liquors, and only on Tuesdays, Thursdays,
and weekends and only after work except on weekends and
Tuesdays and Thursdays when they bicycled into the office,
on which days they never drank before lunch. I have no evidence to support such an assertion concerning this partner
apart from the purple-ness about his nose that might have
been rosacea and a particular smell to his breath that might
have been his mouthwash. I think once he had two scotches
at the airport while we were waiting for a flight back from
somewhere cold in the middle of the country, but it could

just as well have been three and it could have been bourbon, not scotch. Otherwise I never saw him drink, although he was known to have a full bar in his office, which out of sensitivity for all the recovering alcoholics at the Firm he kept in a locked cabinet other than on Thursday happy hours, when the recovering alcoholic partners along with everyone else at the Firm were invited to drink with him. My point is I have little by way of evidentiary support to say he was an alcoholic, but if he was it might explain his lack of effort. Not to say it would justify it, as he was bound by certain professional standards that I managed to abide by, even though technically not subject to them. But one tends to be more sympathetic to those whose failures can be traced to something tragic, such as alcoholism, as opposed to something tragi-comic, such as laziness.

It, by which I mean his supposed alcoholism, might also explain his generally unprofessional behavior toward me, another matter that I won't belabor. It wasn't the first time in my career at the Firm that an older and more established male colleague dropped a memo pad so he could watch me pick it up or put his hand on my behind without the courtesy of at least saying, "I'm about to put my hand on your behind, prepare yourself!" I'll call him Ted, short for Edward and not Ed, the "T" in "Ted" when given as a nickname for Edward being like a human tailbone; in short, something that makes you think of something that isn't there and no longer has a point. Which sums up this fellow as well as anything.

One afternoon Ted and I met in our offices with the young founder of a startup company that had developed a novel weight loss product called HomHunkulus™ (second "h" silent), an oblong emetic manufactured from biomaterials that sprouted cilia-like structures upon contact with certain gastrointestinal fluids, provoking a controlled course of vomiting. The Firm had never represented a startup before due to our rates, which were justifiably astronomical, reflecting the truism in the influence sector that one gets what one pays for. Were I to be completely honest, I'd have to acknowledge that besides the rates, the Firm abided by an unspoken conservatism as far as clientele. Of course, as a biomedicaltechnology firm we favored innovation. But due to the Firm's fundamental conservatism, we preferred familiar innovation.

The founder's name was Cameron but he went by Cammo. What I liked about Cammo was that he had no educational training or experience relevant to his endeavor, just a passion. He showed us a link to his vitae in an online professional database that said only that he'd received his undergraduate degree in entrepreneurial studies from Babson College. His professional background was in fitness. He once owned a gym franchise he'd started with his college roommate and he'd recently branched out into the dietary supplement business. But as he put it—and I can't say I disagreed—the future of fitness is biomedicaltechnology. I should mention Cammo wasn't bad looking at all, for those whose tastes run to the conspicuously fit. His yellow hair was roguishly tousled and his face had a pleasant breadth and openness, even if his eyes were a little small by comparison and had a free range quality, as though at large in the expanse of his midface area. Not that his looks had anything to do with anything except to the extent it was his looks that got under Ted's skin, provoking Ted to cut Cammo short and pronounce the HomHunkulus™ nonviable or with no viable pathway to market or something else just as negative. Whatever it was Ted said concerning nonviability, it rubbed me the wrong way and rubbed Cammo in an even worse way. Imagine being told not only that you faced many obstacles in making your fondest dream a reality, but that the thing you dreamed of wasn't even viable. Of course, I'm in favor of giving an honest read of a client's strengths, weaknesses, opportunities, threats, and so forth, but never at the expense of basic humanity. After Cammo left, I asked Ted to let me personally represent him, and Ted responded with his thoughts on whom I'd need to sleep with to have any success with the nonviable product, and in what positions and where, involving what paraphernalia, with whom watching, and the types of recording devices that would be used, but otherwise didn't try to interfere.

To make a long story short, for the very first matter I handled on my own for the Firm, I devised a novel, untested theory, petitioning the Division of Ingestible Biomedicaltechnology, BoB (this was before my auspicious intervention rechristening, in a secular sense, BoB as the Bureau), that the product wasn't ingestible biomedicaltechnology after all in that its emetic qualities nullified its ingestible qualities, because what good is something as an ingestible if by its very nature it reverses the process, preempting the whole point of ingestion, i.e., sustenance. The upshot was it was neither ingestible biomedicaltechnology nor non-ingestible biomedicaltechnology and thus completely outside BoB's purview. Regrettably, by the time years later that Bureau agents seized shipments of HomHunkulus™ in seven states—purportedly under the direction of rogue Bureau elements—I was in job negotiations with the Bureau and precluded on ethical grounds from being of any assistance to my former client. If I'm not mistaken, the founder sold his company to a defense contractor that had plans for HomHunkulus™

as a countermeasure. But what matters is the Bureau never denied our petition. In fact, the Bureau didn't answer the petition. So you can't say we were unsuccessful.

My portfolio expanded over the years to include many more successes like this one, "success" here referring not necessarily to an outcome but to the triumph of spirit, the moral victory that comes from a principled and defiant stand against nonviability. I soon ascended to the pinnacle of my field. I was esteemed by my "peers," of which I had none due to the esoteric nature of my subspecialty but whom for the purposes of annual peer-rankings comprised non-peers in unrelated fields, accomplished professionals who had no idea what I did but opined I did it better than anyone. Though no non-lawyer and no woman had ever joined the Firm's partnership, the partnership created a special Non-Voting Partner by Assignation designation just for me and later conferred the title on several qualified women who in fact held JDs, further testament to my record of trailblazing. Twenty years went by in a blur of accomplishment and fulfillment.

In fact, it was the afternoon of my 20-year anniversary with the Firm that I received the call that would change everything. My anniversary had gone unfeted due to the recent retirement of the lead administrator, who on her way out the door had deleted the Firm's master calendar. Most likely she was overcome with emotion and deleted the file inadvertently. These things happen. As for why she retired, there were rumors of a golden handshake and poorly-sourced gossip that she'd been asked by the managing partner to arrange a month of business development activities in Kuala Lumpur for one of the firm's associates, freeing the associate's wife (an intern) for rendezvouses with the managing partner, the sort of arrangement certain old school professionals never could get used to. I've never been one to heed rumors, so I have no idea why she retired. All I know was that no one invited me to a steak house under false pretenses where colleagues surprised me with a watch and a Lucite plaque. Instead, I spent the afternoon sitting at my desk, reflecting.

I should mention here that my office at the Firm looked directly into offices on the other side of K Street, including the suite of offices of the Directorate Secretary—or I should say the office of the Acting Directorate Secretary, the post having gone unfilled for two administrations. The Directorate was and remains the sprawling federal department that encompassed the Bureau among numerous other sub-entities, all of them dedicated to the health and well-being of its constituency, i.e. the American public. Which no doubt explains the inability to fill the post of Secretary, the demands of the job being what they were. Rapid expansion to meet the needs of the American people had caused a shortage of office space in the Directorate's suburban facilities that no amount of telecommuting, flexi-place, and office-sharing could abate and so, to set an example of personal sacrifice for the rest of the staff, the Directorate leadership team had relocated to K Street, directly across from the Firm.

As I was reflecting, I peered absently into the offices across K Street and observed an imposing thickset fellow pick up his phone. A moment later, my line rang. My assistant informed me that the Deputy Secretary for Operations for the Directorate was on the line. I asked her to put him through.

"I'm looking at you from my office," I said, and let fly a friendly little wave. I didn't know for sure whether the fellow across K Street was the same fellow as on the line but the risk seemed one worth taking.

"That's something!" he rejoined enthusiastically. He waved back. "You look like someone who can handle adversity."

I was no stranger to the Directorate, even if I'd never seen anyone from the Directorate before. I had worked with the Directorate from time to time, generally when a client had a grievance with the Bureau that could only be resolved by resort to a superior entity. To stay silent in the face of grievances of the sort so often encountered by my clients would be to deprive the government of the opportunity for self-improvement, and nothing so redeems the government to its public as accountability. As often as not, months after the filing of my grievance I'd receive an unsigned form letter from the Directorate's Office of Constituent Affairs promising to investigate the matter. From there it was a crapshoot whether the grievance-causer at the Bureau would (1) call the client and apologize for the misunderstanding; (2) disappear from the client's matter completely never to be heard from again (by the client, I mean, not by the family and loved ones of the grievance-causer; there has never been any credible evidence of the Bureau disappearing critics despite what one sometimes reads in certain slanted outlets); or (3) call his/her elected representative and/or main Justice to initiate a whistleblower action, in which case the client would soon be defending subpoenas and penalties in the hundreds of millions of dollars, jail time, and reputational damage. As I said, it was a crapshoot, but well worth rolling the dice when one considers what the alternative could mean as far as a lack of accountability.

So the call from the Deputy Secretary for Operations for

the Directorate was unexpected. But whatever reservations I might have had due to the surprise factor and the word "operations," which sounded prosaic, were calmed by the Deputy Secretary, whose voice had a chipper quality even when communicating imminent catastrophe.

"We have a small crisis, and we need someone from outside the BoB to manage it. Someone whose background will bring a high degree of credibility to the situation," he said, cheerily.

"Can't BoB leadership handle your crisis?" I looked across K Street to see if his demeanor gave anything away but he'd turned his back to the window and was slouching, so I could see only the half dome of his bald head over the back of his chair. I knew the answer anyway, as did anyone who worked with BoB to any meaningful extent. The answer was no, BoB leadership couldn't handle the crisis, whatever it was. Not because BoB leadership was ineffective, although it might have been. No one knew whether BoB leadership was effective because whether BoB leadership was effective was a matter too important to leave to chance. BoB leadership came and went, but BoB wasn't going anywhere. As a consequence, those in an oversight role, such as the legislature (upper and lower chambers), the courts, the executive, the Directorate, regulated entities (who funded BoB through Fees for Regulatory Service (FFRS)), and derivatively the American public (who bore ultimate responsibility for all of the above including even the regulated entities, whom the American public could have made a lot more uncomfortable with their decisions affecting all the other overseers if they wanted to) ensured crises involving BoB were always referred for resolution outside of BoB, even if it meant bringing someone from the outside inside to create the appearance of self-governance. The outsourcing of BoB problems was a perfect example of how the Bureau parlayed its passivity into wile. Come to think of it, the comparison of BoB to a lowly fungus whose masters tread, unaware, atop its vast underground root system, with an appearance of subservience that belies its wherewithal for survival and its cunning wasn't completely off-base. In this case, though, outsourcing was more than just a reflexive response to crisis. There were rumors that the BoB Director was unpredictable if not ineffective. I never heeded those, having at that time never met the BoB Director. In short, I found the BoB Director to be nothing if not predictable in that she was predictability in absentia. Otherwise all I knew about the BoB Director was that my clients sometimes referred to her as "the Common Law Director," which I assumed said more about their benighted response to women in positions of authority than it did about her.

"The delicate nature of the crisis calls for someone of your skill set. You're aware of the Purge, and it has Cabal fingerprints are all over it." His voice crescendoed and became livelier with each word, so by the time he said "all over it" his voice was booming and he sounded like he was in great spirits.

"So I've heard," I said, referring to The Purge and the Cabal, which were hardly news to followers of the Bureau. The Purge and the Cabal were matters of catastrophic concern to my clients, always referred to by the intentionally ambiguous short-hand "the Cabal of Five Situation." The Cabal of Five Situation was longstanding but ill-defined. The confiscation of HomHunkulus™ and tabling of the PPPD-SP were just two examples of the rumored mischief of the Cabal, central command of a loosely affiliated Bureau faction known for its hostility to biomedicaltechnology and believed to have powerful influence not only everywhere in the Bureau, but at the highest reaches of government. Metaphors for the Cabal were many, perhaps none more overused than the comparison to an octopus the tentacles of which were so many and extended so far from the octopus' brain that it was sometimes hard to trace the tentacles back to the octopus proper, leading one to assume the tentacles had gone rogue. But the theory that the Cabal was a splinter group of a global underground network of anti-technology (and everything else) malcontents sometimes referred to as N'Aut gave both groups too much credit. I found my clients' fear of the Cabal unsophisticated yet affecting, like a child's fear of a monster under the bed.

As for "the Purge," the term came from the informal and unnamed leader of the Cabal speaking of the level of turnover in the scientific staff, quoted thusly in *Crisis at BoB*, a Maddox Pinker exclusive: *Think of me as the finger down the throat of an organism that purges excrement out the wrong hole.*

Who knows what she or he meant by that! I affected calm.

"Can you make it a political appointment?"

"I don't have to tell you what that entails."

"Hearings?" I said the word as though I were asking a question. But he was right about not having to tell me anything.

(I should perhaps mention here that though I'd long since moved on professionally and in other ways, in the preceding decades I'd learned accidentally and through no effort of my own (apart from the standard media-consuming habits of every well-informed member of the public) of certain developments in the life of Jeremy Sakhdvar. He won his first ever campaign against a sitting district attorney, the woman who looked so reasonable in her picture, and that made a splash. Several years later he lost his campaign for New York A.G. for no easily identifiable reason other than, according to the political rumor mill of the day, he was "a bit of a prick." After that I didn't hear about Jeremy for a while, and with the demands on my time perhaps I'd have forgotten him completely if he hadn't appeared, some years later, as number one on one of those "Most Beautiful People" list. Only he was the number one slot on a sublist, which presumably had a lower bar. It was something like "most beautiful person working for a consumer protection non-profit" or something similar. The year after the list he was elected to the House of Representatives, and a few years after that to the Senate. Through the same inadvertent process, I came to know something about Jeremy's committee assignments (the Biomedicaltechnology Committee, for one), rank on said committees (ranking member of same), pending investigations (BoB processes for producing, non-producing, product experimentation on humans, and so forth), in addition to other things I picked up here and there, such as the amount of weight he'd gained since law school (23 pounds through a diet centered on lean meats and healthy fats), his half-marathon time (one hour and 37 minutes; he had the flu at the time), and the names of his wife and two children (Leilani, Antigone, and Ralph). I mention all this only because, as I listened to the Deputy Secretary's cheerful inflection, I thought, "What better way to reconnect with Jeremy after all these years than to be confirmed to a position of prominence in the agency over which he exercises such vigorous oversight?" There was no innuendo in my thinking of any sort.)

The Deputy Secretary hiccupped. When he spoke he was back to his cheery self.

"What we have in mind is less public, advisory in nature rather than executive. Just as influential, but with less accountability. Unfortunately, there is no position like that in the Bureau. Creating one will require us to call in some favors—"

"What sort of favors?"

"Better that you don't know. I'll be in touch."

He hung up and the blinds went down in his office so I can't say what he did next.

It turned out the Deputy Secretary burned through favors quickly, as I would soon learn from his sad downfall due to the unseemly appearance created by his wife's winning bid for logo contractor. For a time, with no favors left for him to call in, my career negotiations seemed to be at an impasse. I casually floated the idea that I be seconded from the Firm for an indefinite term to serve as Special-Advisor-In-Residence-To-The-Director-Of-The-Bureau-Of-Bio-medicaltechnology, a.k.a. as it would soon come to be known "the Bureau." It was the kind of solution I'd come to be known for professionally: one so simple and elegant that others practically had to invent reasons for not having thought of it in the first place. The plan was for BoB to issue my paycheck to avoid any questions about my allegiance. But the Firm's endearingly lackadaisical attitude toward accounting matters resulted in my collection of paychecks from both employers for the longest time. For all I know the electronic deposits into my personal account would have continued even after, some months later, I submitted my resignation from the partnership on the advice of my publicist, who characterized my affiliation with the Firm as "off-brand." I should mention that by then the Firm was defending itself against a complaint containing vivid and not unbelievable charges brought by several former female employees, so my resignation was a win-win situation for both sides. I felt no small tug of sadness when, a few months after submitting my resignation, I received notice from the Firm of its dissolution. But times change. It doesn't pay to be sentimental about past affiliations that refuse to keep up with them.

I wasn't looking for a new job. I was well-compensated, sought-after by clients demanding the same innovation in matters of influence that they exerted in creating their products, and respected by my "peers," even if I didn't have any. What's more, I understood the proposed elevation would demand of me certain sacrifices, requiring that I give up practices that had kept me from feeling the isolation so common to those whose first love is their work. Nonetheless, I didn't hesitate when made the offer, and have never regretted it since, no matter the sacrifice. As effortless as my transcendence to the upper echelons of my professional milieu may have appeared from the outside, the truth was it came at great cost. But one doesn't lightly turn down such prospects, regardless the costs in terms of connectedness.

THE DIRECTOR'S UMLAUT

That, in short, is how I wound up palpating a bench's quizzical inscription with my rear end one chilly spring day as I read notices concerning a technology destined to transform life as we know it.

I wasted no time. Immediately I put two plus two together, the first two being the ə and the second two being the Cabal of Five. The Bureau was nothing if not predictable (the reputation of its director notwithstanding), but there was nothing predictable about a snake (standing in for the Bureau) gagging (standing in for issuance of the Non-Product Petition Denial) on its own tail (standing in for the ə). And how did privileged information supporting the ə's existence get into the hands of this technology and politics editor at *The Washington Post* with the byline Maddox Pinker? Not to mention the hands of Senator Jeremy Sakhdvar. Clearly something was afoot.

But just because one puts two and two together doesn't mean one arrives at four. I like to think it was my ability to avoid that sort of tautological thinking that brought me to the attention of the Bureau's hiring committee. I saw immediately that an investigation was necessary. On my second day at the Bureau, I marched into my office—officiousness of the air be damned—and prepared to take one of my most consequential actions as Special-Advisor-In-Residence-To-The-Director. I hit the button on my phone beside the words "executive assistant." The phone rang across the hall from me and a young man appeared in my doorway.

"I'm your executive assistant."

I was looking at a cherub, with fetching blond curls held in place with just the right amount of product and a plump lower lip curling over a slightly receding chin. He was as light and airy as a cloud, in dress shoes of oxblood leather and skinny denim that looked like it had never been washed, a conspicuously fashion-forward choice for the Bureau. But the collar of his blue shirt was officiously anchored by a pair of twin white pearl buttons, signaling he wasn't above making a small sartorial concession to his environs.

"So it would seem," I answered, a little suspiciously.

"The Directorate Secretary detailed me from Office of the Chief Counsel. My job is to make sure you get what you need to bring down the Cabal. And whoever's behind them."

"Former Directorate Secretary," I corrected him.

"Touché!" He was a little flippant. "I've followed your career."

I enjoy flattery as much as anyone, but I know better than to let it cloud my judgment. I'd seen my share of young go-getters in my day, and found they so often put their own ambitions ahead of the needs of their superiors, too immature to appreciate that the two were inextricably intertwined. I'd hoped for a battle-axe as my executive assistant; one of those war-hardened women or (less common but not unheard of) men of many years' service and unquestioned loyalty who rise by dint of their labors to execute orders from an organization's pinnacle. Yet I recognized the ageism in my reaction and vowed to give this young man a chance.

"Then you're aware of my exacting standards," I said. Here was his chance to prove himself. "Get me the Office of the Inspector General. I want to order an investigation."

"OIG contact information is classified."

"Then how is one supposed to order an investigation?"

"This is to prevent interference in investigations by targets. Every Bureau employee is potentially an investigation target. So—"

"Well that places me in a bit of a pickle. Which means you're in a bit of a pickle. By delegation."

"What do you suggest I do?"

"Suggest? Oh, I don't know, drop something in the suggestion box?"

"Brilliant!" He clapped his hands together and tapped his fingertips. "The suggestion box is part of the 360-degree accountability program. The outcome of every suggestion is recorded in an annual report to Congress."

And just like that he dispelled every unfair assumption I'd had about him. I scribbled my suggestion and contact information on a piece of Bureau stationary and handed it to him.

"Drop this off for me, would you? And by the way, who is it that is supposedly behind the Cabal and that I'm supposedly taking down?"

"I read the same newspapers you do."

"The newspapers I read don't have anything to say on the matter."

"That's why I get my news elsewhere. Some say they're part of an international conspiracy of anti-technology radicals."

"Then it must be true." I found his credulity touching, even as I recognized I'd have to dispel him of it if our working relationship were to have a fighting chance. "And what did you say your name was?"

"Hieronymus Glick." With that he left.

I didn't order an investigation lightly. I understood intuitively that in an organization like the Bureau, known for its orderliness and its hierarchy, such an action demanded vetting through the chain of command, even if only in the sense of an ex post facto vetting. The last thing the chain of command needed was to know about something controversial before it happened. No one benefits from a culture of toxic accountability, which only deters the best people from seeking high public office. But the chain of command liked to be brought in on things in due course to feel included. My point is when I decided to let the one person in a position of superiority to me in on my decision to authorize an investigation, I wasn't looking for her imprimatur because the investigation had already been ordered. I just didn't want her to feel left out. I'm speaking, of course, of Bureau Director Jorg. No umlaut.

I planned to disclose the investigation at my first meeting with Director Jorg. Yet something prevented me from knocking on the closed door of the office next to mine. I should have felt an affinity given her groundbreaking tenure as the Bureau's first female director. Instead, whenever I imagined knocking on her office door, introducing myself, and sharing news of the investigation, an itch broke out along the perimeter of my skull and my neurons agitated. The logical assumption would be that the rumor of unpredictability caused the initial disquiet in my feelings toward Director Jorg. Personally, I think it had more to do with the missing umlaut. I didn't know what to expect, but the situation with the umlaut made me think whatever I expected, I'd get something different. I resolved not to expect anything, yet incredibly I had my expectations upended. In short, I met Director Jorg before she met me. I can't put my finger on what I mean when I say that I think this asymmetry affected our relationship.

It was my third day at the Bureau when I met her. I'd given appropriately deep thought to my appearance on my first days in the office, which precedes one whether one wants it to or not. On my third day, I wore a brown pantsuit engineered from polyester microfibers with an unusually small diameter, then all darted and tucked in an invisible origami of tailoring. It was the sort of suit that leaves an impression of being on the outside of an in-joke at first and only secondarily one of engineering and mastery. The fibers had a snug stretchiness that was invigorating and comforting at the same time. It made me feel supported. Not that I'm vain, but I like to make an impression.

The all-hands memo announcing my arrival went out two days late, resulting in my displacement by a maintenance crew from the well-appointed space facing the machine sculpture on its plinth. The crew had come to hang the letters of commendation and plaques I'd accrued over the years with the Firm and organize the Code of Federal Regulations on my shelves. The crew's appearance in my office gave me a bit of a culture shock; maintenance at the Firm was conspicuous yet invisible, as though the Firm regenerated its gleaming facade and orderliness on its own each night, after the lights went out in every office. At the Bureau, maintenance happened in broad daylight and on its own schedule, a visible reminder that oversight of biotechnology was an all-hands-on-deck deal, built on the backs of laborers as much as on the cerebral cogitations of elites.

Once the memo went out, they made a huge deal over me as though to compensate for being a little late. This "they" arranged for a sequence of introductory appointments over my first several days with my executive assistant (whose appointment we skipped as I'd already taken the initiative to make my introduction), an executive secretary, the director of executive benefits, and several others who were part of an entwined network of executive supports. I can hardly explain how satisfying this was to me, to enjoy all the accoutrements of executive-ness, without having to execute things. Which is not to say I didn't execute things. To the contrary, in time I came to feel that I was the only one in the Bureau with the gumption to execute, even if as an advisor I didn't have the authority to execute anything. It just meant that because I was executing derivatively, for the director, I didn't have to bear the heavy burden of accountability, which is what generally stymies executives from doing things in the first place. By the way, I'm not sure who I mean when I say "they" apart from some person or persons with the combined or singular authority to make the gears in different bureaucratic mechanisms turn all at once. One thing is for sure and that's that "they" weren't Director Jorg. Director Jorg never made a big deal over me. She didn't even meet me when I met her.

I was placed for the day in an interior office that was unoccupied for most of my tenure except for a three-month period when all of the window offices were taken by CEOs from the Regulated-Entity-in-Residence-with-the-Regulator program, but I didn't complain. The temporary office had a kidney-shaped desk and one of those chairs that has an exoskeletal quality, like a squatting cockroach. The lighting was fluorescent, naturally, and one of the bulbs was flickering. I mention this only because it may explain why when I remember what happened, it's as though I'm remembering an old movie on a projector that doesn't work so the movement isn't right and the lighting flickers, instead of remembering something that happened to me. Everything seemed to slow down so you could see the dark spaces in between one thing after it ended and the next thing before it started.

At the time, the executive IT support specialist was engaged in a somber monologue on the matter of data loss. He never intimated that I would lose data or treated me like I might be a careless person who couldn't be trusted with something of value, namely data. He simply started from the assumption that data could be lost, no matter how careful one is about one's data. He was bear-like, with a beard that was full in a way that seemed oddly exuberant. His left arm was extended along the thoracic part of the exo-chair and the right reached for the mouse on the kidney-shaped desk, so his arms made a big C that encompassed me. His right hand kept clicking the mouse to open folders nested inside a series of other folders where the "lost" data might end up being just hard to find. He clicked and clicked and the nametag that was dangling before my eyes stopped rotating on the lanyard around his neck just long enough to snap me out of my trance with the name "Linus" when Director Jorg appeared, squarely in the center of the unoccupied office's doorframe.

"My drive is behaving erratically. Can you come to my office at 6?"

In the moment that followed three things happened in succession:

1. I started to rise to introduce myself;
2. Linus gave the thumbs up; and
3. Director Jorg left in the direction opposite from the direction she'd come from.

My behind dropped back into the exo-chair and my mouth contracted, involuntarily, into a hard minus sign.

That was how I met Director Jorg, and when I shook her

hand just two days later, she said she was glad to meet me. So you could say our relationship was founded on asymmetry.

I returned to my office that evening, after my plaques and award certificates were hung and my books arranged on my shelves. Immediately I buzzed Hieronymus and once again he appeared in my doorway.

"Tell me what you know about the Director," I said.

Hieronymus placed his hands in the pockets of his pants (creased khakis this time, as though his efforts to crack the fashion code of the federal workforce had brought him a little closer to his mark, but not there quite yet.) He extended his lower lip almost to the bottom of his chin then whistled and exhaled at the same time.

"How long have you got?"

"Forever, if that's what it takes."

He took a chair from my conference table and put it down facing my desk. He exhaled again, sat, and began.

"Call her 'Director Jorg', no umlaut. She'll ask you to use her first name. Don't."

"What's her first name?"

"Unknown. She uses the initials J.K. But assume it's a trap to smoke out distrust for authority."

"Of course."

"'Jorg' could be an Anglicized version of a name impossible for an Anglo tongue to pronounce, or it could be the surname of an ex-husband descended from the quote/unquote Flemish diaspora."

"Which is it?"

"Unknown. She's floated both versions. The director herself is from a small South American country known for its poets and its ancient, violent history."

"The exact country is also unknown I assume," I started to think I'd given Hieronymus too much credit.

"Correct." He moved his chair closer to my desk. "You're aware of the rumors about her?"

My curiosity was piqued. I wasn't expecting to find a rumormonger behind this young man's facade of professionalism. But I didn't want to appear to encourage idle gossip.

"So far I'm hearing nothing but rumors."

"Her background is neurosurgery. Plus, she had a stint on Wall Street. Then one day she shows up out of the blue *sitting in this very office.*"

His shoulders and head leaned halfway across the desk between us now, upon which he tapped his fingers to emphasize each syllable of 'ver-y-off-ice.'

"She was brought on by Director Stan, her predecessor—"

"Ousted due to conflicts, if I recall."

Of course I knew perfectly well what had happened to the previous director, one of those governmental types who chased the spotlight more than was seemly. Director Stan was always publishing articles and opinion pieces about things like "science" and "public health," a practice that didn't sit well with the premier biomedicaltechnology industry group (the rather unimaginative "Association of Biomedicaltechnology Manufacturers," initially shortened to AssBiTech, which had too many syllables and so briefly became AssTech, which created other problems. Eventually they went with AssTec with the "Ass" part pronounced "Az" to give the connotation of ferocity, a connotation in no way inapt). AssTec complained to a powerful senator that the director's obsession with the public health distracted him from their needs and that took care of that.

"You're almost right."

The response was a little cocky.

"Stan made a deal. The senator would accept his resignation without hearings, conditioned on one thing: Director Jorg would succeed him. You can imagine the fun the rumor mill had with that," he said, leaning back and looking at his extremely clean fingernails with a brow arched to telegraph his innuendo, as if I could miss it.

This may be as good a time as any to mention a circumstance that while awkward to acknowledge was impossible to ignore, despite Director Jorg's drab suits worn sometimes under a lab coat (which was eccentric but easily understood as a gesture of solidarity with her scientific staff) and occasionally, such as on the Friday after Thanksgiving and on the Jewish holidays, under a ruana (which was excusable because of her cultural heritage). Not that it is in any way relevant to the woman herself, her accomplishments, or her character. Yet it may in some part explain the unsettling reaction she provoked, equal parts awe and unease, attraction and avoidance; a hard nut of apprehension in the gut fighting the impulse of seduction. In short, Director Jorg was magnificently zaftig, insolently rounded in a way that projected cheeky joie de vivre, a challenge to her sensible gray flannel suits to repress what was fundamentally irrepressible. I deeply regret speaking of someone of the director's achievements in terms of her zaftigness. Believe me, objectification is the furthest thing from my mind. I use the term "zaftig" in the spirit of scrupulous fidelity to consensus opinion. Still, even in the spirit of shared confidence I was enjoying with this canny young man, I wouldn't be drawn into speculation spurred by the director's anomalous allure.

"Trailblazing women are often the subject of speculation

designed to knock them down from the professional heights they achieve by their own wits," I said.

Hieronymus pursed his lips in a way that neither affirmed nor denied my comment.

"The understanding was she'd take over on an acting basis, until they found the right fit. But one by one, every other candidate was compromised. The usual issues: faked medical degrees, bribery, plagiary, employment of sans papiers, ill-considered tweets accusing the opposition party of running pederasty rings, a 'wide stance,' et cetera. So you know what that meant."

He raised his voice as though looking for a response but didn't look up from his fingernails. I left him hanging. As was my prerogative.

"Accession-By-Tribal-Law." He pronounced the words in an exclamative whisper.

This was news to me. Accession-By-Tribal-Law was a succession planning innovation under which any Bureau official serving in an acting capacity for more than five years officially assumed the position, a process long observed as a matter of tribal law but considered so just and efficient that the Bureau had it codified. Unfairly, a cloak of illegitimacy hung over Bureau officials who obtained their posts through the Accession-By-Tribal-Law provision, which explains why I didn't know about Director Jorg: while the appointment of a Bureau director through the usual channels was a front page above-the-fold affair, Accession-By-Tribal-Law happened on the down low; it was treated as an unseemly backdoor to advancement, a black mark against both the process and its beneficiary. It also explained how she came to be known among my former clients as the Common Law Director, an aspersion that seemed more offensive in light of the rumors about Director Stan's interest in her. But those in positions of great authority always have detractors.

"Hm," I sniffed. "Anything else I should know?"

"Her date for the holiday party three years in a row was a fantastic-looking Norwegian woman who worked at IMF." He did something like jazz hands when he said the words "fantastic-looking," which seemed out of character. But he checked himself and settled back down. "Since the year she became permanent director, no date. The skinny is she ended the relationship to avoid scrutiny."

"Surely as a people we've evolved past such petty biases."

"If there's one thing that can kill a career in this town it's association with a globalist."

Hieronymus paused.

"That's all I know."

He exhaled, as though relieved of an unspeakable burden, then nodded towards Director Jorg's office.

"Good thing she's doing her 'of the people' thing."

"Pardon me?"

"She's the keynote at the Meet the Regulators forum, you know, where 'the public' aka the psylocibin-and-Birkenstock set gets to say 'you suck' and alls anyone can say back is 'your perspective is a valuable one.' Ever been?"

"Never."

I stood to signal the conversation had ended.

Shortly after Hieronymus left my office I prepared to leave for the day. I saw the director had left her door open a crack, an infraction under the building security rules. I couldn't resist poking my head in, half-wondering if I'd find a photo on her desk of her ex-husband or this Norwegian woman or who knows, possibly even Director Stan. But the only picture Director Jorg kept on her desk was of a mixed breed dog—one of those mixed breeds where the mixing is between the head of one breed (something shepherd-like with pointy ears, solicitous eyes, and an outsized tongue lolling out over its left jowl) and the body of another breed (something terrier-like with wiry hair and bowed legs, the rear ones skewed out to the right under its rear end, as if to keep the dog from toppling left-wise from the weight of that enormous tongue) instead of a uniform mixing resulting in a head and a body neither of which resembled any particular breed but that seem perfectly congruent with one another.

I pulled her door closed and put my head down, then scurried past my office and Hieronymus's office, the only one in the corridor in which the lights were still on.

The following evening I was back at my desk, staring at the director's closed door diagonally across from mine and ruminating over everything I'd learned about her when I received a call on my office phone the caller ID feature identified only as coming from "unidentified caller." The caller had a heavy accent from somewhere in the North, perhaps Canada, which would suggest it was feigned: Bureau security concerns dictated the most stringent of personnel rules for hiring non-nationals. On the other hand, it could have been an accent from Minnesota given the Bureau's popular exchange program with the biomedicaltechnology industry in that state. The conversation went something like:

"This is —— ——." The blanks aren't to protect anyone's identity. I just couldn't make out what he said. "OIG."

The OIG part was clear, but only because he said each letter emphatically, as though he were spelling a word.

"I've been expecting your call," I said.

OIG's call was the last thing I'd been expecting. Not because I'd left my name off of the slip of paper I'd given

Hieronymus for the suggestion box. I'd included my name, title, room number, email address, phone number, and signature (next to the words "for Director Jorg" as would become my habit), notwithstanding the adviso that all suggestions be submitted anonymously to avoid retaliation. If there was one thing the Bureau would not tolerate it was retaliation, so as a matter of official policy the Bureau avoided situations that could lead to retaliation, even if it meant most suggestions were unactionable because the sort of identifying information needed to follow up on the suggestion had been left off. But retaliation was a concern for staff, not for someone at my level in the organization. The call was unexpected only because I had assumed the OIG would have commenced the investigation without further involvement from me. I was miffed to be quite honest. He asked me what he should do.

"Investigate . . . ?"

" — ?"

Whatever he said next it was a question. That's all I know.

"Surveil their personal email accounts . . . ?" The words slipped off my tongue, even though I hadn't given much thought to how the investigation would be done. It was early in my tenure, and I wasn't yet used to the degree to which others at the Bureau turned to me for guidance and leadership.

"Whose . . . ?" It's possible he said "woo!" After all, my suggestion was provocative. I doubled down.

"The personal email accounts of every known or suspected member of the Cabal. And deploy the Drone Team while you're at it!"

Then I hung up for dramatic effect rather than because I was genuinely annoyed by the question (although I would have been annoyed by "woo!" which would have been overly informal). The OIG caller's confusion was completely reasonable. Among the many confounding circumstances concerning the Cabal of Five was that no one knew how many were in the Cabal of Five, the number five being a hypothesis. The actual number was rumored to significantly exceed five, but no one could rule out the possibility that the number was fewer. A popular theory among Cabal skeptics was that it was a single person, meaning it wasn't even a cabal, which gives you an idea of the depth of skepticism. The upshot was it was difficult to know whom to surveil when there was no knowing how many, much less who, were in the Cabal. On the other hand, it was the OIG who was asking, and it's not too much to ask that the OIG know how to investigate, including hiding-in-plain-sight things like the number of people in the Cabal of Five. I ordered the surveillance in the full expectation that it would reveal a few rogue actors imperiling the good work of a dedicated federal workforce. I planned to tell Director Jorg as much at my first opportunity, which came on the day after my call with OIG (two days after I met Director Jorg) when she wandered into my office looking for a paper clip. Only once again, she threw me off my game.

"So you're one of the CEOs?" Director Jorg asked absently, after I gave her the binder clip off of a stack of ONDABO-BiPs, which was a little loose but did the trick after I inserted the piece of polyethylene foam from the box containing a lapel pin of the new Bureau logo, a gift included with the Bureau orientation package.

"I'm your lead advisor."

"What issues are in your portfolio?"

It sounded like a trick question. I noticed a faint itch around my cranium and a tingling in my nerve endings.

"All of your issues are in my portfolio."

Director Jorg seemed thrown off, as though the beat she expected to be missed was instead right there where it should have been. I hoped to capitalize on the moment by initiating the sort of intimate tête-à-tête that has launched so many enduring professional relationships. But she didn't give me a chance.

"OK. So super-duper to meet you." Here she shook my hand. "Call me by my first name, OK? Maybe we'll speak sometime."

Maybe we'll speak sometime! Only in retrospect is it possible to appreciate the discordance between the life-changing events ushered in by our meeting and the nonchalance of the words marking the occasion.

The next day was a Saturday and I was at home resting after what surely was among the more consequential first weeks on the job in the history of the federal bureaucracy when my phone rang. The area and first three digits indicated a call from the Bureau campus.

"It's me," the caller said. "You know this Sordid guy. The founder with the umlaut."

"The umlaut?" It was as though a phalanx of red ants were crawling up my spine and across my cranium.

"It makes you feel better."

"You must mean the ə."

"Yes. I think so. Anyway, this guy calls me up and he says 'so sorry lady but I have to sue you it's nothing personal also let's meet so you can show me how to do a non-file.'"

"I expected as much."

My ambiguity was intentional. It was true the lawsuit was to be expected. No matter how favorable a leak disclosing the ə's emission of sound waves at a frequency inaudible to humans was to the position of Glottal (and, by extension, Sorel Dern) that the ə existed and was therefore more like a Product than a Non-Product, a principle was at stake. Confidential means confidential and if you can't trust the government to keep your confidences, the word "confidence" has lost all meaning. But besides that, Bureau stakeholders were always suing the Bureau. It was almost a rite of passage. In that light, Sorel Dern was quite right that there was nothing personal about it; the lawsuit could be seen as an affectionate embrace of Glottal's role as a regulated entity. But the meeting request came out of nowhere. It felt intimate and a little bit threatening.

"Then there's this other guy Sakhdvar."

Her flawless pronunciation threw me for a loop. Besides that, the level of intrigue packed into a short phone call had become almost unbearable. It took some effort but I kept my head about me.

"You must mean the senator."

"Yeah. Senator Bigshot-I'm-Gonna-Do-Oversight-On-Your-So-Sad-Ass-If-You-Pervert-Your-Scientists guy.

"I believe the word he used was subvert."

"Let's do this meeting. We'll see what Bigshot has to say about that. You're my advisor, right? So why don't you be there. You can advise me not to tell the kid to scratch himself with a broken bottle like they say, OK? Then when I want to kick myself for not saying it, I'll tell myself it's your fault."

She hung up and to my credit I didn't faint. After all these years, I was being drawn, ineluctably, into Jeremy's orbit. There was no point resisting. If Director Jorg wanted a meeting, there'd be a meeting and I'd be there. It would be the first and one of the last times Director Jorg ever asked me to do anything, not because Director Jorg didn't need things from me. To the contrary, in her way Director Jorg was rather needy, even if no one could say what she needed. That was precisely Director Jorg's problem as a leader. Whether it was Bureau staff, the overseers, or the Cabal of Five, no one could put a finger on where Director Jorg was coming from, and as the saying goes, it's hard to be led somewhere by someone else when no one knows where that person is coming from in the first place. But Director Jorg wasn't one to ask for advice and I wasn't one to offer it, never mind my title. I have too much respect for the autonomy of others to infringe on it with advice. Consequentially, when there was something that needed to be done at the Bureau, I did it for Director Jorg to avoid having to advise her to do it. I soon learned to do everything that needed to be done to keep the Bureau functioning smoothly without ever having to be asked. And though her neediness kept me on my toes, I can't say it was unwelcome. Who among us doesn't welcome the feeling of being needed? I daresay few.

It was because of the unique and successful working relationship built on Director Jorg's neediness and my reluctance to dispense advice, the upshot of which was that Director Jorg never stopped needing me because she never got exactly what she needed, that I can say that I know Director Jorg in ways others do not and cannot, even if we weren't exactly close in the usual sense. There are things about Director Jorg you'd never know from watching her televised testimony. She never looked like herself in that milieu, with her hair more or less orderly and an aura of insouciant professionalism, as though born to assume the role of the highest ranking official in the agency that regulates the Products that touch every American's life, even while being interrogated by hostile congressmen. Those outside the federal workforce might describe this woman as middle-aged and maybe a little frowzy, unaware of the combination of prowess and physicality that asserted themselves in her Bureau environs and that had lit the collective loins of the entire regulatory cognoscenti on fire!

For that matter, Director Jorg doesn't much resemble the picture of her in the lobby of Building 1, where the highest ranks of the Bureau have their offices. Director Jorg's picture was on the far end of four dignified portraits arranged to reflect the chain of command: the President of the United States (when his portrait wasn't down for its monthly cleaning per internal Bureau policy, reflecting the high level of support the President had among the Bureau's policy writers), the Vice President (whose portrait wasn't subject to the procedure and as a consequence was a little dull-looking), Secretary of the Directorate (the portrait of the last permanent Secretary remained up to avoid reminding staff of the uncomfortable situation at the top of the Directorate; namely, that there was no one at the top of the Directorate, even on a tribal law basis), and lastly Director Jorg. The photographer focused on Director Jorg's chin in taking the portrait, so the other parts of her face seemed like the kind of things that end up in a photograph because the photographer couldn't get a good shot of the thing the photographer wanted to focus on without all the other things and planned to Photoshop them out later. The overall impression was one of defiance. Or that she had an underbite. On second thought, the picture was a good likeness in that it was confusing. Otherwise not.

The actual Director Jorg is hard to describe except that she was unlike these other versions of her, or like them only to the extent these versions were also hard to put one's finger on. One might say Director Jorg's zaftigness distinguished her but not if one focused above the neck, which is where all the action was as far as Director Jorg went. In that vicinity, Director Jorg had a quality of averageness that resisted adjectives, but she was never average in the same way. Her eyes changed color depending on what else was nearby, such as the whiteboard or the carpeting. They could be brown or hazel or in between, but they were never deep brown, never bright hazel, never too much in between. Though she was average height, sometimes when I stood next to her I felt oddly short. Other times I had to slouch to avoid an advantage that could be taken for insubordination. To this day, the first thing I think about when I think about Director Jorg is the thing I can't put my finger on. Call it a misalignment or an asymmetry. I can't describe it, but perhaps an anecdote will be illuminating:

On the Sunday following my first week at the Bureau, I went to the discount gourmet deli to get pickled beets, pâté, and rye crisps. The burden of the responsibilities of my new life weighed on me, and I was looking for something comforting. I wasn't used to having the American people with their varied needs and anxieties to worry about. I was leaving with my meal when I saw her, outside the automatic door, rummaging through a grocery cart of specialty day-old breads. It was mid-morning and her hair hovered about her head like a black and gray cloud; a sweatshirt hood hung over the collar of a shaggy magenta coat, which I found incongruent in a way that made me itchy. What was remarkable was that it was the Sunday of the leadership retreat, where all the agency heads within the Directorate were to meet in a hotel to share insights on the topic, Leadership: Tools in the Toolbox. But instead, Director Jorg was outside the discount gourmet deli rummaging through day-old bread.

I thought about approaching Director Jorg to follow up the promising inroads made by our conversation of the day before with a quip about European deli foods. Despite the asymmetry, I'd allowed myself to hope that our relationship could transcend the purely professional. Not that I had romantic aspirations in case anyone's wondering, though Director Jorg's unusual allure wasn't lost on me. The American people have certain expectations of their bureaucrats and I had no intention of letting them down. Besides, I wasn't about to be caught on the wrong side of the Bureau's Best Practice Against Fraternization. So I had in mind only one of those purely platonic relationships one encounters in the workplace that are so concordant and fruitful that everyone assumes there's something going on even if there isn't. (When I say "one encounters in the workplace," I'm including those one encounters in televised dramas about the workplace, but only because my exposure to the conventional workplace was limited to the Firm, where purely platonic relationships weren't part of the culture.)

Despite those hopes, I couldn't approach Director Jorg to say hello. Something repelled me. I mean in a physical sense, like the opposite of a magnetic pull. It was as though Director Jorg's center of gravity had dislocated, so it existed outside her body. I felt unnerved and itchy around my cranium.

I'm not sure the point of the anecdote except it seems to lead back to the thing I can't put my finger on. It characterizes Director Jorg in a way words can't. It's as though the thing she wasn't best describes who she was. In other words, she was an outsider.

THE SIXTH MEMBER

I approached the meeting with Sorel Dern with the serious-
ness it deserved. As in other professional matters, I relied on
my habits from the Firm to guide my actions. If I'd learned
anything at the Firm, it was that the key to successful inter-
actions with leaders of biomedicaltechnology companies
was to feel a sense of connectedness to their biomedicaltechnology. I resolved I'd learn all I could about the Ə in
the time before the meeting took place. Helpfully, this Sorel
Dern had a schedule even more demanding and erratic than
the director's. The meeting took weeks to schedule. In the
interim, I became an expert.

I called Hieronymus from my bed the morning of the second Monday of my Bureau gig to seek his assistance. I asked
for the complete Bureau file on the NPPD; files covering
similar precedents; all regulations and policies pertaining
to the non-filing process; all internal correspondence, press
clips, and Wikipedia pages related to the Ə, Sorel Dern, or
Glottal; and anything else a person might want to see before
meeting with Sorel Dern to discuss non-filing. I thought it
would take him a week but that afternoon, as I was leaving
for the day, Hieronymus appeared in my doorway with several thick binders of materials fastidiously organized behind
color-coded tabs. He dropped the binders on my desk and
pointed with his jaw to the sculpture outside my window,
on which a wiry middle-aged man sat cross-legged, his chin
resting on his clasped hands.

"That's Dr. Hrbek," he said, as if "Dr. Hrbek" should have meant something to me. "Director Stan's *other* advisor."

"I'm supposed to know that?"

Though I was deep on Bureau history, policy, and procedure this was inside baseball and frankly a little below my pay grade.

"He was a shoo-in for director until an operative with industry ties wrote an infamous memo dubbing him 'the Bureau's flamboyantly ethical medico.' He has a rap as (a) brilliant; (b) meticulous; and (c) a pain in the ass."

"Sounds like he would have been a disaster for morale."

"Have a look at his ring finger."

We were five stories up, his left hand was clasping the fingers of his right hand, and both were obscured by his beard. So of course I couldn't see his ring finger.

"He's still wearing his wedding band."

"And?"

"His wife left him for the koi breeder who stocks his pond in Bowie. Two years ago. The speculation is all over the place. Some so obvious that it gives speculation a bad name—e.g., that he misses his wife. Other speculation you can't call that because it's been confirmed by the Drone Team—e.g. the ring is a ruse to throw everyone off his romantic involvement with a Cabal of Five member."

Hieronymus paused then leaned in and whispered in the conspiratorial manner that had begun to endear him to me. "He's a known sympathizer."

"I see," I said, feigning disinterest. But the gears were turning. "Let's make him the medical officer in charge of the re-review of the ә's Non-Product Petition. Have him lead the team in preparing a briefing package for the Director." Meticulousness was just what the task called for. And I assumed any biases in the package due to his so-called sympathies would give us just the amount of rope needed to garotte the unsuspecting fellow, whatever it was he sympathized with. "By the way, what's a sympathizer?"

"There are known members of the Cabal, then there are collaborators and sympathizers. But you know what they say."

"Do I?"

"Everyone is presumed to be the Cabal's sixth member."

Then he left me to my binders.

The ə posed novel but by no means unprecedented challenges to a committed student, foremost of which was that it didn't necessarily exist. I don't mean in the philosophical sense but rather for regulatory purposes. Hieronymus had unearthed the entire Bureau file on ELFDELF, including the petitions I'd filed on behalf of the Firm's unidentified client. It was hard to know what to make of the Bureau's handling of the ELFDELF petitions but one things was clear: no one ever thought for one minute that existential nonexistence closed the book on ELFDELF's regulatory existence, a topic of furious debate to this very day. So existence in the usual sense was neither here nor there. I decided I'd focus on what the ə did.

I began by perusing files on the core features of the ə.

The core features of the ə were already well known and consisted of the standard things one expects from one's technology to facilitate a contemporary lifestyle: camera; video and audio recording; cloud storage; internet; email; messaging; phone; voicemail; step tracking; calorie counting; peak fertility; peak infertility; indices concerning one's body mass, sociopathy, erogenicity, and other indicators of desirability and sociability along with notifications, alarms, and warnings concerning one's body mass, sociopathy, and erogenicity; games; news; gossip; entertainment; emergency alerts—codes yellow, blue, red, and others depending on your country, region, state, municipality, and zip code; heart rate; mood; daily insights; horoscope; tarot card readings; calculation of nondiagnostic propensity for diabetes II, heart disease, Alzheimer's, breast, colon, pancreatic, prostate, and brain cancer, allergic response to pool chemicals, taste for cilantro, Brussels sprouts, and Coca-Cola vs. Pepsi, and similar conditions; personality inventories; sociopathy scores; pulse oximetry; likes and dislikes and notifications, alarms, and warnings concerning proximity to one's likes and dislikes; navigational tools; GPS; surveillance system; locator systems for sex offenders and certain religious minorities; similar information concerning one's neighbors and loved ones; and so forth. These standard features were non-controversial, and while as a regulatory matter each of these features was a Product by virtue of its status as a Potential Product, long before my tenure the Bureau had adopted an official policy to allow such features on the market without Bureau permission. In other words, the Bureau agreed to treat Potential Products with lifestyle-facilitating features as though they were Non-Products, as free as the wind from pesky government intrusion.

The policy was surprisingly controversial. I learned just how controversial one afternoon as I sat with my laptop on The Bureau Insists Reality Matters bench enjoying a break from the stressful grind of my new life by searching the names of past and present colleagues, associates, and lovers. One of the first hits was a news article in which Senator Sakhdvar, again sticking his nose into the Bureau's business, accused the Bureau of abdicating its responsibility to protect the public from "quackery" (his word, not mine). I wasn't sure how I felt about his constant attention to the Bureau. The knowledge that our every action fired across his synapses, provoking a reaction of some sort was titillating. But it was also a little hurtful that he didn't seem to trust us to do our jobs. That afternoon I called Hieronymus into my office, showed him the article, and asked him what he thought.

"I've read he's a monoglot," he commented. At first, this seemed like a bit of preening to me, as Hieronymus claimed fluency in French, German, and Chinese. Then I realized where he was headed.

"You don't say," I said.

He left my office and returned 20 minutes later with a document prepared for my signature (next to the words "for Director Jorg"), an all-hands memorandum directing Bureau staff to refer to the permissive policy for lifestyle facilitating Products only by *Politique De Douce Insouciance* and demonstrating again my assistant's nimble deviousness. Incidentally, in light of the *Politique De Douce Insouciance*, some might ask why the Bureau even kept files on the ə's lifestyle-facilitating features for me to review, as under the policy such features were outside the Bureau's regulatory reach. To which the obvious answer is that the *Politique De Douce Insouciance* exempted lifestyle-facilitating features from regulation. It didn't exempt lifestyle-facilitating features from surveillance. How was anyone to know what was and wasn't regulated unless one surveilled everything?

Had the *Politique De Douce Insouciance* exempted the new feature of the ə from regulation just as it exempted all the standard lifestyle-facilitating features, that would be that, so to speak. The ə would have remained the concern of ə consumers and tech bloggers (along with the Bureau Drone Team, but it was generally accepted that the Drone Team was going to do what the Drone Team wanted to do), and that would have been fine with me. Believe me, I've never been one to court controversy. Nor have I ever run from it. Glottal had developed a new feature, which was different from the core features. The new feature didn't fall under the *Politique De Douce Insouciance* because it claimed to do more than merely enhance one's lifestyle. In short, the ə sponsor, Glottal, proposed to add to the use statement listing the lifestyle-enhancing uses of the ə the clause: "cements feelings of connectedness to oneself and others."

The Cementing Connectedness Clause (as it came to be known) was a problem for the ə. It wasn't just me who didn't understand how the ə cemented connectedness. My absence of understanding was appropriate but irrelevant. I wanted to know everything about the ə. I didn't care whether I understood it. I was an advisor, after all, not an engineer or an MD or any other manner of personnel who owe their employment to understanding things. In fact, I'm not sure how the engineers and the MDs would have responded had I understood how the ə cemented feelings of connectedness to oneself and others. The gulf between our understandings helped us communicate in that each knew where the other stood as far as biomedicaltechnology goes; namely, they generally understood how it worked and I generally didn't. My relationship with the engineering/medical staff was built on this fundamental expectation concerning understanding on their part and the lack of understanding on my part. And because in all things at the Bureau I stood in for Director Jorg, and Director Jorg stood in for the Bureau, it's fair to say the well-being of the entire organization rested on our respective understanding/lack of understanding as far biomedicaltechnology goes. The problem was the engineers didn't understand how the ə cemented feelings of connectedness and so forth, and the engineers understood it better than the medical officer.

"I'm wholly confounded by this vexatious gadget," is how Dr. Hrbek put it when he appeared in the doorway of my office weeks into our effort to schedule a meeting with the elusive Sorel Dern. It was noon sharp on the day that happened to be the day that I had my office hour, which I held at noon so I could have company while I ate. Of course, as often as not I ate my lunch at the cafeteria, for the same reason. Frankly, the whole concept of an office hour seemed to me unduly restraining. Even if I didn't have to get lunch, I didn't necessarily want to be tied to my desk. I preferred to interact with staff on my own terms. On this day I'd gotten in late and hadn't yet left for the cafeteria or anywhere else. So that was how I met Dr. Hrbek, the medical officer, and his first words to me were a rhetorical flourish.

This was my first face-to-face encounter with a reputed Cabaler, or at least someone on the Cabal fringes. I inspected him closely. Dr. Hrbek's facial hair was unruly, as though he were making a proud point of letting his freak flag fly in this one area while observing the usual rules of federal office place decorum in all other ways, from his canvas boat shoes to the short sleeves of his dress shirt hanging loosely just above his elbows. One of his eyes was blue and the other was blue with just a little brown, which didn't make talking to him any easier: one was always shifting one's attention from the brown part of his eye, which seemed trustworthy, to the all-blue eye, which was detached and analytical. He wasn't bad looking incidentally not that it matters.

Putting aside feelings about rhetorical flourishes, it was easy to see why Dr. Hrbek might call the Ə "vexatious" and why he was "confounded," even if he might have used words that were less showy. Believe me, I felt the pathos that lunch hour as Dr. Hrbek, a man who'd made it his life's work to understand relations between biomedicaltechnology products and human beings, told me he was wholly confounded about the Ə, despite the data submitted by the company in files titled "Mechanism of Action," "Bench Data," "Animal Data," and "Clinical Data." It was highly unusual to find such files in a Non-Product Petition, as in its review of such filings the Bureau is looking for a concise statement of the petitioner's argument—more of a zinger than a treatise, the sort of thing that would compel even the most skeptical scientific reviewer to reluctantly mutter Q.E.D.! Data tended to confuse matters. I'd also perused those files, so I knew that despite the wordiness of the submission, the Mechanism of Action file was only a sentence long: *The Ə uses the latest advances in bioengineered neural networks and astrolinguistics to cement feelings of connectedness to oneself and others.*

This left Dr. Hrbek flummoxed.

"There is no validated cementing-to-oneself-and-others scale," he said. "How can you know whether you're cementing connectedness to oneself and others when you can't measure connectedness to oneself and others? As scientists we lack units to quantify it, either before or after exposure to a connectedness-to-oneself-and-others cementing device. At least not in any validated sense."

Before leaving my office, Dr. Hrbek handed me a briefing package with a sticky note affixed to the document on top of the stack, a memorandum signed by him in which he recommended that the Bureau deny permission to file a non-filing petition and uphold the NPPD, retaining the Non-Product status of the ə. His memorandum was concise and scientific, with no emotional content. Each time I read it I found the objectivity off-putting. What mattered was his conclusion and his reasoning to the extent it supported his conclusion, which it did in the usual sense. As I've indicated, the memorandum was scientific and a bit of a snooze. I won't go into the particulars; it boiled down to the following:

1. The Bureau's authority is limited to Products.
2. Products affect the condition of man; things that do not affect the condition of man are Non-Products.
3. The condition of man is one of deviance, measured in symptomatology of disease, suffering, and pestilence.
4. The cementing of connectedness to oneself and others does not relate to deviance, disease, suffering, and pestilence in that anyone can have his or her connectedess to her or himself cemented, including someone who is perfectly healthy.

I can't say I enjoyed reading Dr. Hrbek's memo. There was something controlling about his use of logic, as though he didn't want anyone to arrive at their own conclusions about things. It was not as though I disagreed with points 1-4, per se. Points 1-4 were indisputable. But included in the packet Dr. Hrbek handed me was another more persuasive memorandum that came to a different conclusion. The memo of the Neuro-Psychological Engineering Team (NPET), the team to which the new ə feature had been assigned in consultation with Dr. Hrbek. The memo was divided into sections with the titles "Risks and Benefits (Including Risks And Benefits To Society At Large But Excluding Any Benefit Of

A Speculative, Hypothetical, or Conjectural Nature Such As Purported Benefits To Humanity That Flow From Greater Connectivity)," "A Word on Neural Plasticity," "The Coming Epidemic: Contemporary Theory on Technology-Induced Socio-Cognitive Dissonance," and others. Punctuating each of these subparts were diagrams and equations that presumably supported the existence of issues concerning the risks relative to benefits, effect of the Ə on neural plasticity, and the potential for epidemic levels of dissonance, if not the existence of the Ə. I couldn't make heads nor tails of them, yet was not immune to their impact on some visceral level. In short, the NPET recommendation was in favor of Producting the Ə to retain the Bureau's oversight. Things could get messy when the engineering team disagreed with the lead medical reviewer but, not surprisingly, it resulted in a better read. The memo didn't dispute points 1-4, which were indisputable, but it had passion. Which made it persuasive.

Or at least points 1-3 were indisputable. Point 4 was a matter of opinion, but one so uncontroversial as to be all but indisputable. As for point 3, the most that could be said against it was that it was an overstatement. The NPET memorandum made the strategic decision not to address points 1-4 at all, thus avoiding the traps set by Dr. Hrbek's reliance on logic. In fact, apart from the passion the avoidance of logic was the high point of the NPET memorandum, even if the avoidance was for reasons having nothing to do with whether the Ə was a Product. The reasons of the NPET for not addressing points 1-4 had to do with hypothetical risks, such as a population-wide rewiring of human cognition to reinforce hedonistic behavior without commensurate benefits (apart from the benefit of connectedness, which the NPET review team deemed speculative). In short, the NPET was uninterested in the ho-hum question of the Bureau's legal authority, and addressed its memo to other matters that, it's fair to say, held more human interest.

I should probably mention here that the NPET was a known hotbed for Cabal of Five activity. Their disagreement with Dr. Hrbek may seem counterintuitive considering Dr. Hrbek was a Cabal of Five sympathizer, but there's no reason dissidents can't disagree with one another just because they are all in disagreement with whatever the person or thing is in relation to which they are dissidents, which in the case of the Cabal and its collaborators and sympathizers was of course the Bureau and, by extension, biomedicaltechnology. In fact, the opposite is true; dissidents by their nature are disagreeable and thus as likely to disagree with one another as with everyone else.

To help Director Jorg make sense of these diverging views, I included a brief cover memo with the briefing package prepared by Dr. Hrbek and the NPET. I noted that science was one thing and intuition was another, and any concern she might have about interfering with the integrity of a scientific review decision didn't carry water so long as she based her decision on intuition rather than science. In summary, I wrote, as a matter of science, public health, law, philosophy, public relations, and internal Bureau harmony, there was no clear answer as to whether the ə was a Product or a Non-Product. Were the decision mine to make, I wrote, I'd leave myself open to persuasion and decide, on a whim if need be, at the last possible moment. But of course, I concluded, the decision was hers and hers alone.

I walked in on Director Jorg in my office the week after I'd submitted the briefing package with my cover memo, which happened to be the evening before our meeting with

Sorel Dern. We'd finally scheduled the meeting to coincide with his fortuitous attendance of a Phish concert in the D.C. area. I'd just returned to my desk after taking a call from the rooftop of our building, where I went when I couldn't find a free bench on the campus. I could see most of the buildings from the rooftop, laid out at odd angles amongst landscaped walkways and courtyards, and sites cordoned off for excavation due to irregular performance of Geiger counters in proximate labs. From there I could observe and note the irony in the spectacle of Bureau employees departing and arriving at all hours in their unpretentious vehicles while limousines carried captains of industry and secured vehicles deposited delegations from sister agencies around the globe, all of them here to seek the ears of the humble sedan-driving bureaucrats. Unlike the usual case with irony, which almost by definition is one of incongruity, the VIPs in their status-announcing chariots supplicating themselves before my co-workers, who in their vehicles as in all other ways eschewed status, made me feel strangely apropos. In short, the rooftop gave me a feeling of cohesion that I have to admit was sometimes lacking from my professional life.

It was unusual to find Director Jorg in my office when I returned from the rooftop to collect my things and leave for the day. She was seated at my desk, slumping absently.

"I'd appreciate your point-of-view," she said. "About a thing that makes everyone hot in the collar but might not exist."

It occurred to me at first that she perhaps hadn't read my memo. That seemed unlikely; by that time she'd grown increasingly reliant on my singular talents. I decided instead that even with her facile intellect, the subtlety and inventiveness of my reasoning had thrown her off her guard. Perhaps she sought my calming presence to steady her as she absorbed my analysis, which in its own way was destabilizing.

"This Sorel Dern is a feckless imbecile I think."

Not what I was expecting her to say. But I can't say my research into the ə and its founder contradicted her assessment.

"But if he wants to call this Thon gadget a biomedicaltechnology Product, it's OK by me! As long as I don't have to think about it too much because it makes my brain feel shitty. Can't we just Product it and send him on his way to another Swish concert?"

"It's the ə. Thon is an early gender-neutral pronoun that has fallen into disuse."

"You use it to feel connected, correct? So it's almost the same thing."

I felt I'd met my match. A swelling of pride rose inside of me to be the trusted second to this brilliant and enigmatic woman.

"And it's Phish." One of the hardest things to do when in a position of trust with a superior is to correct him or her, or thon for that matter, when thon or she or he gets something wrong. To eschew this responsibility, however, would be the height of delinquency. I got the correction out of the way so I could get to the rub. "My suggestion to you is that you listen to your heart."

Director Jorg cocked her head, as though considering my extraordinary advice carefully, then stood up and tugged the bottom hem of her lab coat so it straightened over her behind.

"Yeah I think I'm gonna do that," she said. Then she left.

I had no idea what it would mean for the director to follow her heart when it came to the ə. Concerning Producthood, Director Jorg's inclinations were a matter of dispute, though her Product decisions were noteworthy for reliance on extenuating circumstances—the absence of any known purpose, sales at a loss, the lack of mass—that always weighed against a finding of Producthood. It was Director Jorg's questioning of whether something without mass could be a Product that raised the hackles of the Bureau rank and file, who understandably believed the matter had been settled when the Bureau stood up its Division of Massless Products (DoMP). On the other hand, the Bureau never could fill the position of DoMP Director, perhaps because the idea of regulating the massless required an imagination and subtlety of intellect not every bureaucrat can claim. The position was filled on an acting basis by someone who went by V.—apparently a shorthand for the mononym neVin, the cryptic entry that appeared beside DoMP Director in the Bureau directory—who rose to his post via the Accession-by-Tribal-Law provision despite his suspected ties to the Cabal.

As for me, I took no satisfaction in the prospect of disappointing Sorel Dern by telling him his ə wasn't a Product, even if he did seem full of himself. But one doesn't ascend to the highest ranks of the Bureau unless one has a strong stomach for the disappointment of other people. I prepared myself in the days leading up to the meeting by supplementing my research with materials about Mr. Dern personally to see if he was the type of person who took disappointment well. Overall it seemed not, in that he had made a habit of calling his interviewers "tools" and walking off sets when asked about the Bureau petition response, in one case tripping on the mic wire before ripping off the mic and throwing it at a podcast host. On the other hand, surely a man of his worldliness would know better than to resort to such behavior in a meeting with the highest-ranking Bureau officials.

I also came across articles about him that showed his other side, meaning the side other than the one that assaulted journalists. Naturally I was interested in his parentage, but the only thing I found in that regard was an early quote from him claiming not to have parents. That was preposterous, if never disproven. A retired actor from a popular 1970's sitcom who'd made his fortune late in life on a widely-broadcast infomercial for a versatile potato peeler claimed on Twitter to have fathered Dern in a crack den; the mother, he claimed, had died tragically young of an overdose. An alternative theory held that this woman was a small-time scammer who had reinvented herself as the wife of a prominent televangelist, though both the wife and the televangelist strenuously denied it. Dern threatened a multimillion-dollar defamation suit against the potato peeler peddler but he wouldn't relent. A week or so into the public dispute, Dern posted to YouTube footage of the proclaimed paterfamilias in one of those home porn movies from a more innocent time, where everyone kept their dress socks on. This led to a retraction and a public apology, followed by the two of them becoming friends and steadfast supporters of one another in many a social media feud of the sort that dog famous people.

What put Dern in a position where he was around podcast hosts he could assault and lesser luminaries claiming parentage was his quest for contact with extraterrestrial life, the pursuit of which had led to many useful innovations later adapted by the military and makers of smart home appliances. Interestingly, Dern wasn't the petitioner behind the ELF-DELF petition, which had been filed anonymously. In fact, Dern had filed a Comment in Opposition to the ELFDELF petition, as granting the petition would have given the intelligence agencies a leg up on Producting ELFDELF, intelligence agencies being the only ones generally assumed to have ELFDELF in their possession to the extent possession of something not known to exist makes any sense at all. For that reason, it was generally accepted that the intelligence agencies were behind the ELFDELF petition. I gleaned from my preparations for the meeting that ə technology was an outgrowth of Dern's efforts to communicate with life from other planets, an endeavor in which he claimed to have succeeded.

"They speak in clicks of the 'tongue' or their anatomical equivalent, which is hyperextensible," was one of his intriguing quotes on the matter. "They can produce one billion times the distinct phonetic sounds we can, meaning they can say exactly what they mean. Miscommunication is unknown to them. Ditto lack of connectedness. On the other hand, the neutral vowel sound is unachievable for them as a matter of anatomy."

Sadly, he was unable to repeat contact, causing a downward turn in the public perception of him, which had otherwise followed a remarkably unidirectional trajectory, threatening Glottal's bottom line. One tech writer captured Dern's perception issue pithily in an article titled: *Tech Visionary or Fruitcake? Wunderkind's Barmy Claims of Extraterrestrial Contact Spook Investors.* A week or so after that article appeared, Dern made the comment about platforms and everyone forgot about the whole E.T. diversion, thus proving the power of provocative ideas to turn around all manner of troublesome situations.

I had all of this information under my belt when another cache of information about the ə fell into my lap the night before the meeting, after Director Jorg left my office. The evening shift mail clerk delivered the cache to my inbox, bound together with a piece of twine. The twine wrapped around the document lengthwise and widthwise then tied in a bow, which was a nice bit of improvisation. It made the document stack look like a gift from one of those stores where when you ask them to gift wrap something they put whatever it is in twine and brown paper, except there was a pink sticky note on top of the stack that said:

```
To: N--
the results of our surveillance.
                          --from: O.I.G.
```

I raise the cache not because there was anything worthwhile in it about the ə but because it included a nice puttanesca recipe. The puttanesca recipe was tucked in the so-called results of OIG's surveillance, a stack an inch or so high of emails with the names of the senders and recipients crossed out with a black marker. For example, the first document was an email from someone or another to someone or another with a re: line that said "?" There was no text in the email, but there was a handwritten asterisk beside the blacked-out name in the from field and another handwritten asterisk at the bottom of the page followed by: *Membership in the Cabal of Five is a matter of hypothesis and conjecture (and similarly sympathizer and collaborator status). Thus, we have removed identifying information to protect the innocent.*

Most of the emails were similar in nature, so I'm not exaggerating when I say the puttanesca recipe was the most significant thing in there. The puttanesca recipe called for three pounds of peeled tomatoes, but I wasn't going to spend the night before a meeting to decide the fate of groundbreaking biomedicaltechnology peeling tomatoes. Anyway, I'd never peeled a tomato, and the whole endeavor sounded like a classist twist on a wholesome dish of proletarian origins, like using peeled grapes to make a grape, endive, and Roquefort salad. Fortunately, the European deli where I'd once sighted Director Jorg sorting through loaves of bread had puttanesca in a jar. Only the puttanesca in a jar had anchovy paste from real anchovies unlike the puttanesca from the recipe, which proposed using kelp extract, something that purportedly could be found at most "better health food markets and gourmet pantry stockers." The deli also had farfalle and though the recipe called for orecchiette, I thought farfalle was the right choice for a puttanesca, a hearty sauce that could make for an overbearing meal when paired with a chewy orecchiette. Obviously, others may feel differently. Even if I didn't use the recipe to make puttanesca at least the reference to puttanesca inspired me to eat puttanesca and avoid the trap so many busy professionals fall into of neglecting sustenance when workplace expectations most demand strength and focus.

There were a number of other emails from someone or another to someone or another with nothing in the email and a re: line that said something like "Huh?," "When?," "6:30," ":-)," ":-(" "cinq-a-sept …?," and so forth; there were emails forwarding science articles about nematodes and anti-quark, which didn't surprise me; one email forwarded a review of a literary book, which did. I had no idea there was that sort of activity at the Bureau, even among the dissidents. Separated from the others at the back of the stack and affixed with a paperclip to a photograph was an email from Dr. Hrbek, with his name left unmolested except for the handwritten asterisk beside it, referring one to the handwritten asterisk at the bottom of the page followed by: _KNOWN_ *sympathizer.* This email was unlike the other emails, in that it had nothing in the subject line. But it did have a short message:

> We can all agree that what the thing is named
> for exists in that it appears in a number of
> useful words, including decubitis (də'kyo⁻
> obədəs), spumante (spə'mäntē), and, as you
> point out (and here I've been very clear
> that I don't disagree with you), hendiadys
> (hen'dīədəs). We're both sophisticated enough
> to agree are we not that this tells us
> nothing about whether the thing itself exists
> and frankly that you would argue otherwise
> makes me question your good faith, something
> I'd hoped to never have to do but now feel I
> am left with no choice.
>
> --- yours, Les H.
>
> P.S. Our difference of opinion on this
> matter affects my romantic feelings for you
> not in the least (even as I question your
> intellectual honesty). I remain emotionally
> and erotically in your thrall. Please call me.

The attached photo was a black and white aerial shot of a suburban home and what appeared to be a petite black-haired woman exiting the back deck. She was otherwise unidentifiable due to the gratuitous pixilation, which had been applied only to the woman and to the license plate of the original Volkswagen Beetle she was walking toward. The photo was time stamped 5:13 a.m. and the light of early dawn shone across the surface of a koi pond.

As I said, the puttanesca recipe was the most useful thing in the entire stack, although at least the email from Dr. Hrbek reminded me to pick up a sparkling beverage to drink with my puttanesca and farfalle.

THE REVERSAL

I didn't call in to the meeting with Sorel Dern from my preferred bench or from the rooftop. I knew my people skills might be needed to defuse what could be a tense situation and people skills are best deployed in person. I walked in and there was Sorel Dern. He was whistling something.

There were over 30 people in the room, occupying every seat around the conference table and several of the chairs arrayed around the perimeter of the room. The entire NPET team was there at the table in shades of brown and gray and some green and blue, but never blueish green or greenish blue. There was only brownish green and grayish blue. Dr. Hrbek stood with his arms crossed and one foot on the ground and the other against the wall, each planted in its respective location somewhat defiantly. I was tempted to conclude that his deportment was that of someone who'd experienced more than his share of rejection in relationships and had responded by walling himself off from others rather than by examining how his own behavior had contributed to his predicament, but it's possible I was reading too much into the arm crossing and foot placement based on what I'd learned from surveilling his personal email account and home.

The Chief Counsel, a rigidly analytical type, took the seat to the right of the head of the table, which I found presumptuous, but to avoid getting the meeting off to a bad start, I didn't object. Instead I took the seat to the left, across from the Chief Counsel and Sorel Dern. The seat between us was still vacant when a fellow of average height and build walked into the room. He had a peculiar gait and an excessive number of pockets in his pants, all of which closed with Velcro and one of which was hung with a carabiner. His shirt had the dull shine of wicking fibers. That sort of outré outdoorsmanship was out of keeping with Bureau culture and for that reason alone he was conspicuous despite his unremarkable physical qualities. He looked around for a place to sit and, though several seats at the table remained, he took the seat at the head. I cleared my throat and was about to say something, only when he looked at me I forgot what I was going to say. I was expecting to make eye contact to establish a rapport before issuing what might be taken as an admonition concerning his choice of seat. But I couldn't make eye contact in the usual sense because his eyes were darting between the seat he'd been denied and the perimeter of a circle centered on the Chief Counsel's nose. I recognized him immediately as my inscrutable bench mate from my first day at the Bureau.

"This seat is reserved, old chap," the Chief Counsel said. "For Director Jorg."

The strange fellow got up and sat at the other end of the table. Then he took out a piece of paper, wrote something on it, and folded it into a name tent like those in front of panelists at a conference. The tent fell over, the paper not being stiff enough to make a proper name tent, but only after I read "V. (Director of DoMP)" on the front. A young woman with an unruly mane of black hair and a nearsighted squint who was standing behind V., Director of DoMP, kept reaching over his shoulder to set the name tent back up. I recognized this young woman as a member of the communications staff who had approached me after my office hour one afternoon as I was returning from the cafeteria. She'd come to request a detail to my staff. I suggested that she leave me her name and her vitae, then handed her vitae off to Hieronymus, and didn't think about her again before noticing her straightening the name tent of V., Director of DoMP, and, resourcefully in my view, taking what appeared to be a fennel bulb and a Jerusalem artichoke from her backpack and placing the fennel bulb and Jerusalem artichoke under the tent fold so they held it upright. She tapped V., Director of DoMP, on the shoulder excitedly and pointed to the erected name tent then held her hand to her mouth to suppress a giggle.

As for Sorel Dern, I noticed his shirt before I noticed him or even that he was whistling. The shirt was cotton but luminous. Almost iridescent, with the blue reflecting back aqua. The buttons were gray instead of white, which is fine outside of government but unheard of at the Bureau. His hair was sandy-colored and wavy and I suppose that's why he gave me the feeling of being at the beach. It was all a little too much, like the wicking fabric of V., Director of DoMP's shirt. I suppose he couldn't help the hair but the shirt was presumptuous from someone who had come to ask us for something.

Director Jorg was the last person to join the meeting. The Chief Counsel pulled the chair out from the head of the table, but without looking up from rotating her thumb on the joystick of her Blackberry Director Jorg pulled out the chair to the left of me and took a seat, surprising everyone. Neither Sorel Dern nor Director Jorg seemed interested in the other, which made me wonder why we'd gone to all the trouble of scheduling the thing when the two people the meeting of whom was the whole point didn't seem to care whether they met or not. I assumed they were just playing it cool.

"You must be N—," Sorel Dern said as he extended his hand to me. And then:

"I feel like we've met before."

"Sometimes people confuse me with characters in movies," was how I responded.

I didn't give my response any forethought. It just came to me. The response may sound vain but it's a statement of fact. People have commented on it. Not long ago I read a clipping my publicist sent me from a way too long article that used the word "plasticity" to describe the phenomenon, which without the word "neural" in front of it seemed ostentatious. The article was supposedly a review of a book about whistleblowers but was actually more about the author's feelings about whistleblowers. That was typical of this particular publication, which claimed to review books but generally used books as an excuse to talk about whatever the author of the article wanted to talk about in the first place. In my view, anyone who wants to write about topical matters should just write about topical matters and not confuse things by dragging books into it. *The plasticity of her appearance and her affect of nonlinearity telegraph a detached moral locus,* is what the author of the article said about me in what was supposed to be a book review. It was a strange comment for a reputable publication.

Sorel Dern was whistling what sounded like a grunge-influenced cover of "Ain't No Sunshine When She's Gone" by a band from someplace like Stockton that would only play on the late-night broadcast of the college radio station, but it's hard to say. His demeanor was upbeat rather than bereft, which would be incongruous with the song. You'd have to conclude either he was bereft but not showing it, or he was the kind of person who could whistle a song about bereavement without himself being bereft. I.e., a compartmentalizer. More likely he was whistling something else that I can't remember.

It seems to me he stopped whistling just after the note that corresponds to the words "I know" at the end of the sequence of "I know's" more than midway through the song, and that when Director Jorg walked in he'd been repeating the same two notes over and over to correspond to the lyrics I know I know I know I know et cetera. What I remember well is that he stopped abruptly, cocked his head, which made his hair undulate, then looked at Director Jorg and looked at me.

"You must be N—. I feel like we've met before."

"Sometimes people confuse me with characters in movies."

If I repeat myself it's because our introduction went so well, I like to play it over in my mind. Maybe it was because it all seemed so right, and I didn't want to spoil it, that I didn't say anything else for the rest of the meeting.

"I'm a huge fan of the cinema," he said. "We should go some time."

No one had ever asked me to a movie during a Bureau meeting. Like anyone else I've engaged in my share of office flirtations with, for example, superiors, subordinates, members of the public, officials in an oversight capacity, members of the judiciary and their clerks, assistants, the security team, the rangy young man on the mobile scaffold who cleaned my windows twice a year, et cetera; flirtations being an entirely different matter from hook-ups concerning which, as I've alluded to, I avoided even the appearance of since assuming my position at the Bureau. I started to feel differently about Sorel Dern and thought about suggesting something with an NR rating to see how he'd react, but the moment Director Jorg's behind landed in the seat next to mine I felt strangely silenced. Not that I thought Director Jorg would disapprove, exactly, at least not on grounds having anything to do with workplace decorum. The truth is Director Jorg always struck me as a bit of prude, as though she were indifferent to her own inscrutable allure and dismissive of the normal appetites every red-blooded man and woman gives in to at one time or another. Which is just one reason why I never credited the rumor about her relationship with her predecessor.

We proceeded with the introductions, which took a good part of the meeting given the number of attendees and the length of their titles. So I appreciated the Director of DoMP's name tent, which made his introduction highly efficient in that when it was his turn to introduce himself he just pointed at his name tent without so much as looking up. Then the woman next to him who'd been so helpful erecting his name tent introduced herself tersely as "Nym, detailed from the Communications Team." She didn't say to where she was detailed, but I felt reasonably sure it wasn't to my staff.

"What can we do for you?"

Director Jorg had an arm over the back of her chair and was slouching forward on her other arm in a way one rarely sees in women in positions of authority. It was as though she and Sorel Dern were competing for who could be the most casual, only Director Jorg had a lot of ground to make up. She was wearing a gray wool suit, different from the one of the day before and a little snug but equally rumpled, while he was wearing an iridescent cotton shirt. So there really wasn't any competition, even if Director Jorg's suit didn't fit and had a schmutz of something on a pocket flap.

"I feel like total crap about the lawsuit," Sorel Dern blurted out. "I asked counsel 'Do we really have to do this?' and she said 'Yeah, man, we kinda do.' So I was just like, 'That sucks but OK.' As per counsel, that's all I can say about it."

Sorel Dern affected a pouty look.

"It's totally cool," Director Jorg said.

"I knew you'd be understanding," he perked up and looked at her meaningfully but she'd already turned back to her Blackberry. "I'd like to introduce you all to the ə. Midge?"

For the first time I noticed the woman sitting beside Sorel Dern, likely because he had a way of monopolizing one's attention. Midge had the opposite quality. There was a disconnect between her affect, which was outward-looking and sociable, and her hands, which were small and fidgety as though attempting to do something by stealth but lacking the confidence to get away with it. Her turtleneck was more brown than green and her plaid pants were of a somber plaid, not one of those discordant plaids. She was attractive but in a way that deflected notice.

"We miss your good energy," Director Jorg said.

The exchange struck an off-note. I was stuck on the off-note in the way one gets stuck on things one can't put a finger on when a breakthrough unstuck me. I recognized Midge's name as one of The Purged, casualties of the "small crisis" that had precipitated that fateful call to me from the former Deputy Secretary for Operations for the Directorate while I was still at the Firm. Hieronymus had given me the details, as only someone on the inside could, early in my tenure at the Bureau. The Purge was the Cabal's greatest caper, a stealthy coup by which the Cabal would hoist by their own petard Bureau scientists suspected of an industry-friendly bent. The Cabal accomplished its mission by leaking embarrassing internal memoranda by the scientists who would come to be known as The Purged, memoranda supporting the approval of technologies that, once unleashed on the American public, caused suffering and death. The approval memorandum for the Poindexter Pneumatic Arm™ (known popularly as "the Perforator"), in which Midge—a bioengineer who'd risen through Bureau ranks on the strength of her MBA —overruled her staff MDs and PhDs to find that the arm was ALAG (At Least As Good, per the regulatory standard) as a scalpel was widely quoted in the press: *Had humanity allowed a few perforated organs to stand in the way of innovation, we'd have never left the Stone Age,* she wrote.

Midge and her fellow travelers left the Bureau rather than submit to the hearings and investigations triggered by the Cabal's airing of Bureau internal deliberations. So if you ask me, the name "The Purge" was a misnomer: it suggested something coercive, but it referred to something voluntary, like sticking a finger down one's own throat. I had a hard time sympathizing with The Purged even if I generally shared their opposition to the Cabal of Five. The name was a little self-important and not even accurate. Realizing who Midge was sent a warm, unpleasant sensation up my spine, more like a flush than an itch.

Midge smiled and waved at the Director, exacerbating the conflict between her demeanor and her gesticulations in a way that was jarring. It took me a moment to focus on her presentation, even after someone dimmed the lights and Midge did something awkward with her thumb to project the first slide.

The first slide was a white field. One of the best decisions I made as Special-Advisor-in-Residence-to-the-Director was to replace the four small flat screens in the Directors' conference room with a single enormous flat screen that faced the head of the conference table. It guaranteed presentations would make a splash if for no other reason than that they would be very large. Midge's presentation was no exception.

At first all we were looking at was 150 inches of white. Not the white of a piece of paper or a white rabbit. The white of a screen. Gray veins began to separate the white so the white became big soft clouds. Piano-y music began to play. The clouds parted and became wispy and waterless as little black flecks gathered in the shape of a crop circle in the form of an upside down "e". It was a nice effect, but hard to appreciate fully because of the rapid-fire thumb gestures necessary to make the clouds appear, part, and vaporize and then to make coil-like things assemble from pixels. I would have liked Midge to put the control and her thumb with it under the table to lessen the distraction, but I wasn't sure whether the signal would penetrate the wood. At least wondering about the signal distracted me from the thumbs, until the coil disintegrated and italicized words appeared and broke up:

HARNESSING NEURAL-NETWORK LEARNING AND ASTROLINGUISTICS TO PROBE THE MYSTERIES OF THE HUMAN CONDITION AND DELIVER PERSONALIZED INTERCONNECTEDNESS SOLUTIONS

The whole thing ended with another crop-circle type thing, but it was a monster. It took up the entire screen height and a good bit of the 150 inches across. Looking over the engineers, and doctors, the legal, regulatory and communications staff, the leadership, and the worker bees, I could see many were moved. I glanced over casually at the Director of DoMP and saw his fingers were steepled in front of his name tent and he looked as though he wanted to roll his eyes but rolling his eyes was like herding cats, though I knew from experience that it was within his repertoire. The members of the NPET seemed twitchy and furtive, uncrossing and crossing their legs (those who were sitting) and shifting their weight from foot to foot (those who were standing) and, I noticed, shooting glances at the Director of DoMP (those sitting and those standing). On the other hand, Dr. Hrbek's brows met over his nose as though seeking consolation in one another, and Nym was squatting awkwardly beside the Director of DoMP, her shoulder touching his. So at least there was some meeting that was going on, even if it was just things like eyebrows and shoulders. Director Jorg was the only one who wasn't paying attention. She looked up at most once or twice as she fiddled with the button on her Blackberry.

Someone flipped on the lights and as our eyes adjusted, Midge reached down and produced a small box. She took out one of those sport watches that people use to track their steps or remind them when to pop a propofol or whatever. I have no idea what anyone uses them for; my tastes run to haute couture. As though reading my mind, Sorel Dern interjected:

"You can use the connectedness feature on most smart-watches. But we're configuring the ə for use on phones, ear pods, and intimate personal devices. Remember, platform is irrelevant. I'd like to demonstrate."

Midge passed the watch to Nym, who had moved in to get a closer look.

"You mean we're human subjects?" Nym asked.

All eyes turned to Director Jorg.

"No problem as long as everyone says 'sure, no problem, OK, I'll do it—'" Director Jorg began, shrugging to indicate it wasn't for her to interfere in the decisions of consenting adults to be a part of human experimentation any more than in the boudoir.

"It would be better if you just told us about it," the Chief Counsel interjected.

"Too bad. I think it would bring us all closer together," Sorel Dern said. He took the watch from Midge and put it on his own wrist. "I would never proceed without consent. At least not my own."

Sorel Dern smiled out of one corner of his mouth as though pleased, but the joke fell flat. If you were going to try to win over Bureau hearts and minds with humor, the humor had better comport with certain standards. It occurred to me that the comment supported the Director's feckless imbecile assessment but I resisted jumping to any conclusions. Sorel Dern's awkward attempt at humor seemed to me the predictable consequence of Bureau processes, in their somberness and maturity, thwarting the usual outlets for his youthful energy, so when they found expression, it was unsurprising that they were a little twisted. I found his resolve to plunge ahead, unaware of the oceanic depth of Bureau protocol courageous and oddly affecting. Who was I to judge if it produced the occasional malapropism?

"The ə communicates with a sensor that calibrates to galvanic skin response, activating euphonics at an astro-frequency imperceptible to human ears."

"What about my dog. Can he hear it?" I assumed Director Jorg was being irreverent.

"We're still analyzing our canine data," Midge responded before anyone else could say anything.

For a moment, everyone stared at Sorel Dern in silence as he sat with his wrists crossed on the table and his eyes closed. After perhaps a minute he opened his eyes. They were a little moist. He removed the watch from his wrist and put it away in continued silence.

I can't deny that I was moved, despite my professional obligation to remain objective. But I'm only human. Though I wasn't the one wearing the watch, I experienced a level of intimacy that usually kicks in only during that special kind of closeness, generally a one-to-one proposition, but what I felt was more like a group merging, something communal. Not surprisingly the feeling of connectedness was followed by a little surge of excitement.

"This is the first I've heard about astrolinguistics and probing," Dr. Hrbek muttered.

"I doubt it's the first," Sorel Dern said, having apparently recovered himself. Malapropisms were one thing, but innuendo about a member of the scientific team was borderline blasphemy. The comment was like his shirt, but harder to explain away as a matter of cultural differences. Being from California didn't absolve one of basic courtesy.

"I mean in relation to your Non-Product."

The words were cutting. The familiar negative associations I had with Dr. Hrbek began to surface. Midge intervened.

"We didn't mean 'probe' in a literal sense."

"So you guys probe stuff figuratively?" Nym rejoindered.

It's no exaggeration to say that every person in the room looked over at Nym, more than one with mouths agape.

Nym bent her neck so her hair covered her face. She moved back toward the Director of DoMP.

"I want to non-file." Sorel Dern broke the uncomfortable silence, pivoting to Director Jorg as he spoke.

"You have to file a non-filing petition," Director Jorg said, suppressing a yawn as she spoke. Director Jorg's statement struck a note of tension. Having to file a non-filing to undo the initial filing of the Non-Product Petition seemed like an overreach. It went beyond the snake eating its own tail and in a different direction from the snake eating its own tail then vomiting it up. It was like the snake regurgitating its tail, then eating it again even though it already knew it couldn't hold it down. It was a little greedy. Yet, I felt defensive. I was about to say something when the Chief Counsel chimed in.

"It's strictly pro forma," he said.

Those were exactly the words I was about to say, but now I didn't have to.

"Although there are requirements in the Code as to content and format. For example, you have to be granted permission to non-file, and you have to have grounds," he continued.

"But we'll waive them," Director Jorg said in a manner that was still sleepy, but definitive.

Director Jorg was showing a side I hadn't seen before: helpful, even as she was being irreverent.

"Why can't you waive the non-filing petition?"

"You need the petition to return you to a state of Potential Producthood," the Chief Counsel explained, also helpfully but without the irreverence so the net effect was a little pedantic. "As of now the ə doesn't exist for us."

While true, the conclusion struck me as gratuitous. My

feelings were on a rollercoaster, rollicking between the competing demands of public-spiritedness and bureaucratic formality.

Sorel Dern scratched the back of his head. He unfolded the keyboard and stand of a small tablet and began to type, concluding with a dramatic stroke of his index finger.

"I just e-non-filed," he said.

The Chief Counsel cleared his throat. An email notification appeared on the screen of my tablet, accompanied by a pleasant ping sound. I could never remember to turn the sounds off on my devices in meetings but in this case I was glad I hadn't. I was flattered that he had filed the non-filing petition with me but maintained an appearance of objectivity. I simply opened the email and forwarded it to Hieronymus to print with a cover email directing him to bring it to us in the Director's conference room ASAP, which he did cheerily even if the task was beneath his station. He entered the conference room, carefully minimizing any disturbance by softly closing the door behind him, handed me the piece of paper, then shot his eyes discreetly from Dern to me and back. He was wearing a suit and a bowtie, as though he had dressed for the occasion. On his way out he held his hand to his chest.

In its entirety, the Petition read as follows:

I am petitioning the Bureau of Biomedicaltechnology (BoB) to non-file the Non-Product Petition for the Schwa, a product to improve the human condition.
Sincerely, Sorel Dern, CEO and founder, Glottal

Director Jorg looked over the petition, then grabbed one of the stamps from the tray in the center of the conference table, adjusted the date and time dials, and stamped the word "GRANTED," followed by the date and time across the top of it. She inked her initials beside the stamp.

"By the way, it's the Bureau," she said.

"A petition can't be granted until it's been officially received, i.e. the Bureau has to file a petition before it can be granted," the Chief Counsel noted. Pedantic, but he had a point.

By this time, I was overtaken by the spirit of the meeting, the helpfulness and the sense of common purpose, even if it wasn't common to everyone. I could feel the undercurrent of dissent from the DoMP Director and the engineers and Dr. Hrbek: even if they didn't all disagree with the outcome per se, the outcome gave Sorel Dern what he asked for, and not giving others what they ask for is almost the defining trait of a dissident. Yet rather than undermine the feeling of commonality, the dissent affirmed it. Without the dissent reminding us of the dissidents, the rest of us might not have even noticed the feeling of commonality among everyone who wasn't one of the dissidents. In short, the dissenters gave off a bad vibe, which drove everyone else in the opposite direction.

I can't say what caused me to do what I did next. It would be easy to say I was moved by the feeling of commonality. No doubt that played a part, but there was more to it: I sensed that I stood at the threshold of a new day that would ineluctably unfurl, but according to its own logic and timeline, a reversal of fortunes not only for the ə but I daresay for all humanity. I slid the petition and Director Jorg's pen away from her and grabbed a different stamp from the tray, adjusted its dials, then stamped to the right of the word "GRANTED" the word "FILED," followed by the date and time, which was one minute later than the time of the GRANTED stamp. Then I signed my name followed by "by Director Jorg," as was my habit.

And while in most cases, filing is to granting what being alive is to death, a necessary but insufficient condition precedent, it's a little different when granting has already occurred, and the sole outstanding condition precedent necessary to legitimate granting is filing. Under those circumstances you'd have to say cause and effect are pretty tightly bound. Although it's strange to think of something being caused by something that hasn't happened yet.

Following an unusually satisfying sleep, I woke up late the day after the meeting to a feeling of nervous excitement. I showered, dressed, finished the leftover puttanesca (but with gnocchi; the farfalle was done) and made it to my desk during my office hour. I felt better about my desk after the meeting. The officiousness seemed benign, even warranted. After all, it was in an office. I might have sat at it even if I weren't expecting a visit from a Cabal of Five or at least a collaborator or sympathizer. It seemed certain one of them would have a grievance to press with me following the ə meeting, even if the outcome of putting the ə back under the Bureau's thumb was what most of those troublemakers wanted. As I've said, there is a reason they call dissidents dissidents and it's not because they're easygoing.

Which explains why whenever by accident I was present for my office hours, the occasional visitor was always someone who in one way or another fit the bill of a sixth member. They came to talk about things like the Bureau's scientific denialism, or its incrementalist apologism, or corporatist consortship. It was always something that was a noun with a suffix added to it that didn't make it not a noun but made it more loaded. It is a measure of the commitment to my work that I decided on the day after participating in the controversial decisions to file and grant (not in that order) the non-filing petition for the ə that I would remain in my office for the duration of my office hour precisely because I expected a dissident to show up aggrieved about an action

I'd made possible, even if I'd made it possible only after it had happened. So it was a little strange to sit at my desk alone for most of the hour with no visits.

I'd done what I could as far as my responsibility to the public. I was getting up from my desk to go to the roof or to one of the benches when I caught sight of one of two people in the entire Bureau never accused of being a sixth member, believe me. Director Jorg passed my doorway on the way to her office, then stopped. She stopped for a long time, still faced in the direction of her door, which was precisely the sort of thing that ordinarily would cause my cranium to itch and my nerve endings to fire. Instead I sat back down and waited to see what she'd do. Then she turned and did the last thing I expected her to do, particularly during my office hour: she entered my office and approached my desk.

Now that I think about it, the lack of itching might have been because I was distracted by other things, such as the tingle of nervous excitement I continued to feel for one and Director Jorg's smell for two. Something wafted over me as she stood in my doorway, something loamy. My olfactory sense is highly developed. It is perhaps then unsurprising that few scenes in contemporary cinema have affected me as deeply as the one where the infamous cannibal inhales deeply from inside his prison cell and assures the detective that he can't smell her vagina, no matter the crude comment of the criminal in the adjacent cell. It's small acts of decency like this one that bridge the gulf separating people from one another.

My point is that smell makes me feel connected to things, just as smell connected the cannibal to the detective, though in their case the connection was because of the absence of a smell that might have embarrassed her. Similarly, it was only when I noticed Director Jorg's smell that what I would have thought impossible started to happen; that is, I started to feel connected to Director Jorg. I suppose the unexpected connectedness got my tongue, or maybe it was the tingly feeling that had spread from my gut to the nerve endings over the entire surface of my body. Whatever it was, I couldn't speak.

"This teenybopper Derp guy was blowing smoke at us out of his rectum yesterday, would you agree?" I admired her effort to embrace the idiom of her second tongue, even if I couldn't condone her negativity. "Now the 'period period period'"—here Director Jorg made air quotes around 'period period period'—"is our problem."

"You mean the Ə."

"It's a good lesson for the American people not to trust their faceless bureaucrats. Want to celebrate?"

There was a warmth and a depth to the loam smell, like friendship itself. The warm tingle climbed up my spine. It was as though I had to smell Director Jorg to open my heart to her.

"I'm free later."

"Ah, maybe tomorrow," she said after a pungent pause. Then she turned and left me. I was relieved to see that by then my office hour had ended in the sense that it was one hour after the beginning of my office hour as opposed to in the sense that I had decided to quit waiting for someone to make good use of my availability, a commodity that was in high demand and of limited supply. Not that the standard for "ending" matters all that much, such things being notoriously subjective. But not everyone sees things that way, and the Cabal of Five, including its sympathizers and collaborators, could be sticklers for rules. So while I was prepared to take advantage of the prerogative of anyone who keeps an

. . .

office hour to say when the office hour ended, I was relieved nonetheless to see it had ended even if one takes one hour equals sixty minutes as a rule rather than a guideline. Anyway, it was at the end of the hour in the overly literal sense of the word that my phone rang.

"Hello. This is OIG."

It was a different voice this time—female, winsome.

"I've been expecting your call."

This time I meant it. I had a few things to say. I'd asked for surveillance, not the lovelorn semantic and metaphysical woolgathering of a mid-level bureaucrat the object of whose affection wasn't even revealed by the fruits of the so-called surveillance. And certainly not a puttanesca recipe, no matter how helpful the recipe's insinuation into my consciousness of the idea of puttanesca ended up being. Now that the non-filing had freed Glottal to submit a Product application, there was a real risk that whoever from the Cabal was responsible for the other leaks would leak whatever proprietary information it contained. The occasional leak was one thing. If anything it was a morale booster, in that the risk-taking and illegality involved in leaking Bureau secrets made the work of the Bureau seem important and a little risqué. One doesn't mind being caught with one's pants down when what one has under one's pants is a marvel. But a pattern of leaks was a different story. The aura of risqué-ness becomes one of disorganization, which for an organization is a special kind of failure.

"We'd like to meet with you."

She was using some sort of voice distortion technology, but nothing sophisticated. Something like a shirt sleeve over the receiver but made from one of those technical fleeces with weather repellant qualities that squeak.

"I'll decide when and if a meeting is necessary after you send me your stack without the redactions. And extend the surveillance to personal cell phones."

For a moment there was silence, followed by the squeaking noise of synthetic fibers rubbing against each other. Then there was something that sounded like muffled conversation that went on for a long time. I thought I heard her say, *just pour the hot water over the couscous instead of boiling them*, but who knows.

"We feel a face-to-face meeting is necessary —" additional muffled conversation followed "—to establish a meeting of the minds."

"You'll have to work with one of my assistants. I hold unscheduled meetings during my office—"

"Meet us in the meditation/lactation lounge in Building 32, at midnight." Then she hung up.

Like any forward-looking arm of government, the Bureau had meditation and lactation lounges in every campus building, except Building 32. Building 32 was one of the sites of irregular Geiger counter activity, but perhaps because mostly biologists had their offices there, they were more vocal than others had been in demanding action. They requested special dispensation to house both activities in a single lounge so the Building could house a detoxification center in the other lounge. After the request was leaked, certain Members of Congress suggested Building 32 staff should just tough it out but I never entertained such a callous suggestion. I approved the request the same day I read it, which was only a few months after it had been submitted but not before a group of self-starters had set up a colonics kiosk in the meditation lounge. I was about to point out to OIG that there was no vending machine in Building 32 due to a local ordinance prohibiting food sales in any colonics facility. I was getting the vibe that this would be the sort of meeting where one might need a break to get something to eat and restore one's energy. But OIG hung up.

Undeterred, I stocked up on cheese crackers with peanut butter and chocolate-coated wafers from the vending machine in the lobby of Building 1 to prepare for the visit to Building 32, then took a nap at my desk, its officiousness having a lulling effect after long exposure. I awoke feeling invigorated and not the least daunted by the walk to Building 32, a distance that all but the most fitness-oriented Bureau workers generally traversed taking two shuttles or a motorized scooter from one of the scooter stands that had been funded by an excess in Fees for Regulatory Service (FFRS). The scooters thus bore the AssTec (pronounced *az-tek*, I feel I should repeat) logo, prompting certain of the most dedicated scooter-riders, most of whom were rumored Cabal sympathizers and collaborators, to pack electrical tape to block the logo for the duration of their rides.

I arrived at Building 32 early, so I sat down on one of the mats in the meditation area of the lactation/meditation lounge and ate the first cracker from the package of the cheese crackers with peanut butter. I chewed slowly to give myself something to do, as there is little to do in the meditation/lactation lounge for someone who is neither lactating or meditating. By the twelfth cracker I was getting a little annoyed, especially as I realized I had no more crackers left should the meeting be the sort of meeting where one needs to restore one's energy, and might have to move on to the chocolate wafers before the meeting had even begun. On the other hand, I felt I had reserves of energy from the nap and the 12 crackers.

"It's me."

Dr. Hrbek walked toward me from the lactation side of the lounge.

"You must be in the wrong building."

"OIG sent me."

"Why should I believe you?"

"I mean Nym."

"OIG or Nym?"

"OIG is Nym."

"Nym is Communications."

"On detail to OIG."

"Details are approved by me."

"Per the personnel rules, approval of details is delegable."

I had no answer for that. It was irksome for a medical type to be up on his regulations. He stared at me in a way that seemed out of line and confrontational given our respective roles in the organization. I'm not one to take offense at small acts of rebellion against authority figures such as myself, but any management consultant worth his or her salt will tell you one only encourages such behavior by backing down when confronted by it. At the same time, I wanted to avoid the brown part of his right pupil, as I didn't want a false sense of security to lure me into becoming an unwitting agent of whatever subversive scheme had brought him to Building 32. Unfortunately, the brown part was on the left side of his right pupil, making it hard to avoid: it was right of in the middle of things. I settled on the spot between his eyebrows.

"Not only OIG, but Cabal."

The conversation, which had been irritating and bordering on the insubordinate, had taken a turn for the absurd. Everyone understood that the Cabal was for so-called scien-

. . .

tists. Nym was in communications. Ergo.

"A collaborator at best," was all I said. To have shown surprise might have been taken for weakness. His eyebrows moved away from one another and upwards.

"Actually, the Second Member." Then his eyebrows relaxed smugly. I'd had enough.

"Why would someone who is the Second Member of the Cabal, on detail to OIG, arrange a meeting with someone in the highest levels of Bureau hierarchy then send a sympathizer to expose a subterfuge that was no doubt highly advantageous to Cabal activities?" Perhaps I was uncharacteristically strident. But if there's one thing I expected from Dr. Hrbek, it was logic.

"Tense. She WAS the Second Member. The First Member discharged her. For what it's worth, first he dumped her (her words, I wouldn't be so callous in speaking of someone else's relationship, even a manifestly unhealthy one that I also opposed for personal reasons.) Then he discharged her for being untrustworthy. It turns out an interest in fiction is incompatible with a commitment to truth. Surely he must have known she was literary when he made her the Second Member, but wasn't paying attention to how deeply it runs with her, something I understood the first night we spent together, when I read to her from Goethe—"

"If you continue, I'll have to report a violation of the Best Practice Against Fraternization," I interjected. I wasn't being heartless. Just professional.

"I didn't mean to speak about the emotional subtext to this meeting. Nym's bereft and turned to me. She may or may not want you to know that her lover planned to have her draw you into a conversation revealing the Bureau's malfeasance, then share the recording with our overseers.

He sabotaged his own plans by insinuating there was an off-flavor to something she made him for dinner which, as she noted, was just cardamom, but as so often happens in relationships a little thing can bring to a head long-running undercurrents of intellectual, temperamental, and perhaps sensual disharmony that left unchecked simmer between intimates, then percolate and in time erupt into—"

"Share?"

"With the Subcommittee on Biomedicaltechnology." Dr. Hrbek looked at me knowingly. But perhaps I read too much into his look. I found my eyes drawn involuntarily to the brown striation in his right pupil and looked away. "V.'s following extends to an uncatalogued underground network of dissenters."

"V.?"

"His nystagmus is idiopathic and possibly hysterical in my view." I was reminded that Dr. Hrbek was trained as a neuropathologist but resisted questioning his qualifications to diagnose a disorder of the eye. "Before you object, I can assure you I would never use the term concerning a female patient."

"V.'s the First Member?"

I already harbored an unwholesome fascination with Dr. Hrbek's relationship with Nym. The revelation of a love triangle with Nym at the apex and Dr. Hrbek and V. at opposing corners left me stunned and confounded. That a person like Nym, awkward but oddly fetching, would have intimate relations not only with Dr. Hrbek but also with V. was difficult to process. The only obvious commonalities between the two of them were dissidence and that they were both hard to look in the eye due to pigment irregularities (in the case of Dr. Hrbek) and hypermobility (in the case of V.). I

. . .

started to think perhaps this Nym was one of those women who seek out men whose personal traits frustrate connectedness out of her own buried fears of intimacy, a conclusion on its face hard to jibe with her apparently indiscriminate pursuit of intimacy. But as any popular women's magazine will tell you, in fact completely consistent, as the buried fear of a thing so often leads to the brazen pursuit of that very thing to put to rest that fear through overexposure.

Dr. Hrbek only nodded with his eyes half-closed, as though patiently confirming the obvious to a simpleton.

"He has a line to a certain senator."

The nervousness and titillation spread to every extremity and over my skull. Had I been a graffito, my head would have been depicted exploding, possibly with small appliances flying out of it. I remembered my feeling from the day of the meeting that I'd lit a long fuse that, when the spark finally reached its end, would detonate loudly enough for the world to hear.

"And I assume you mean the presidential candidate and United States Senator Jeremy Sakhdvar."

It was a risky move, but I decided to be direct to smoke out whether he knew anything.

"The darkly sensual one. For whom V. will never do anything. If there's one thing he distrusts more than fiction, it's sensuality." I had to give Dr. Hrbek props for acknowledging the appeal of another man, something one doesn't encounter every day in your garden variety heterosexual male. I adjusted my gaze slightly downward from his brow to meet his eyes again, steeling myself for the brown part. They were a little moist. "Would you consider speaking to Nym on my behalf? She speaks highly of you."

"Such as?"

Dr. Hrbek hesitated for a moment.

"She likes your memos to staff. She used the word 'Gogolian,' though she's not actually a Slavicist. I didn't probe—er—press her on it. She's a little thin-skinned about credentials. She was this close to defending her dissertation–on the portrayal of vegetarians in literature–when her advisor broke things off and she left to complete an online course in communications. The combination of intellect and self-immolating tendencies is among her most maddeningly beguiling traits."

I could see that I'd learn nothing else useful from Dr. Hrbek. At the risk of sounding superficial, I had to question the emotional intelligence of someone whose lover left him for a humorless ascetic in wicking fibers.

"I won't give you a third warning," was all I said.

"Of course. Can I give you a ride to HQ on the back of my scooter?"

"No, thank you, I'll walk."

The charge of energy that had begun in the morning as a flicker then surged like an electrical fire over the course of the day had exhausted me. But I needed time to myself. I took the long way back through the little worn system of secondary pathways hidden by shrubbery that ran between buildings in a network known only to a select group of Bureau leaders for use in the event a disaster rendered the primary pathways unsafe. No one could think of a disaster that would jeopardize the primary pathways and leave the secondary pathways intact, leading to the common assumption that the secondary pathway, obscured as it was by dense foliage, was a hedge against the Drone Team, whose funding through FFRS led many to suspect its allegiances. By the time I got back to my office it was almost light out.

. . .

I tried to sleep but had too much to think about, never mind the lulling effect of my desk's officiousness. I tried to think about what I would say to Director Jorg about the events of the night before, but when I imagined sitting across from her, perhaps twirling a swizzle stick in a prosecco and kir presented with a cross section of starfruit floating atop as she knocked back shots of ouzo (I knew nothing about Director Jorg's drinking habits but this seemed plausible), I drew a blank. I'd never gotten around to mentioning the surveillance of the Cabal to Director Jorg, an oversight that was the unavoidable upshot of the Director's unsettling effect on others, however unwitting. Telling her now that I'd inadvertently suggested a clandestine surveillance of the Cabal to a Cabal deputy on detail to the OIG seemed like it would only cast a shadow on what was otherwise a time for savoring our triumph, even if the nature of our triumph was, according to her, in confirming the American people's worst suspicions about faceless bureaucrats. I feared it could derail our blossoming friendship. But I didn't know what else we would talk about. Hence the blank.

I didn't know what to make of the blank. It wasn't like one of those blanks onto which one can project whatever one wants. It was a fulsome blank, like a computer screen radiating bright pixels. Thinking about the blank wasn't altogether pleasant, even if it was better than thinking about what to say to Director Jorg. I decided to do my hair. I thought about the attributes of nonlinearity and plasticity and decided it was past time I embraced them. So I did my hair in way that appeared undone, like something out of retro erotica, a refreshing counterpoint to my otherwise career-forward presentation. I thought, perhaps, Director Jorg would comment with an observation just decipherable enough to pass for a compliment, then she and I would bond as so many other professional women have over shared tips for passing in a male-led workplace without ever sacrificing one's identity as a woman. I was winding a messy chignon around the top of my head as the workday drew down when someone appeared in the doorway of my office.

"Not everyone is happy about how things went at the meeting."

The point was obvious if the negativity was roundabout. It should go without saying it wasn't Director Jorg, who was direct with her negativity. I dropped the chignon and tried to think of something to say. The scoop that not everyone was happy was less surprising than most things. In fact, it wasn't even as surprising as that the visit I'd been expecting during my office hour took place outside my office hour, more than a day later. The person who appeared in my doorway was V., by the way.

"Speaking as someone who prefers to blow the whistle on atrocities that exist, I personally think it went well," he continued.

"Perhaps 'atrocities' is a little over the top," I suggested. A short silence ensued, during which the weight of my comment landed and I congratulated myself for putting V. on his heels. Even one given to overstatement can hardly defend an analogy between the ə and war crimes. Or so I thought.

"The problem with you is that you've been desensitized to your own commodification like a crab crawling along the bottom of a pot not even knowing when the flame's been lit, its lifeforce bubbling to the surface, blup, blup, blup, vaporized and snorted up by our malfeasant tech overlords who use it to create a more docile liege, a better consumer, a more debased receptacle of manufactured wants meander-

. . .

ing down every blind digital alley, thinking the next click-bait you click on is going to restore the humanity you left lying on the ground like a used rubber in a data sewer. We're Onans of our own humanity–"

"I think you mean a frog." His imagery was getting out of hand. We were in the workplace, after all. Nonetheless, his volubility opened a small crack in the Cabal's impermeable fortress of secrecy. I sought to exploit it. "Anyway, I didn't know the Cabal endgame was a masturbation ban."

The eyebrow over his right eye tried to knit but the left one wouldn't budge, as though each were taking a different cue from his eyeballs, which flit in unison from the middle of my face to somewhere behind my head. His eyes rolled upwards, as they had the day of our first meeting on the stone bench, while still flitting. The flits were at a diagonal, the journey upward a series of hairpin turns instead of a leisurely roll. The effect was a little flirtatious, as though at the break of each upward interval his pupils paused for a moment to make sure I was still with them, to wave me along. For a moment it occurred to me that I had seen a glimpse of what the unfathomable detailee Nym saw in this otherwise rather severe fellow and just as I was pondering this unexpected revelation, something more remarkable still happened: V. leaned in, placed his palms on the far side of my desk with his fingers spread and he made eye contact with me. With both of my eyes. At the same time. He leaned in closer still, his eyes locked on mine as though heeding an unspoken dare so I couldn't possibly look away. When he spoke it was in a hoarse whisper.

"Tell me, when it's gone, will you notice? Will you even miss it?"

What happened next was so improbable, so astounding, to

this day I struggle to believe my own memory. Yet the image is etched there as decisively as the letters on the bench where I first encountered this singular man. In short, beneath his protuberant and now preternaturally immobile gray pupils, fluid pooled, welled just to the brink of brimming over. First, a whiff of attraction; now, an appeal to our shared humanity. I wasn't prepared to have an emotional connection to my professional nemesis. I had to think quickly.

"I think we'd all be at sixes and sevens if masturbation was completely off the table."

Immediately the tears receded and his pupils wandered furiously from my face to the blank white board behind my head to somewhere outside my window (possibly the sculpture) as he erected himself. When he spoke again his voice was steely.

"You'll know our endgame when it becomes your new reality."

"I applaud your ambition. Maybe you really are part of a global underground network of anti-consumer-slash-capitalist-slash-patriarchy malcontent agitators to the extent anything can 'really' be something that doesn't exist but what do I know."

"N'Aut exists the way the ə exists. Proof of its existence is in the suffering it causes. At least one of them targets the right people." Before I could respond I was distracted by something earthy. Some may say it's implausible that in the instant Director Jorg flitted past my doorway from her office, closed her office door, then flitted away—all of which I observed behind V.'s shoulder—she could have imparted her loamy essence. I'm not contesting the implausibility. I'm just telling you what I smelled.

V. glanced over his shoulder, then straightened himself

out again. I noticed that his posture was outstanding and perhaps it was my new awareness of his unusual appeal that insinuated a strange thought into my mind, though I think it was something deeper, and having to do with his undeniable passion: I found myself wondering for only a brief moment, were I not a leader of the entity that ushers biomedicaltechnological invention safely into the waiting arms of a grateful public, and were he not essentially a Luddite engaged in subverting my lifework, if we might have been friends.

"Your hair looks different," he said.

After he left, I continued unplaiting and re-plaiting the chignon. I had stopped caring about the effect and was more focused on the unplaiting and re-plaiting. The unplaiting and the re-plaiting made me think of the blank. The blank I was anticipating ended up being exactly what I got in that Director Jorg never connected with me to celebrate the non-filing. So at least I didn't have to figure out what to say to her. And while not completely fulfilling, the blank was better than other things, like for example an itch on one's cranium.

A POSTCARD, A THUMBDRIVE,
AND AN INQUIRY

When next I encountered Director Jorg, I didn't have to
pretend nothing had happened because nothing had happened. I could be myself around her as much as I could ever
be myself around her, which I couldn't. Let's just say the
blank returned things to the status quo ante. But the next
time I encountered Director Jorg, I was so preoccupied I
didn't feel like myself anyway. So it would be unfair to blame
Director Jorg, even if she was uniquely dislocating.

I'd taken a week off work to recover from an unusually
intense couple of days. The Bureau was famously generous
with undeclared leave, earning it a spot on one of those lists
of top federal employers for working families and others
with needs that take them away from the office. It was one
of the lower spots, due to the workload and public scrutiny that were acknowledged to be crushing and withering,
respectively. I never particularly noticed the workload or
the scrutiny. Had I been asked the major downsides of work
at the Bureau, I'd have said something about my cranium
and the difficult relationship with my desk, which reasserted
the antagonistic edge to its officiousness after I sat at it for
two days. Leave it to the popular media to focus on only the
most obvious detriments to workplace quality of life, without mentioning the other, more subtle detractions that end
up being harder to live with if you ask me.

When I returned to my office, I was greeted by a mailer in
the middle of my desk. I opened it immediately, not because

I cared what was in the mailer but because the clutter was out of whack with the officiousness. I could put up with one or the other but not both. In my haste, I neglected to first confirm it was addressed to me. The mailroom was always giving me Director Jorg's mail and occasionally giving Director Jorg my mail, though much less often for the simple reason that I didn't get as much mail. So there was nothing unusual in not confirming that the mailer was addressed to me. To whom Bureau mail was addressed was something I generally only bothered investigating after I'd opened the mail because, generally speaking, it didn't matter to whom the mail was addressed. I was the one who was going to have to do something about it.

The mailer held a thumb drive, which was common enough, only it turned out the mailer was addressed to me, which was unusual. The American people were always mailing thumb drives to Director Jorg, but never to me. But those in decision-making roles are so often immobilized by the awesome responsibility of having to make decisions, which is precisely why they have advisors, whom in many cases it would make as much sense to call deciders except that it would ruin the illusion of accountability. Anyway, I didn't think much of the thumb drive. What was odd was that there was a note with the thumb drive. A postcard, to be precise, with one of those pictures of the beach that immediately creates the desire to be at the beach. The sky was blue but it was glowing, like a blue screen. The water advertised its own wetness. But I think it was the black rocks that made it all so alluring because you knew they would be hot, making the water all the more attractive. In other words, the postcard was perfect, complete in that it created a desire and sated it at the same time. Or at least it put you in the mind of satedness. I could tell from the black rocks that it was a California beach. The note said:

> Dear N--This drive holds information that will
> demonstrate the benefits of the Schwa in improving
> the human condition.
> I know I can trust you with it.
>
> —S.D.

I was taken aback. Not just by the picture of the beach and the note, but also by the claim for the ə. I'd never thought about it that way. The note neutralized those like Dr. Hrbek who claimed the ə couldn't be a Product because it didn't treat a condition. If one couldn't treat the human condition with Products, it was hard to know what the whole point was of the Bureau. I was so taken aback that I didn't notice that Director Jorg had entered my office, in fact had been standing not more than three feet away. She had been looking right at me, yet I'd had no awareness of her at all. I hadn't even smelled her. It was as though the tables were finally turned and we were even. I felt a little smug.

Director Jorg was holding a multi-page letter in her right hand and the pages fluttered a little in the space between us, distracting me from the postcard.

"What's that?" I asked. I was trying to sound carefree, raising my voice up a little as I pointed at the fluttering pages, which she'd given a decisive shake so she could grasp both sides of them to stop the fluttering. Not only did she not reciprocate my playfulness, she didn't even answer my question, which in microcosm goes a long way toward illustrating the problem in our relationship. It was as though there was always a time lag between the response of one of us and whatever the other was doing that demanded a response so that even once we had evened things out and the number of responses equaled the number of things that needed responding to, we still weren't in sync.

"What's *that*?" she asked, pointing to the open mailer. The question was frustrating for all the reasons mentioned. I reached behind me for the thumb drive and placed the postcard from Sorel beach side down on my desk.

It was then that I noticed an undernote of loam. The undernote might have been welcome, might have revived the fellow feeling that had surfaced between us the day after the meeting. Under the circumstances it was unwelcome precisely because it was distracting. Occasionally the workplace calls for uninterrupted concentration.

"You didn't answer my question." This struck me as just the right response on my part. There's nothing like a non-sequitur to derail a line of questions prompted by other questions.

"It's an inquiry from the chairman and the ranking member of the Subcommittee on Biotechnology into our filing for the Ə. And also the granting. It wants to know which came first." It was just then, as Director Jorg gave the letter a shake and handed it to me, that the letter unfurled, revealing the signature blocks on the final page.

I wasn't surprised. I felt I'd been waiting for the moment forever. Still, I couldn't completely master the surge I felt, emanating from my solar plexus to every part of me. I crossed my legs.

"Er."

"Also there's this business about surveillance." She flipped through the pages until she found what she was looking for then read whatever it was to herself. "Why would I surveil people who are so boring?"

It may sound incredible but in the next several minutes Director Jorg said more to me than she'd said in our entire relationship up until that point, not so much in the sense of word count as in the sense of content. It seems to me much of what passed between us in our professional relationship fell into the category of non-sequitur. The quality of non-sequitur no doubt was one of the many things that made our relationship such a profitable one for her, the Bureau, and by extension the American people. By that I only mean that had we been able to follow each other—had we been in sync and able to meet at the same time for once instead of one after the other—I'm not sure our relationship would have lasted. Her outsider status would have grated on me, and I think she'd have had a hard time with certain deficits in my character, even if I couldn't do anything about them, not having had a good role model in life.

"They're saying I have a 'flagrant disregard,' for science. I'm OK with science but what's it got to do with a doodad like the—the—"

"The Ə?"

"That! I'm going to tell them 'So sorry I spied on our scientists even if I don't remember but sometimes I get bored and oh yeah I got the order mixed up with filing and granting but neurosurgeons can't remember which stuff comes first—do you slice open the skull before or after you get the tumor out? Who can remember?' Anyway 'disregard' is bullshit. Avoid, maybe. There's a lot of intimacy in the scientific process when you're up close to how things work. It threatens these guys. Sakhdvar wants a hearing. We have ten days. The topic is this so-called scientific integrity. They're asking that guy Fennel, too. Please handle. By the way, this guy Sakhdvar seems like a real prick."

You can imagine that got my attention. When I say "that," I mean multiple "thats," including, but not limited to, allusions within close proximity to one another to "intimacy," "Sakhdvar," and "prick." The sensory memory of something pressed against my thigh hurtled back to me from decades ago and with it a rush of fealty. There was an awkward silence, which Director Jorg interrupted by tapping a finger on the back of the postcard, then leaving my office abruptly.

My attention turned back to the mailer and the drive and the responsibility with which I'd been entrusted. I placed an intra-Bureau call using my private phone because one never knows who might pick up.

"Les here."

"I have new information concerning the Ə."

"Please continue."

"An entire file. The Product application has been submitted. I thought you might be interested. By the way, we might wish to broaden the indication."

"I wouldn't call cementing connectedness to oneself and others narrow."

"There's reason to believe the indications go beyond that."

"Is that so?"

"I'm calling because I've come upon information that could decrease your sense of discomfort with the filing, if not make you 'happy,' which after all, only you can do."

"Is the information scientific in nature?"

A difficult question to be sure, but not unanswerable.

"It's a scientific characterization in fulfillment of a legal standard."

"Eh?"

I could see I was losing him so I cut to the chase.

"Would you agree the human condition is a condition of man?"

"In the sense of a disease?"

"In the sense of something that responds to products."

I couldn't see Dr. Hrbek in those few moments and he was speechless for longer than was comfortable. Nonetheless, in the silence of those few moments, I pictured something that had been closed opening up in him, like the jaws of one of those meat-eating plants before they clamp down on a fly, only in reverse.

"Perhaps I should see for myself."

"One should always see for oneself."

I'd made my point. After disconnecting our call, I saw to it that Hieronymus made a copy of the drive and hand-delivered it to Dr. Hrbek for his review of full scientific reports supporting Producting of the ə. With that, I felt I'd discharged my responsibility to Sorel Dern and derivatively to those who stood to benefit from improvements in the human condition, which is to say, humanity.

I WAS GOING TO ROLL MY EYES
BUT I COULDN'T

Ten days flew past in a whirl of preparations. There were long lists of questions and answers, but the questions were more like commands. Things like, *Director, tell the committee what scientific integrity means to you.*

It should go without saying that I wasn't the one to prepare the questions and answers. That would be like spending my time peeling tomatoes for a puttanesca the night before an important meeting when I could get a perfectly good puttanesca from a jar. We had legislative staff to draft the questions and answers, which I then had Hieronymus revise and read aloud to me so I could dictate additional revisions to reflect my unique experience and perspective. I had him strike anything that came across as analytical or detached that might give the impression that the director thought about scientific integrity as though it were an abstraction, like a vision or value, as opposed to something relatable, anthropomorphic. Hieronymus and I had grown close, close enough that at times he gave voice to my words before they could leave my mouth. It was he who came up with the perfect answer to the first and most basic question, riffing: *scientific integrity is the lifeblood coursing through the Bureau's veins.* Director Jorg was less impressed and said only *OK, if you say so.* Anyway, she didn't object.

Our preparations ran late the night before the hearing. Director Jorg was nowhere to be found so without a witness to prepare, I suggested to Hieronymus that we watch old

C-SPAN footage of Jeremy grilling his usual targets—rapacious pharmaceutical executives, derelict regulators—to see what we could learn. We had the A/V team set us up in the conference room, where Jeremy's head beamed across the enormous screen. I was riveted. And a little jarred. Perhaps it was this unsettling effect combined with exhaustion and our growing familiarity that led to an uncharacteristic lapse in Hieronymus's professionalism.

"He looks familiar," Hieronymus commented, leaning back a little so Jeremy's whole head was in focus. "Omar Sharif?"

Though he was decades younger than me, Hieronymus often seemed like someone from an earlier era.

"Who was the actor who played Fortinbras in that Hamlet adaptation?" I commented with studied nonchalance.

"Rufus Sewell! I never thought of that but now that you mention it . . ." Hieronymus squinted at Jeremy's face as the camera moved in. A few distinguished silver hairs salted his hairline about his ears and he wore little wire rim glasses on the tip of his nose. But his jawline was as lean and delicate as ever. Looking up from his jawline to his eyes, a thought came to me that had been dancing about on the threshold of my consciousness: *what will I do when our eyes meet?*

"Too bad he's a self-righteous dick."

Neither of us said anything for a moment. It was one thing for the director to call Jeremy a prick. He was disrupting her important work with this hearing while raising the sort of allegations that can end a career. Besides, she was the director. But Hieronymus was speaking out of turn.

"He's a United States senator and may be our next president," was all I said.

"Of course."

He crossed his legs and placed one hand over the other atop his knee then continued watching the gigantic image of Jeremy's head in silence. Looking again at Jeremy's eyes, focused downward over the tops of his slightly officious spectacles at some hapless official, Jeremy's pupils dilating like a cartoon cat that sees a little bird, the answer to my question came to me like a revelation: I'd look away. Yes! I'd blink, then I'd look away but in an upward direction. The gesture would be equal parts averting and rolling of the eyes, a message and an affirmation that said at once: *If you're looking for validation of this spectacle, which is doing nothing more than keeping dedicated public officials from the business of the American people, I'm afraid you won't find it here* and *I've moved on.*

The next morning, I pulled the third-from-the-top button on the menswear-inspired dress shirt through the third-from-the-top hole and wedged the shirt's shirttail into the snug waist of a navy skirt. I practiced my eye gesture while flossing my teeth. Just before I left, I pulled from under my bed the slender attaché I'd used in my early years at the Firm, repurposed to hold the few mementos I'd kept from my past life. From there I retrieved the old newspaper clipping about Olf. Looking at the picture of Jeremy as a young crusader for justice for the first time in so many years, I thought I felt something mobile and uncomfortably fuzzy, like a tarantula crawling up the back of my throat. I swallowed hard and I was fine.

I arrived at the hearing on time and took a seat behind Director Jorg, in the pit beneath the elevated dais in front of the senators' seats. Director Jorg was seated at a long conference table; directly ahead of me but higher up was an empty seat behind a plaque that read *Mr. Sakhdvar.*

I had much to think about, but the intimidating environs made it hard to focus. The elevated dais for the senators was just one small example of how the whole hearing was set up to make the person testifying feel like they were being punished, even if they hadn't done anything wrong. Why else put the witnesses in a pit relative to the senators? If the senators were just one half of the whole reason for the hearing in the first place, then witnesses should have been treated as just as important, possibly even more important. No one would tune in to watch just the senators asking their questions, but I'm pretty sure they'd tune in to watch the witnesses answering, even without the senators asking, if that were possible. It's the senators themselves who always say, "we want answers." The senators never say, "we want questions." Perhaps putting the witnesses below the members of Congress was a way of getting back at the witnesses for being more important than them. That sort of a power play seemed familiar to me, and for no more than a second I wondered whether the elevated dais was Jeremy's idea.

No, I wouldn't let myself take things personally. I could hardly begrudge Jeremy and his compatriots for having questions about biomedicaltechnology. It's often said that biomedicaltechnology brings people together and the saying never felt truer. We were called there because the senators were just as much in the dark about biomedicaltechnology as everyone else, so it was like we were all in it together. My indignation began to subside, as a sense of connectedness came over me, knowing we were all bound by a shared oblivion.

I was trying not to fidget, but the suit's snugness made me want to adjust and pull on the fabric and zipper and so forth. I thought about the cameras and resisted. Fidgeting is the behavior of a guilty person and I wasn't guilty of anything, except perhaps filing a petition after the petition had already been granted contrary to Bureau regulations, something that was only a violation in a chronological sense. As for the surveillance, I felt not the least bit of guilt. I was sent to the Bureau to do a job and had no intention of accepting blame because I did it with a verve one doesn't encounter in every member of the federal workforce. I was studiously not fidgeting with the suit, rehearsing the movement of my pupils from the unoccupied seat behind the plaque with *Sakhdvar* on it to some point in the back of my head when Sorel Dern appeared in the field of that trajectory, only more to the side.

"I feel better knowing you're here," he said, leaning over the empty chairs to my left, a little more closely than called for, then grabbing my hand and clutching it instead of shaking it. His hand was smooth and warm and neither big nor small, like the hand of a hand model. He was wearing a suit ironically, by which I mean not that it was ironic that he was wearing a suit but that he was wearing a suit in a way one can only describe as ironic. The pants were tight at his ankles and a little short. It was the shrunken look, and he wore it well. A consequence of his wearing the shrunken look was you could see his dress socks, as if he were trying to make a point about wearing dress socks. It was as though the socks were saying, *Observe, we're socks. You probably didn't expect to see us here.*

Strangely, Sorel Dern looked less out of place in his suit than Director Jorg, who wore a suit every day and often the same one. Director Jorg's head had turned all the way around on her neck to inspect Dern, then watched him as he walked over to the seat next to hers. I thought for a moment I smelled something loamy, but it was probably just an association. They shook hands without any clutching.

The director was on her own now. I had matters to attend to. I was rehearsing looking upwards in a way that alluded without committing to an eyeroll when instead of seeing an empty chair behind a plaque marked with *Sakhdvar* in the spot where my eyes began their upwards trajectory, I saw Jeremy. I didn't see his face, which was turned to a staffer who was handing him a binder as he pulled his chair out, swung one leg over the chair, and thrust his groin forward, possibly not in that order. He sat down and raked his fingers through his hair in a way that seemed to be making a point, such as, *I regret that the actions of my witnesses have diverted me from the nation's business but such actions being what they are an accounting is unavoidable,* or something similar. The gesture seemed a little showy, as if directed at all the balding male senators on the subcommittee and the one woman, who had the sort of coif that repels raking. Just like Jeremy to sacrifice the feelings of others when he wanted to make a point. He followed the raking with other mannerisms that had a different effect, including rubbing his bottom lip with his index finger and staring resolutely ahead of him.

Shortly after I saw Jeremy and he took his seat, one of the other senators from some place that always seems like a state and not like a place called the hearing to order. He had a few things to say first about implantable biomedicaltechnology products, beginning with the sort of sad stories one so often hears at these hearings: first about a constituent who had to fly to Bolivia to have his implantable implanted; second about a constituent who was only marketing her implantable in the EU due to the onerous US regulatory requirements; third about a constituent who wanted to study implantables but had to go to China to study implantables because of the tireless and ultimately triumphant efforts of the Communist Party to corner the global market for non-human primate testing of implantable biomedicaltechnology. I should say it wouldn't have surprised me in the least to learn that the implantee, the entrepreneur, and the researcher were notional. I know better than most that we lead the world in implantables whether you want them for implanting, selling, or testing on non-human primates. But the point of these discussions wasn't exactly "truth" in the usual sense. The point was more to line up the senator with something positive, like implantables, so by contrast the Bureau would appear negative because of whatever the Bureau was doing that supposedly resulted in less of the positive thing.

When he was done, a different senator from a coastal state, one of the thirteen colonies that no one ever remembers when naming the thirteen colonies, started talking about scientific integrity, but again mostly he was talking about its absence and blaming Director Jorg and the Bureau. Like the first senator, the second began his remarks with a story, this one a real heartbreaker involving the malfunction of a lifestyle-enhancing wristband, excluded from Bureau regulation under the maligned *Politique De Douce Insouciance*. The wristband sent an alert after rather than before his constituent's narcoleptic episode, or I should say former constituent due to his untimely automotive-related death. It's not easy being blamed for the problems with things everyone is in favor of, like implantable and wearable biomedicaltechnology, and, of course, scientific integrity. All there is to do is to maintain innocence, or at least the appearance of innocence by not fidgeting, no matter how snug the suit.

Eventually the first senator asked Sorel Dern if he had prepared remarks, and he surprised everyone by saying he didn't have anything prepared. I felt a little badly for him, knowing he would be compared unfavorably to Director Jorg, whose prepared remarks I'd written myself—by which I mean I'd asked the legislative staff to write them and Hieronymus to rewrite them then read the rewrite aloud to me so I could leave my mark. They were, of course, excellent. But before I could decide what to make of Sorel Dern's shocking admission, he proceeded to give remarks off-the-cuff.

"I'd like to begin with a simple question for the subcommittee: Have any of you ever suffered?"

Sorel Dern paused for a long time until the female subcommittee member started to raise her hand, then brought it down before her colleagues could notice. He continued with a litany of questions, exactly the opposite of what was wanted from him.

"Of course, we've all suffered, some would say suffering is the human condition. What if I told you, we could change the human condition, that the human condition is one that responds to intervention?

"What if I told you, we could neutralize suffering and replace it with something else?

"What if I said instead of suffering, the human condition could be one of connection, of balance, proportion, and symmetry?

"What if I told you, we have the technology now?

"Would you quibble about whether or not that technology is a Product, whether or not a Product has to have mass, whether a Product can be more or less imagined as opposed to produced?

"Would you ask me whether it worked chemically or physically or metabolically?

"Or would you say, 'let's get this technology in the hands of people so they can feel connected instead of suffering'?"

He went on like that. I assume there was more to it, by which I mean more questions, but one gets the gist. I should have been riveted by this testimony, which combined my twin passions of connectedness and biomedicaltechnology. Riveted wasn't the word. Perhaps it was the questions that threw me off because, as anyone would who came expecting answers then getting nothing but questions, I started to tune out. Sorel Dern finished; Director Jorg went, and the real questioning began. When Jeremy began, I felt his voice reverberating in the chamber before I realized what was happening, that for the first time in so many years, Jeremy was speaking, in person.

I should perhaps mention the strain of being alone. I bring this up only by way of explaining how little I remember of the hearing as it progressed, how the questions and answers blurred into a uniform background miasma. One might otherwise wonder how I came to be "flummoxed" in the words of the author of that profile of me in that women's magazine, the magazine known for mixing serious content with sex advice about how to orgasm during a PowerPoint presentation without interrupting the presenter and the like, advice one struggles to imagine an audience for—any professional worth her salt knows perfectly well not to interrupt a PowerPoint presentation unless you have something incredibly clever to say. She asked, *Were you concerned when Senator Sakhdvar threatened to refer the ə matter for an investigation?* I wasn't flummoxed at all by Jeremy's threat. When he made his threat I was thinking about something entirely different. With the word "ə" hanging in the air and the talk of technology and connectedness and Jeremy, rubbing his lower lip with his index finger as he looked down at his witnesses, it's perhaps unsurprising where my mind went, somewhere that couldn't have been further away from an investigation. My mind went to a hot white beach with black rocks, the sky bright, and Jeremy right there with me, pressed against the surface of my body, as porous as lava rock but pliable like a loofah. He muttered about Vesuvius as the loofah pores created a suction and tried to open up even more, and the suction drew in Jeremy, and the linkages that held everything together started to give out and everything behind them started to leak and then gush from the open pores of an exhausted loofah as we fell, buffeted by the hot sand, an inseparable tangle of breath and limbs . . .

At first there was a ringing in my ears, but that died down as all my atoms exhaled, noiselessly, and a low "AAAAA" in a baritone took over. When I looked up to where the "AAAAA" was coming from, my eyes met Jeremy's. He squinted for a moment, then opened his eyes wide without looking away. I forgot about the whole rolling my eyes business and our eyes remained locked for I don't know how long.

Yet the questions didn't stop. They were the sort of difficult questions Sorel Dern had asked himself earlier. With Jeremy's gaze fixed on me, it was as though he was asking his questions directly of me. Only Director Jorg answered.

"What is a ə?"

"Senator Sakhdvar, I commend you for getting to the heart of matters with your question, one that is so deceiving in its straightforwardness that I regret I can only answer with reference to arcane areas of scientific and metaphysical—"

"Is it a Product?"

"You are asking me a legal, regulatory, scientific, and one might say, metaphysical conclusion we've had no opportunity to reach."

"But you'd agree it exists?"

"Er . . ."

"What does it do?"

"The standard things everyone expects from technology to facilitate a contemporary lifestyle: camera; video and audio recording; cloud storage, internet; email; messaging; phone; voicemail; step-tracking; calorie-counting; peak fertility; peak infertility; indices concerning one's body mass, sociopathy, erogenicity and other indicators of desirability and sociability along with notifications, alarms, and warnings concerning one's desirability and sociability; games; news; gossip; entertainment; emergency alerts, codes yellow, blue, red, and others depending on your country, region, state, municipality, and zip code; heart rate; mood; daily insights; horoscope; tarot card readings; calculation of nondiagnostic propensity for diabetes II, heart disease, Alzheimer's, breast, colon, pancreatic, prostate, and brain cancer, allergic response to pool chemicals, taste for cilantro, Brussels sprouts, and Coca-Cola vs. Pepsi, and similar conditions; personality inventories; sociopathy scores; pulse oximetry; likes and dislikes and notifications, alarms, and warnings concerning proximity to one's likes and dislikes; navigational tools; GPS; surveillance system; locator systems for sex offenders and certain religious, ethnic, and gender minorities; similar information concerning one's neighbors and loved ones—"

"Does it have proven benefit vis-à-vis any condition?"

"It has a hypothesized benefit—"

"Did you grant and then file, in that order, a Non-Filing Petition for the ə?"

"Unfortunately, we have members of scientific staff who were unhappy with the filing, but when was the last time everyone was ever happy about something? The most you can ask for in life is that more people would be happy after whatever I do than were happy before it. In fact, if just one person can be moved from the unhappy column to the happy column, or from a lot unhappy to not so much, we've won the ball game. Unless others were moved in the opposite way. So who knows who's the big winner."

"Who ordered the surveillance of the so-called Cabal of Five?"

"Eh—that was a dead end."

"Did you or didn't you order the surveillance?"

"Yes, I think maybe—"

It was obvious what was happening. Director Jorg wasn't the sort of person to respond to having her goose cooked by removing her goose from the threat. Director Jorg was the sort of person who would prepare a port sauce to give the impression she'd come up with the idea of cooking a goose in the first place to hold on to the appearance of control, if not the actuality. Ordinarily I would be sympathetic but this was unforgivable. It would be logical to think that, in response to her testimony, I tensed up and the atoms reclaimed their spillage, reorganizing themselves in orderly linkages, et cetera, et cetera, but I remember things differently. After a long time, Jeremy looked away, and I experienced a disintegration of a different sort. Similar in the experience of linkages breaking down and cell contents spilling out but without the gushing. I felt like I was evaporating.

Soon, the questions weren't just coming from Jeremy. Other members were asking equally pointed questions, and not just about the ə. They were questioning the Bureau, its leadership, and its mission. The questions kept coming long after the answers had run out, so the hearing outlived the reason for having a hearing in the first place. It was one of those asymmetries that under other circumstances might have made me itch but the discipline of not fidgeting also kept me from scratching.

After everyone had run out of questions, Jeremy stood up and walked to the back exit without shaking hands with his witnesses or otherwise doing something to make everything feel less tense, which was pretty typical of Jeremy, who had always been more interested in creating tension than relieving tension. Director Jorg stayed seated after the senators had left, scratching the back of her head as though she were having a bad reaction to her own outsiderness. But there wasn't anything to be done about that. Sorel Dern bounded out of his seat toward the exit without speaking to the spectators who'd started to throng him.

As he passed my row he winked then leaned over and gripped me in an awkward embrace while I remained seated and immobile due only in part to my snug suit. He produced a rolled-up document from his interior suit pocket and handed it to me.

"A report of our canine data," he whispered.

"Regulations require you to turn this over to our scientists," I whispered back. "Not to mention the principles of scientific integrity that were putatively the reason we all sacrificed the last few hours of our lives to be here and that we'll never get back." I thought I saw alarm flash across his normally unworried features. But it lasted only a moment.

"You were fantastic!" He exclaimed, somewhat loudly. Then he left.

I folded the report and stashed it away in my purse then promptly forgot about it. The Ə's problems concerned humanity, not dogs, and I refused to fall into the trap of reverse anthropomorphizing lower mammals, no matter how fetching. That was a job for scientists, like Dr. Hrbek. Besides, I had other things on my mind.

I snuck out of the hearing room without congratulating Director Jorg on her testimony, the polite thing to do even when the testimony is catastrophic. Though it was late in the day and Director Jorg would be headed to her home (whatever unusual circumstances the word conjured in her case, which I never could imagine), I went to my office instead. It's hard to imagine now, but at the time, I imagined calling Hieronymus into my office and telling him everything, from the moment I'd first seen Jeremy's head bobbing above a sea of patrons at a meat restaurant up to the present. But incredibly, when I passed his office, there was no light streaming from under his door. Hieronymus had gone home for the day.

I entered my office, closed the door, and approached my desk, which seemed to me as stolid as an old colleague, the sort one would never mingle with outside of work hours but whose shared experience nonetheless bred a feeling of common purpose. A low "AAAAA" echoed in my head and when I closed my eyes I had the experience of something momentous focused on me, bearing down with the weight of human history, awaiting my next move. But I wasn't inhibited. To the contrary, the sense of being surveilled was motivating. I felt invigorated, as though unified in purpose with the furniture, the walls, the very air of Building 1.

I suddenly knew what I had to do.

From my office I composed a short note, a challenge without my trusty second to do the writing part. Word choice and tone were a struggle. It was important that the tone not be overly eager. The tone needed to be casual, yet

respectful. Above all, credibility was key. In the end, I wrote
the following:

Dear Jeremy:

I write with your interests and those of the American
people at heart. It is of critical importance that we
speak. I obviously mean in person.

Our diverging view concerning matters of
biomedicaltechnology was (and for you, may remain) a
subject of some delicacy. Yet I ask that you consider
my perspective before you do anything rash. I'm
speaking of the "investigation" you alluded to today,
which would only uncover the diligence of the Bureau
workforce and the entrepreneurial spirit of our
stakeholders. Even if your current diet allows you the
occasional oeuf en cocotte, that doesn't mean you
want egg on your face.

Nice seeing you today, as always.

I remain,
Yours truly,
N.—

PS Rest assured, our rich erotic history is forever
safe with me from prying public eyes. I'm nothing if not
discreet.

I read it over once and weighed an overt reference to the
Olf matter to illustrate a time when our views had diverged.

Perhaps, with the passage of time, Jeremy had come to see things for how they were: that is, I was right about Olf, and he was misguided. On reflection, twenty years seemed a pittance, a drop in the well when it comes to disagreements based in fundamental life philosophies between one-time intimates. Any mention of Olf could get us off on the wrong foot. Similarly, I feared, at first, that an allusion to his reformed dietary habits might hit a nerve, as though I were suggesting he was ethically fickle. But I'd made my share of concessions to his dietary preferences in our relationship only to have him abandon them when I could no longer benefit. Plus, 'oeuf' was lexically not unlike 'Olf," potentially insinuating the Olf matter into his consciousness without rubbing his nose in it. I'd found the perfect solution. My final edit was to put the word 'rash' in italics. The emphasis made the word hard to ignore, like an actual rash. It was another triumph of the subliminal.

My most difficult conundrum concerned the postscript. Without the postscript, I could leave the note with one of his staffers to pass it along and be done with it. Sure, the staffer might read the note, but without the postscript, I couldn't care less who read the note. But the postscript was the most important part. For one thing, it reminded him of who I was. In a word, discreet.

I folded the note and dropped it into my purse. I'd already written the words that would reset our relationship. Getting the words to him was a task for another day.

SPILL!

I took leave from work to focus on my conundrum.

It is a truism that those most indispensable to an organization are well-advised to absent themselves in times of greatest need to give others an opportunity to rely on their own wherewithal. Besides, I couldn't be asked to save the Bureau from Director Jorg's outsiderness. When I said that all of Director Jorg's issues were within my portfolio, it should go without saying that I didn't mean issues of a psychological nature.

A week went by and no solution to my conundrum came to me. I decided to call upon my trusted second. I'd wanted to get to get to the bottom of Nym's detail anyway, so a call to Hieronymus was overdue. He picked up on the first ring and I thought, *That's my boy.*

"I need something from you."

"Er. Did you get my voicemail?"

"Your what?"

"On your work and home numbers."

Retrieving voicemail from Bureau phones was a complicated process, involving multiple option menus, a password, a PIN, automatically generated tickets to the IT department when one couldn't remember one's password or PIN, electronic passcodes and secret questions about old boyfriends and mother's maiden names that always made me sad. So I'd never successfully retrieved voicemail from my Bureau phone. Concerning my personal phone, I hadn't bothered checking. The only person who called my personal phone was Director Jorg, and I was avoiding her. But I had no time to explain all that to Hieronymus. I had to think on my feet.

"I haven't been checking. I've had a spell of vertigo," I said.

"I've been avoiding email for delicate matters because, well, you know."

"I'm not sure that I do." It was almost as though he was using his knowledge of my vigorous pursuit of the Cabal against me to justify his dereliction in getting across whatever this communication was about which he was being so cagey.

"So I left a note in your inbox . . ."

"It seems you've been busy."

" . . .tendering my resignation."

I let out a small gulp that I assumed was inaudible.

"I'm going to work for a presidential campaign," he continued, cockily inflecting the "dent" in presidential.

"I thought you were no fan of the senator." I rejoindered. I was trying to make sense of what I was hearing.

"I'm a huge fan. Of the other guy."

The other guy! He was referring, of course, to the crass fellow already dismissed in polite circles as a grotesque but harmless joke. As a public servant, I prided myself on nonpartisanship. But that didn't make me blind. I weighed prevailing on my young charge to consider the impact on his future of associating with this figure, who by then was known to have no prospect of winning. I refrained. Hard lessons are best learned by experience.

"I wish you every success."

"You're too kind."

"By the way, before the opportunity to ask eludes me forever, could you refresh me what you did with the vitae of that young woman—"

"The Cabalist and N'Autie! I planted her in OIG." For a flash the old enthusiasm for deceptively effective hijinks that employed his unparalleled Bureau savoir faire reminded me of our budding friendship and I felt a pang. Then it occurred to me he had confessed to nothing short of sabotage.

"I was relying on OIG to conduct an investigation."

"To expose the Cabal! Which they did for you, with your fingerprints nowhere near the crime scene."

He wasn't wrong. But I couldn't condone his methods.

"Don't thank me," he sniffed.

"Let me know if you ever need a reference," I said, then immediately regretted my words. I wasn't prepared to commit to putting my credibility on the line by vouching for this young man, whose judgment I now had to question. But he hung up before I could qualify my offer. Still, we parted more in sorrow than in anger. At least on my end. What was in the heart of this crafty but misguided young man was a mystery to me.

With Hieronymus gone, I didn't know where to turn. Then I realized the answer was right in front of me. No member of the Bureau communications team could succeed without deep ins in the staffs of pivotal members of congress. I had to find Nym.

I didn't know her last name so I entered "Nym" in the online staff directory and two names came up, one of whom had just taken his leave in a somewhat testy exchange with me. The other was Naomi "Nym" Pham. I assumed this was my target and dialed without hesitation. Only my call to Nym went unanswered, not even by voicemail. This was almost certainly a violation of the Bureau Best Practice on Accessibility, which, in Nym's defense, was widely ignored unlike the one on fraternization, fraternization being considered the greater threat to good order than inaccessibility. I let the infraction slide and sent an email instead, only I received a bounce-back saying Nym was no longer with the Bureau. The forwarding address was Nym@Echt.com. To learn, in the space of 20 minutes, that the Bureau had lost two of its bright young lights was disconcerting to say the least. But not surprising. The Bureau's struggles with retention of its young talent were well-known. I had commissioned a study of recently-departed young staff to determine what led over half to leave within the first year of employment. The study confirmed what everyone suspected, namely, that young Bureau employees were fickle, a result that was too inflammatory to release. Instead, the results informed a new personality inventory for job candidates to assess loyalty. Lest anyone accuse the Bureau of discriminatory intent or wasting taxpayer resources on unproven pseudoscience, the inventory was administered to all candidates, regardless of age, and resulted in several useful referrals to the intelligence community. In any event, I'm not one to be swayed by intergenerational prejudices, including those based in truth.

I wasn't the least perturbed by Nym's past affiliation with the Cabal. I felt certain she was of fundamentally sound character but led astray by her questionable judgment in affairs of the heart. With those romantic ties severed, I had no reason not to believe she could be an indispensable ally in my quest.

Nor did Nym's departure dissuade me. Everyone knows relationships are between people, not organizations. And if anything, her affiliation with Echt.com seemed like one that would enhance her access to powerful people. I had every expectation that Nym would have me in to see Jeremy in no time.

Echt.com was one of those online outlets that catered
to the popular interest in politics and the popular interest
in sex, but with a subversive edge to its presentation that
gave off a vibe of exclusivity, a vibe the URL capitalized
on by using a word few people ever actually use in a sentence. I myself had to look the word up online, having never
encountered the term in any vocabulary-building exercise,
including the "exercise" of a long career at the pinnacle of
a profession in which use of exotic terminology to establish
one's pedigree is the norm. I composed an email stating that
I needed her help with a matter involving Senator Sakhdvar
and two minutes and 53 seconds later she emailed me back
and asked if I'd meet her for lunch.

Nym suggested an Ethiopian coffee house and workspace
that was on the same block as an arms dealer and three auto
repair shops in a neighborhood where many young Bureau
staff bought their first condominium before marrying into
a different federal agency, having children, leaving the government for a consulting firm, and moving to Bethesda. (We
recruited heavily from Bureau staff at the Firm, where the
term "revolving door" had none of the pejorative under-
tones that sometimes color its usage, but simply referred to
the idea that we were all spinning on the same axis.)

I stepped inside the café and surveyed the tables hosting
single, young-ish men in hoodies or windbreakers staring
into their laptop screen as they sipped their beverages when
my eyes were diverted by an artwork hung on an exposed
brick wall, a colorful rendering of a rat winking under a
balaclava as it emerged from a manhole cover with an automatic weapon held in the air, the strap running diagonally across the rat's torso or whatever you call the part of a
rat's body closer to its head than its tail. Squinting, I could

make out the writing on the index card beside the painting: "Ratatatathole. Rodin(t), Early period, $1200." This seemed fortuitous. Or perhaps not. I never knew what to make of Jeremy's Rodin(t) collection, although, in retrospect, his offloading of them was easy to understand. Obviously, his elegant wife-to-be was less understanding of her spouse's interest in rat-themed street art than some women would be, if only for the sake of marital harmony. For all I knew it went the same way with his veganism.

Two hands like agitated pigeons flapped at me from the back wall, where Nym had taken a table. She was wearing Buddy Holly-style glasses and had cut her hair in a short coif that exposed her nape and shoulders, revealing an endearing roundedness.

"Call me Nym," she said, knocking a recording device to the floor as she extended her hand, then bonking her head on the table's edge as she retrieved it.

"The Bureau canned me for a violation of the fraternization best practice," she volunteered before I was even seated.

I suppose she was trying to put me at ease by answering an awkward question before I asked it, but instead I tensed up. Although I hadn't approved her firing, it was possible that I'd delegated her firing with one of my blanket delegations for personnel matters. The personnel actions for noncompliance with the Best Practice against Fraternization were termination or counselling, but termination was reserved for the senior-most infractor. Dr. Hrbek and V. exceeded Nym by over a decade as far as years-in-service, but no one cared about years-in-service. The Best Practices Manual determined seniority the same way reserved parking spaces were awarded, by stature within the organization. And members of the Communications Team were second only to Director Jorg and her Special Advisor In Residence to the Director of the Bureau of Biomedicaltechnology as far as stature within the organization. Everyone knew what was in store for a violation of the best practice, so one could say Nym had it coming to her. But that sounds unsympathetic.

"I was hoping you could arrange a meeting with Senator Sakhdvar."

"Pfft."

"Pfft" was unexpected. I saw I'd have to elevate my game.

"I'm concerned he's about to do something *rash*. Concerning the Ə."

Nym flinched and scratched herself all over for a second. Then she collected herself.

"It's not exactly a secret what he's going to do. He's going to investigate. But there's no there there. Or is there?"

She arched an eyebrow pointedly. That's when I remembered. I dug into my purse and extracted the report Sorel Dern had handed me after the hearing. Nym's eyes widened and she reached across the table to grab the report, but I pulled it away, flipped past the pink sticky affixed to the cover and went right for the results:

"Canine subjects were randomized to test and control groups. Test subjects exposed to the Ə were twice as likely to attack lab technicians as controls, which were exposed to a Dvorak sonata.'"

"What kind of a bastard would do that to a dog?"

"It seems to me the lab technicians bore the brunt."

"I wouldn't count on the American people making that distinction. I assume Hrbek has the data?"

"Of course." I had no idea if Dr. Hrbek had the data. But I'd told Sorel Dern what to do with the data and was accustomed to being listened to.

"Because he's the type to comply with a government sub-poena."

"Only if he gets one."

"I'm not sure what you're suggesting."

"It's as I said, I need you to get me to Jeremy." I wasn't planning to play my ace in the hole so soon. But she left me with no choice. "I'd be interested in your views on a some-thing."

I dug into my purse and extracted the note I'd drafted for Jeremy, then unfurled it for her. Her eyes flitted across the note in a nanosecond, and she started scratching herself again.

"That is, if you can you be trusted."

"Spill."

"Where shall I begin?"

"At the beginning."

And so I did. I spoke for nearly an hour without interrup-tion, except when Nym reached for her coffee and inadver-tently brushed against her recording device, dropping it to the floor again so I had to repeat that Jeremy ordered sauce verte with his mashed potato, the significance of which didn't seem to register with Nym, but I didn't mind repeat-ing in the least. It's easy to forget how good it can be to be listened to, especially for those of us whose station in life is more to listen to others as opposed to vice versa. I was sur-prised to learn that Nym wasn't the least bit prurient. She was polite enough when I shared with her the kind of inti-mate detail from my relationship that brings a story to life. But I expected her to have more questions.

"Feel free to interrupt if you'd like me to go deeper on any of this," I offered. "Although there's much more to come."

"You're not almost done?" This was my second exchange

in two days with an impertinent young person. My patience was tried.

"I hope I'm not boring you."

"I need more to work with."

I was aghast. It was as though she was implying I had an ulterior motive.

"I was sharing this as a friend and former colleague. Not as a source."

"Because if you wanted to get the attention of a former screw-buddy riding his high horse to the People's House THE LAST THING you'd do is spill his private peccadillos to a hungry journalist writing for a sex-obsessed online political rag." Nym rolled her eyes so vigorously it hurt to watch. "Anyway, if you were really a friend you'd have gotten me a detail on your staff."

I stared at this woman in stunned silence. I'd never encountered such insolence from a subordinate. Former subordinate. But still. At the same time, what she was suggesting wasn't crazy.

"You can't work with somnophilia?"

"Somnophilia is like apple pie."

"What about ungulate-philia?"

"I'm listening."

I continued and she listened without comment.

" . . .and that's when it's fair to say he erupted like Vesuvius over a little au lait in his café au lait." Nym perked up.

"So he's lactose intolerant?" she asked.

"He was a vegan. He's always been ahead of his time."

"But you gave him café au lait?"

"I had other things on my mind."

"Is he still a vegan?"

"He stopped being a vegan before the last time I saw

him, which explains why one always hears about his looks and his interest in justice and less about his eating habits. As far as I know, they're unremarkable these days. He's never described by his prick either for that matter, but maybe that's because no one's asked me. I'd be happy to tell you anything you want to know about that—"

"Maybe he's a vegetarian now?"

"I assume we'd know for reasons I've already mentioned."

"Ovo-lacto?"

"That Maddox Pinker fellow at *The Post* would have said something about it." I thought Nym looked a little annoyed when I mentioned Maddox Pinker and *The Washington Post*, but maybe she was annoyed because she dropped the recording device again.

"Freegan?"

"That's all I've got as far as his eating habits."

Nym seemed disappointed.

"We need to do a shoot to accompany the article. Something intimate, preferably where you live. What do you have to wear?"

"I have an extensive wardrobe."

Nym looked at me skeptically.

"Don't worry. I'll come early tomorrow and help you find something."

I tried not to be obvious as I surveyed her attire, a maroon and gold bowling shirt over plaid pants. I'd grown accustomed to always having to make difficult decisions on my own. But female friendship was among the things I'd had to sacrifice to my career. I was touched. Perhaps it was because of an unexpected surge of fellow feeling that I broached a different matter.

"What do you think of the artwork?" I gestured with my hands to the two or three other Rodin(t) artworks hung against the back wall of the café. Though I'd unburdened myself to Nym, I withheld a few details. I hadn't said anything about Jeremy's Rodin(t) artworks. I was interested in her unvarnished aesthetic opinion.

Nym raised her nose, bringing her lips up with it in an expression signifying neither approval nor disapproval but a complicated backstory that precluded a simple response on aesthetic grounds.

"Those were V.'s."

"V. is Rodin(t)?"

"Please. A second alias would be quote/unquote self-indulgent," she flattened her voice to mimic V. "Plus, he hates puns."

"His Bureau salary can't keep him in bushcraft?" I felt our relationship had progressed to where I could risk a little humor at the expense of her former paramour. Her response was neither encouraging nor discouraging.

"He bought the art twenty years ago as a hedge. Against what, you might ask? 'If you have to ask what it's a hedge against you haven't been paying attention.'" With the second sentence, Nym opened up her left eye while squinting with the right one so it was half-closed and pronounced the words in a deep uninflected monotone. "He used to print an underground newsletter out of his apartment in Alphabet City that covered jailed Marxists, street artists, anti-patriarchy agitators. Called N'Aut."

Nym raised her eyebrows and stared at me, as though expecting a reaction. I wasn't going to give her one.

"Oh, like the underground global decentralized network

of anti-technology/capitalist and so forth agitators that might not exist? Interesting coincidence," I said, coolly. If Nym was trying to bolster the Cabal's influence by tying it to N'Aut she'd have to do better than that. So V. had created a newsletter called N'Aut. Who's to say he hadn't likewise invented an organ of the counterculture with the same name? "Also I think he used to screw her."

"Her?"

Nym took out her phone and pecked at the keys, then turned the screen to me. On the screen was a sylph-like woman with fuchsia hair wearing green lowriders, a magenta coat that looked like it was made from shag carpeting and was somehow familiar, and rust-colored patent leather boots standing outside a clothing boutique with Rodin(t) spray painted across the storefront window. She looked winsomely into the camera with long eyes. So besides being a depicter of anthropomorphic abusers and an anti-technology anti-capitalist, Rodin(t) was an owner of an upscale boutique who liked to take fashion risks. And a woman. She seemed complicated.

"He offloaded her stuff right after he dumped me. According to him, she's quote/unquote degenerate." She did the same thing with her eyes and the monotone again. "Irony is also quote/unquote self-indulgent." Then she shrugged.

With that we parted until the following day, when Nym arrived at my condominium with two large lambic ales in bottles with corks, one cassis and one boysenberry flavored. She unwound the wire that I surmised was keeping the cork from popping out on its own, then pulled the cork out of the bottle with her teeth, which seemed dangerous, but apparently she knew what she was doing. The cork popped out with a few light-hearted jerks of her neck from side to side as she pulled downwards on the bottle. Then she handed the bottle to me and, not wanting to snub her, I took a quaff. One doesn't further oneself in the professional world with a blinkered fixation on sobriety, particularly when it comes at the price of rejecting an overture of friendship.

"Where do you store your togs?"

From lighthearted to business-like, just like that. I wouldn't have pegged Nym as having that kind of range.

Perhaps because demands of the workplace had left me little time for the sort of annual closet culling urged by lifestyle coaches, much of what we found was unexpected. We approached the choice rationally and systematically, as you'd expect from two professionals and soon narrowed the options to teal separates made of silky fabric and a PVC bustier.

"Do you care if people take you seriously?" Nym asked.

Perhaps I should have been offended by the question, but I was too surprised by it to be offended. It had never occurred to me that I could be taken in any other way.

"What's the alternative?"

"You can play this two ways. One ends with you competing against fifth stringers for a degrading reality TV gig dancing the flamenco, the other has you parlaying a sit down with a major news magazine, a strategic print piece or two, a few serendipitous pap shots, and a book deal into quasi-cultural icon status."

"The second sounds more up my alley."

In the end, I wore only the top half of the teal pajama-like separates, but over a pair of men's jeans we found in my closet. Who knows what the story was with the men's jeans. They were tight and a little long, as though they'd belonged to someone lanky.

I was tipsy by the time Nym packed up her equipment. But more importantly, I felt Nym and I were now bound together by friendship and meaningful shared experience. I ventured a question.

"Your exposé going live will change the dynamics, would you agree?"

Nym shrugged.

"I mean vis à vis Jeremy and me as regards prospects for a face-to-face rapprochement."

"Maybe his office will issue a statement," Nym said absently. Then she exited my apartment.

Echt.com broke its story three days later. The story appeared under the same picture of Jeremy that Maddox Pinker would use for so many of his articles, a picture of Jeremy from the hearing with his Adam's apple looking unusually prominent, only Echt.com did something to make him sepia colored, and pasted him to one side of a purple capitol building. I was also cut out and reclining on the chaise lounge I had in my living area, so I looked comfortable, then pasted on the other side of the capitol building. In short, the graphic had just the right combination of irreverence and depth. If I had a minor quibble, it was that I wished they had made more of an effort to put me and Jeremy together, even if they had no photo of me and Jeremy together. They could have cut out a picture of him sitting and put it next to the picture of me on the burgundy chaise lounge or something. And I can't say I agreed with the headline, which read "PERVY VEGAN!" in large caps across the top of the graphic. While the vegan part was just factual, it was in the past. And the pervy part was judgmental.

I was thinking about calling Nym to suggest a different direction, if not for the piece already published then for future pieces, should our collaboration be ongoing. But the phone rang and I had to redirect my attention. It originated from within the Bureau.

"Les here."

Perfect! I thought, but I didn't say anything. Though I'd always assumed it was the brown spot in Dr. Hrbek's eye that made talking to him so difficult, I realized I felt every bit as uncomfortable with him over the phone. I started to think that perhaps it was his attachment to logic that created the gulf between us.

"We have a dilemma. We need to bring you in."

"To the office?" I started to wish I hadn't picked up.

"Of course not. That would make everyone uncomfortable. Jorg's under pressure from above to act quickly on the ə."

"Pressure?"

"Forces within the Directorate want it out. It's a case of regulatory capture."

"I find that hard to believe," I said. I was irked that Dr. Hrbek hadn't bettered the paranoid tendencies that made him easy prey for the Cabal in the first place. I couldn't resist needling him. "Why don't you PPPDSP it?"

"Because the Provisional Product Pending Data Supporting Producing is a chimera without regulatory basis, as I think you know. The window for action on the ə closes if the Senator resolves his—er, situation. For now, he's distracted."

"Perhaps he's crafting a statement about this dilemma you speak of."

I'd hoped to engage Dr. Hrbek's fine-if-tightly-coiled intellect in speculation on how Jeremy's might respond. But he wouldn't have it.

"You don't know about the canine data."

"Au contraire."

"How—"

"I like to keep up on things."

"No matter. I assume you have your sources. But it creates new problems for the cementing-connected-ness-to-oneself-and-others indication, which I could never get behind anyway. Without a validated cementing-con-nectedness-to-oneself-and-others scale the indication is unprovable. But that doesn't mean it can't be discredited when your beagles attack your lab techs."

"How about something simple, something like 'improves the human condition.'"

"The human condition is ill-defined and amorphous."

"What about its sequelae?"

"Sequelae of the human condition are legion, even if quantifiable in theory. You can't design a study big enough to support the indication."

I knew, given an opening, he'd resort to logic. Fortunate-ly, I was prepared.

"Tell them to pick three sequelae and design a bridge study to support the rest." I didn't know what a bridge study was and assumed Dr. Hrbek knew I didn't know. Which made it hard for him to object when he didn't know what I meant in the first place.

"I never knew you and your ilk to be so concerned about the ə or, for that matter, the Director," I observed, casually.

"I care only that our decision be grounded in science. And I would think you of all people would be wary of the perils of judging others by the company they keep. Besides, I've cut those ties. As for the Director, her mind is unknow-able. Yesterday she asked me what I have against caveat emptor as a guiding principle for the regulatory state. Her contrarianism focuses my intellect in a way no one has before. Our exchange has been as provocative as it has been productive—the spoils of our having been thrust into the roles of perfectly matched ideological opposites in a spar of cerebral repartee will go to the American people. Her only reward for her singular brilliance is to have landed in everyone's crosshairs."

"I'm not one to tell people what to do, but if it was me I'd get right on it before a certain senator's office issues a statement and next thing you know he's got nothing but free time on his hands to think of new ways to distract the American public from his intimate history, which isn't what's going to win the hearts and minds of voters no matter how gripping from a human interest perspective."

With that, I hung up.

It was only with my time away from work that I appreciated the strain of keeping in check the difficult personalities and unremitting conflicts in play at the Bureau. So it was with a deep sense of relief that I resolved not to take further calls originating from Bureau offices. An hour after my resolution, I received yet another call. It was from Director Jorg's office. Out of respect I listened to her message immediately.

"Holy cow, you've got secrets," she said; and "So sorry for calling Senator Sakhdvar a prick;" and "He's a freakshow in the sack, eh? Hey, that guy Sorghum filed a request for Permission for Human Experimentation. The n is American consumers. He's going to start the study unless we deny permission but I don't know how to deny permission. Let me know how this rubs you, OK?"

For a moment I felt something warm and not particularly

welcome creeping up the back of my head, which I assumed was my sense of professional responsibility. Certainly, I wasn't troubled by the prospect of allowing human experimentation to commence on a scale never before implemented. The Bureau was notoriously laissez faire in its attitude toward human experimentation. And allowing the release of the ə for investigational purposes with the imprimatur of a producing decision seemed the perfect ploy to elude the overseers while preserving all options. There was nothing for me to do but let it happen. I erased the Director's message and ordered in bulgogi.

PFFT

When I woke the next morning the first thing I thought about wasn't the ə or human experimentation or even the notoriety I had decided to embrace. It was Jeremy's statement. The lack of one, that is. I sat down to leftover bulgogi and thought about how to change that.

Once again, my phone rang. I didn't recognize the number.

"Am I speaking to N—?"

It was a man's voice with a casual air that transported across the telephone lines, as though it was of no consequence to him at all to whom he was speaking.

"In fact you are."

"This is Pinker." Zero bells rung.

"Maddox Pinker. With *The Washington Post*."

Just as Nym had predicted. I was leaving my mark on the communal psyche.

"I've been expecting your call."

"I wonder if you'd answer a few questions for a profile I'm working up."

"Name the time. I assume there'll be a shoot?"

"We have photos of the senator."

"If it's the senator you're interested in—."

"Let's talk over drinks."

I realized this was just the opportunity I was looking for.

I felt so good about the teal pyjama shirt and the jeans that I ended up wearing them to the hotel bar where Maddox Pinker suggested we meet. He was a middle-aged man with a raffish stubble and a nonplussed affect, an affect I assume he cultivated to disarm his sources. I won't belabor the details of our conversation, except to say it was a different experience entirely from talking to Nym. He wasn't the least bit fumbly for one thing, and he was refreshingly prurient. I told my story again over two Negronis, again without interruption. Pinker leaned sideways with his cheek propped up by his fist until I was done. Then he straightened up.

"What's his deal with the ə?" Pinker drew a pad from a nylon backpack and stationed himself over it, ready to go at a moment's notice.

"I haven't a clue who put that bee in his bonnet."

"Speculate. As a professional journalist I'm giving you permission."

Of course I'd do no such thing. Anyway, I'd never asked myself such a question. It was like introspection, only directed at someone else.

"Have I mentioned Jeremy's eating habits?"

He looked at me quizzically.

"Perhaps metaphorically." Who knows what he meant by that.

"What can you tell me about Sakhdvar's father?"

I wasn't going to let a curve ball throw me off of my game.

"Quite a lot, it so happens."

"Name one thing."

"I thought the practice was to read a book before one reviews it."

"You mean his memoir? It says his father was a hapless schmo who married his mother a few weeks before driving his vehicle off a bridge."

"Which bridge?"

"A lesser bridge. In New Jersey, I think. Or Queens? Who knows."

"But you've confirmed a bridge was involved."

"There are contemporaneous newspaper clippings, saying he was survived by a wife and son."

"I'd like to go on deep background," I said. He put aside his notepad and clasped his hands in front of him.

"He was fathered by a member of the clergy with a background in zymurgy." Maddox scribbled the word zymurgy on his notepad then looked at me and struck a line through it.

"Sounds like a limerick."

"If you can rhyme 'fornicator' in the short lines."

"'Senator' almost works."

"I'll have no further comment on the matter."

Maddox Pinker went in an entirely different direction from Nym in a piece published under the title, "Sakhdvar, Unplugged." It ran under a three-quarters shot of Jeremy looking up from his wire reading glasses all the way down at the bottom of his nose, as though he was itching to bed whoever was taking the picture but with his forefinger fussily pressed into his chin, as though he was trying to hold himself back. The article was all over the place, with quotes from a dozen sources, named and unnamed, and bolded subheadings like *The Man Who'd Take Your Tech* and *A Multifarious Career Spinning with Ramrod Constancy on Near-Oedipal Antipathy to the Pleasures of the Tech.* Yet the only mention of me at all was an oblique one, under the rhetorical subheading *Is Sex Still Relevant?,* one of those questions intended to poke fun at everyone who assumes the answer is yes, and not to bring anyone one iota closer to the truth. But nonetheless, I read it all the way to the end. I admit, the question drew me in with the hope against all experience that the article would end with an answer in the affirmative. Instead, it ended in the back pages abutting a short article by one of Pinker's colleagues titled, "The Roots of American Zymurgy." Like Pinker's article this one was also accompanied by a photo, only this one had a doozy of a caption:

The man sometimes called the father of American zymurgy was a prominent cardinal believed to have fathered dozens of his parishioners' children. He was 88 years old when he died in his sleep earlier this year.

The photo showed a fellow with a little skullcap on his head and a cape-type garment buttoned to his chin; he was in three-quarters view looking up from wire frame readers from long eyes. He looked not unlike Rufus Sewell.

I was disappointed. This wasn't the piece that was going to elicit a reaction. Like a request to meet. Or even a statement. Other than one from Nym, who called as soon as the article ran.

"You spoke to Pinker?"

Her tone was accusatory.

"Last I looked it was still a free country but let me know if something's changed," I said.

"He didn't even name you. He's undermined your credibility. Listen, you need a gatekeeper. More than that, an image guru." Nym could be a little blunt, I'd discovered. "Someone who can coax your most echt self out, then dupe the public consciousness into thinking the invention is primal, a collective memory or the embodiment of a universal yen."

"You may be getting a little ahead of me."

"You need an ally who's equal parts confidante, life coach, and image consultant, wearing the mantle of a publicist. A word-lover and media-savant who also knows your background, who can mold you like a lump of clay into the willing vessel of the public imagination."

"Craigslist?"

I knew exactly what she was suggesting. I didn't want to hurt her feelings. But one's publicist so often stands in for oneself and I didn't want my stand-in dropping things. I said I'd hire her on a trial basis. Then I never looked back. Her rate was high to make up for the loss of income when she quit Echt.com to commit herself full time to my needs but she earned every penny. From then, she spent many working hours at my apartment.

One afternoon weeks into my leave-taking from the Bureau, gripped by a foreign spirit concocted from the stress and ennui and my singular situation, I shared my frustration. I was no closer to meeting with Jeremy. And he still hadn't issued a statement.

"We need to turn up the heat."

I didn't know what she meant, but I liked the suggestion. It sounded intimate and participatory. I perked right up.

"Let's write an editorial."

That wasn't what I had in mind. Three days later, Nym texted me a link to my editorial in *The Washington Post*. Having other people's words in something with my name on it was hardly new to me, or for that matter having my words in something with someone else's name, even if the words were actually written on my behalf by someone else. But usually there was an effort to make the words seem as though they could have come from the person whose name was attached to the words. The first time I had Hieronymus write something for Director Jorg—I think it was an Op Ed on nano-ingestibles or something equally provocative—I gave him written instructions to compose a first draft by orally explaining the topic to someone completely unfamiliar with it, transcribing a tape of the explanation, then using a thesaurus to replace all the nouns with synonyms rated less relevant than other synonyms and adding modifiers that were evocative but ambiguous. This did the trick. The Op Ed was a little jarring and hard to put a finger on, so even if it didn't sound like Director Jorg it made you feel like you were inside Director Jorg's head. Nym went in a different direction. For one thing, I doubt I would title my editorial "Seitan as Metaphor." She called four minutes after her text.

"What do you think I meant when I wrote 'Over our first dinner he hungrily devoured my adulation and his seitan'?"

"Meaning isn't the point. You used a zeugma. I promise you his head is spinning." A silence followed, as though she was giving me time to ask the obvious question. That would only encourage her sesquipedalianism, which I found ostentatious.

"It seems awkward."

"You're a regulator. No one expects you to write well."

"Though your memos to staff were masterful," Nym added after an uncomfortable silence.

"He ordered a baked potato with sauce verte," I pointed out. I didn't mean to be critical, but my credibility was at stake.

"'Baked Potato as Metaphor' wouldn't have worked. With or without the sauce verte."

"We were at a steak house."

"A vegan meeting you for a date at a steak house isn't credible."

"Seitan wasn't even a thing then. Perhaps we can impose upon them to issue a correction . . ."

"All the better New York City vegan restaurants served seitan then same as they do now. You can't impeach me with 'but you were too young to go to vegan restaurants in New York City back then,'" (here Nym spoke in a stilted high register). "I went to more than a few vegan restaurants during my years of graduate study and the better ones had pictures on the walls from the 90's of their celebrity guests eating seitan dishes. So I think I know a thing or two about it."

The memory of kelp extract flooded my consciousness.

"Here all along I'd assumed the puttanesca was for V."

"V. lived on egg whites and ostrich jerky."

"Dr. Hrbek?"

"A vegan sympathizer."

"Then you're the sympathizee?"

I was pleased with myself for a moment. Then I thought of chimpanzees and I felt unsettled.

"Anyway, for what is seitan a metaphor?"

Nym gasped in exasperation.

"Sex! Hypocrisy! Senator Suckmydick going Medieval about a pissant process foul over a piece of quackass boondoggle gadgetry but poking his bareback tofupup into his snoozing sidepiece's sprout salad without a by your leave. Anyway, the metaphor's not a one-to-one kind of thing. Stop being so goddamn literal. My metaphors are multidetermined. And now, so are yours."

I'd always admired Nym's passion, even if it expressed itself in ways I found inscrutable. Yet I detected an undercurrent of self-loathing that had to be called out. The first step to overcoming something is to confront it.

"Would you agree there's something, shall we say, anomalous about your anger towards vegans?"

"*Former* vegans. The poster children for the kind of all-things-in-moderation, including slaughterhouses, establishment, mealy-mouthed, heuristic hypocrisy Sakhdvar represents. But anyway, I'm not the editorial's target audience. The American public is, and if there's one thing that sets the collective canines of the entire American public on edge . . ."

She paused.

"Veganism?" I ventured. Having never harbored any such hostilities, I had to wonder whether Nym was suffering from a persecution complex. To say I could hear her eyes roll over the phone would be an exaggeration. Yet I can't remember the conversation without imagining Nym's pupils hitting her upper eyelids with a little "plink" sounding just before Nym hung up on me.

Though the reckoning with Nym's complicated demons would have to wait until another day, she was right on the money as far as Jeremy's head spinning. Two days after the fictionalized editorial ran (if you want to call it an editorial), Jeremy's office issued the following:

> Senator Sakhdvar has never met the quixotic fabulist who has made false claims concerning his intimate life. He categorically refutes her allegations and, for that matter, a history of exotic eating habits.

It was more like a comment than a statement. But it was something. There were more words but the rest was filler, wasn't even part of a comment. I was a little hurt by "false allegations." At the same time, "quixotic fabulist" seemed to come from a place of affection. Nym called after texting a link to the comment, or whatever you'd call the whole thing given that only part of it qualified as a comment.

"It's almost a zeugma."

I said nothing.

"Words lie but the mode of expression never lies. We've penetrated his consciousness."

That got my attention. But it didn't satisfy me. I still need-ed to meet with Jeremy. I knew what had to happen first.

"In light of our history of intimacy it seems to me the least one could ask for is that whatever he says—e.g., comment, denial, refutation, veiled admission, and so forth—when he says it, he should refer to me by my name," I mused.

Something splashed on the other end of the phone line and there was a clanking sound as though Nym had dropped the receiver into a bowl of something then knocked over the bowl while getting the receiver out. Out of politeness I pre-tended not to notice when Nym dropped things and never would have asked a question that presupposed her tendency in that regard. But my conjecture was entirely plausible, and not the sort of thing Nym would have confirmed one way or the other perhaps because she too was sensitive about her tendencies. In any case we were disconnected, whether by the contact of the receiver with whatever was in the bowl, or by the bowl itself when it was knocked over, if either of those things happened. What was strange was Nym didn't call right back the way she usually did when we were discon-nected by her dropping the phone, but instead called back a day or so later.

"I got you a meeting with Jeremy," was the first thing she said, before even "hello," and while it's possible she said oth-er things after the first thing I couldn't focus on what they were.

"How–?"

"He's starting to feel the heat."

Then she hung up the phone without dropping it.

Days went by. To distract myself I read commentary on

the comment and the editorial, which generated quite a bit because it confused everyone. #Aquixoticfabulist trended, and I became something of a cause célèbre as a woman unfairly derided for speaking truth to power. Still, the commentary generally focused on the wrong things, like whether sex was relevant, and whether Jeremy's exotic appetites in that regard were related to his dietary issues, giving rise to speculation on certain nutrition blogs about the effect of protein deficiency on one's sexual urges. On the other hand, with so many articles the odds seemed favorable that Jeremy would read one of them, including my name as it appeared in the articles. Closing my eyes and concentrating as hard as I could, I was able to imagine his eyes floating across N—, and his mouth moving to say it aloud as one sometimes does to drive home the actuality of something in print so stunning that the initial response is to require audible proof of what was read. When the time came, I decided I was as ready as I'd ever be.

"I've made all the arrangements," Nym said. "There'll be a gray Volkswagen Beetle parked outside your building. An unmarked gray Beetle. You'll find the key under the weigela. Get the key 15 minutes after you get off the phone with me, but only after you've made sure no one is outside. If anyone is outside, go back upstairs and come back down 15 minutes later, and so on until no one is there. If the same person is there more than once we'll have to think of a plan B."

"Where's the weigela?" Again, I wasn't going to ask the obvious question. But I thought she might volunteer it.

"It's in the quadrangle with the clematis and the phlox," Nym paused. "Plants."

Nym claimed to have memorized an encyclopedia of botany to enrich her experience of Shakespeare. Her knowledge of plants was not unlike her knowledge of hendiadys and zeugma in that it was a little showy.

I peered out from behind the drapes of the street-facing window in my front room to identify the gray Beetle. If Nym was one of those people who called things gray that anyone else would call slate or smoky-loden colored, I needed to know that ahead of time. But the closest thing to a gray Beetle were a few silver sedans that besides not being gray, plainly weren't Beetles.

"I don't see a gray Beetle."

"Don't worry about that. It'll be there by 9. At 9:15, take the key you got from the weigela, then once you're inside, look for instructions. They'll be in the glove compartment or underneath the seat covers, which have a Dalmatian pattern. I haven't decided yet where to put them except for that they'll be inside, not under the chassis or anywhere where you might need special tools to gain access. By the way, step away from your window."

I was a little put off by the level of detail I was expected to memorize. I view life more as an improvisation than a list of instructions. It was helpful that the instructions would be in writing, but first I'd have to find the instructions and I wasn't even sure if I could find the weigela.

"Follow the instructions to a T and they'll take you to Jeremy," Nym concluded before hanging up, again without dropping the receiver, at least not before we were disconnected.

As it turned out, the weigela was easy to find and the gray Beetle was gray. The weigela had a plastic tag around one of its branches like the sort of tag a farmer puts on a chicken's foot, only the tag said "weigela" instead of the chicken's name or whatever farmers write there. Not only was the gray

Beetle gray, but it was right in front of the quadrangle with the clematis and the phlox so I could hardly miss it even if I wanted to, which of course I didn't. The instructions were on the passenger's seat, on top of the Dalmatian-patterned seat cover and they were incredibly user friendly. In fact, "instructions" was an overstatement. There was only one instruction, so Nym could have just told me to look for the instruction. On the other hand, that might have seemed condescending, as those of us who've spent our lives in pursuit of our best selves always seek out instruction, even if we find instructions off-putting. When I read the instruction, I knew exactly what to do.

DRIVE TO THE TIDAL BASIN
THEN PARK BY THE TREES

You could say there were two instructions, one related to driving and one related to parking, but they gave an illusion of unity and singleness of purpose. And any disconnect from having two instructions crammed into a single sentence was more than balanced out by the other quality of the instruction, which was the quality of something completing itself. There could be no better place to see Jeremy in person and unobstructed after decades of seeing Jeremy only in print or on the television or behind a name plaque. One hates to resort to clichés, but it was as though we had come full circle.

The night was perfect. The sort of night where occasionally a breeze would blow the few petals left on the trees off of the trees, but one noticed the petals, not the breeze. It was perfect weather for the teal pajama-like top and men's jeans that I wore in my initial photo shoot, even if that's not why

I wore them. I wore them because that's what I was wearing when I was reintroduced to Jeremy through the media, and what one might assume I was wearing when I penetrated his consciousness. I was leaving nothing to chance.

Just as I pulled the parking brake and was about to exit the gray Beetle, I heard a tapping noise against the car roof.

"You look different in person." The voice was basso profundo, unfamiliar.

I couldn't think of anything to say but congratulated myself for the teal separates, which presumably looked the same.

Initially the head of the person tapping on my car roof hung diagonally outside the window of the passenger's seat as he rested his left elbow against the roof. He stopped tapping but didn't say anything else for long enough that I was unnerved. I couldn't see his features because his face was darkened by the streetlamp behind him. I squinted and put my forearm over my eyes, but neither helped. All I could see was the black cutout of a head that didn't look quite like Jeremy's head. The head disappeared and I heard the tapping again. Then he reached in to unlock the door and let himself in.

Up close his head blocked the streetlamp so once my eyes adjusted I could see his features as long as he stayed still. He was a young and extremely tall but pale and a little soft, as though he didn't get out much. His features were hard to make out due to the light shining through puffy, sagging os in his ears, like sad little mouths pouting for the accessory that would have kept them round and firm, if only this young man had been more committed to a certain lifestyle. Plus, he had a cowlick or perhaps it was just that the part of hair on the back of his head remained upright from his head hanging upside down outside the car window even after he'd straightened his head out and all the rest of his hair clung to his head. It was hard to tell.

"You're not Jeremy."

"I'm Zed."

Zed opened the glove compartment, flipped the window visors, felt under the seats, emptied my purse and finally patted me down all over, which I can't say was unreasonable.

"We asked to meet with Jeremy."

"I was referring to how you look in print." Zed extended his hand, which I shook out of common courtesy. "Good to meet you. I'm on Jeremy's campaign staff."

"My business is with the senator."

"We thought it was best this way, for your safety. The senator has powerful enemies."

"Perhaps I should speak to them."

Zed reached into his shirt pocket with his forefinger and middle finger, then pulled out a piece of paper that had been torn from a notepad. The notepad paper had a series of handwritten bullet points on it but no sentences, which I could tell from the lack of punctuation other than bullets. Zed studied the notepad paper for an unduly long time but naturally I was impatient, so perhaps it just seemed like an unduly long time. Zed cleared his throat.

"'The senator has never forgotten you and thinks of you often. He commends your accession to a position of such prominence at the Bureau especially in light of the discognizence—er—discordance with your quote/unquote past self. To the extent your current foray into the public sphere with revelations of certain matters that if true would be of a highly personal nature are an effort to influence outcomes vis-à-vis the Swab Matter, he is of the view that there is a role for communication between and among our (his and your) respective staffs to reach a rapprochement among the interests of the public, the Bureau, and the scientists who have bravely, though perhaps without full information, come forward to—'"

"Are you certain you're part of his campaign staff?"

Zed stiffened. The streetlamp shining through the holes in his earlobes was like a second set of eyes, only I couldn't see the first set.

"I'm on temporary detail while he deals with a staffing issue."

"I see," I said.

He crammed the paper back into his shirt pocket for emphasis, who knows what of.

"I'm extremely fucking competent in my usual role, but this one's a first for me and way the fuck outside my portfolio, which is asylum policy, or I should say my portfolio as a staffer before I took on campaign staff duty, which now apparently includes dealing with the consequences of the senator's junior member of Congress taking asylum in Randompussytown—"

"One wouldn't say random. Jeremy answered my ad," I clarified.

Zed relaxed again and the shift in posture resulted in his collar covering the backs of his earlobes so the streetlamp didn't shine through them. I felt safer with his features visible given his hot-headedness, which I could only imagine was counterproductive for the sort of job that places one in regular contact with high-pressure situations. But Jeremy always was one to reward passion over everything else, such as skills for coping with explosive matters.

"Anyway, Jeremy's cool with letting bygones be bygones

but to be very clear he won't stand for retaliation as regards the whistleblower shit—," Zed continued.

"You mean the Cabal of Five. Whistleblower is a legal conclusion."

"We know of at least 20."

"The Bureau doesn't tolerate retaliation. And I believe you mean the ə. Surely that isn't the only reason the senator called me here to meet with his second."

"Jeremy would like you to issue a retraction."

I scooted back in my seat to try to get Zed's head in front of the streetlamp, but there wasn't enough room for me to move far back enough to make any difference. I was able to straighten my posture though, which didn't affect the relationship of Zed's head to the streetlamp enough to block the streetlamp but gave me a boost of confidence.

"That's not what I had in mind." I cleared my throat. "It's fair to say our relationship, by which I mean mine with Jeremy, was an unusually significant one for each of us. I'm the last person to psychoanalyze the motivations of another person but Jeremy's wheelhouse is justice. One need not have a knack for analysis to question the provenance of Jeremy's interest in the ə, or should I say the Bureau's oversight of the ə, and the Cabal of Five and related matters, matters the investigation of which would lead unavoidably to me in my role as one of the nation's leading biotechnology regulators and, not to put too fine a point on it, oversight of me, which given our history is hard to think of in a purely platonic sense."

By that time my eyes had adjusted somewhat to the streetlamp, so I could make out Zed's features enough to see when they were moving. He was pressing his lips together so his mouth shrunk up as if there was a cord running through his lips and someone was pulling the cord.

"Jeremy says you guys fucked like twice."

"The physical was just one dimension of our connection and 'fucking'—your word not mine—was just one element of the physical side of things, which in our case was highly varied."

Obviously, Zed had no response to that.

"What do you want?"

"It was three times, by the way, as far as intercourse goes, which I've already made clear is the wrong metric. Not that it's your business but for sake of clarity."

I squinted again to see if his mouth was puckered, but all I could see of his face were his lashless gray eyes, and one of the holes in his ears, the other being invisible with him at a three-quarters angle.

"I'd like Jeremy to issue a comment acknowledging the intimacy of our relationship. In consideration of the situation as far as Jeremy's wife and other constituents and, of course, his life goals, which I commend him for by the way (although I'm not prepared to issue an endorsement), you don't have to say anything about sexual intimacy, but whatever you do say about intimacy I prefer there not be any ambiguity concerning with whom the intimacy was had, i.e., me, as in N—. This as a prelude to a meeting, where I believe I can convince him of the appropriate posture a man in his position should adopt as far as the ə."

An awkward pause ensued.

"What Jeremy says about his eating habits is his business, by the way."

I was about to continue when he straightened up, put his

hand on the passenger door handle, and turned his head so it completely blocked the lamplight. The darkened o shapes at the sides of his head again seemed disappointed at the same time the cowlick was indecently upright.

"In the event we weren't able to reach agreement on how to move forward, Jeremy asked that I relay a special message." Zed again withdrew the crumpled paper from his shirt pocket and consulted it, then looked up.

"'You're a SO-CI-O-PATH,'" Zed said, but he said it as though there were an accent on every syllable of the word "sociopath." It sounded more like a cheer than an insult. "His words. You seem nice to me."

Zed opened the car door and got out. I saw my window was closing to turn this meeting around, to say something that would show Jeremy the folly of frustrating my eminently reasonable request to meet.

"I can think of numerous reputable journalists who'd find time for a sit down to get the scoop that the man who may be our next president was fathered by a notoriously fornicative former man of the cloth."

Zed paused a moment with his back to me. Yet I heard his response perfectly clearly.

"Pfft."

LA FIN DE L'AFFAIRE

I slept in the next day. Late in the morning I dreamed the phone was ringing and it turned out my phone was ringing. I was certain I knew who it was. An apology was the least I could ask for.

"You don't know me."

"I believe I do," I corrected, still groggy. "Better than most."

"By my art. That's not what I'm talking about."

It was only then that I realized the caller couldn't possibly be who I thought it was. The person I thought it was had put art behind him. And he wasn't a woman.

"I'm a fan of the arts," I said, leaning into my skill for hair-pin course corrections.

"When can we meet?" the woman demanded. I found her insistence strident.

"First I don't know you now it seems I'm obliged to meet you. Choose one why don't you?"

"Someone important to you is about to be set up."

My thoughts raced, then hit a wall. No one fit the description and this seemed sad. I wanted to take a moment to nurse the wounds bared by this reminder of my solitary existence. But I knew not to let down my guard with this mysterious caller.

"I'm an island."

"Sakhdvar."

I sat upright, my back as straight as a rod. My intuition about the caller was almost right. Even if Jeremy wasn't the one making the call, it seemed he was the reason for the call. An old protective instinct kicked in, quite against my will.

"I have a hard time believing anyone would want to hurt someone who's life work has been the protection of the American people from fraudulent products and other injustices. Even if he sometimes takes things too far."

"Listen to me very carefully. You know V."

She didn't sound like she was asking so I felt no obligation to answer. I decided to disarm her with an absurdity.

"I added him to my contacts. In case I misplace my carabiner."

"He's plotting to take Sakhdvar down."

I'd been outdone on the absurdity front. I didn't know whether to be impressed or offended.

"That's ridiculous. Their interests are aligned. That is against the ə and anything else for that matter that gives the rest of us a little bit of distraction from the humdrum of our daily existence. I concede their motivations are different."

"V.'s making a powerplay to show the strength of Cabal. He needs to take out both: the ə to show his dedication to the cause and Sakhdvar to show his ruthlessness, his refusal to collaborate with establishment agents. It's the opening salvo in his bid for leadership over all of N'Aut."

"I was starting to think you had something to say before you brought up the global anti-blablabla conglomerate that would be totally a big thing we should all lose sleep over if it weren't an overwrought figment of perfervid imaginings."

I had been spending a good deal of time around Nym, and her showy vocabulary was starting to rub off on me. For a moment there was silence, I gather because the caller was digesting my words. Which I concede had some bulk to them.

"I've said too much already. We need to meet."

Despite my dismissive remark, this woman had captured my attention. I felt I had to meet her.

"If you say so. But I'm doing this for the senator, whose only transgression is that he cares too much. If we're going to 'take people out' for that (as you put it), none of us is safe."

"There's a hookah bar in Adam's Morgan. It has a private room in the back."

"I know it well."

"I'll be there at eight."

"How will I know it's you?"

"I'll be in the private room. Duh. Plus, my hair is magenta."

"That narrows things. Barely."

"With orchid low lights."

"How do I know you are who you say you are?"

"I haven't said who I am."

"Touché."

"Sakhdvar's my half-brother."

"You should have led with that. Had I known you were motivated by filial affection—"

"He's also a prick."

"Then what exactly is your motivation?"

"My motivation is irrelevant. I go by Rodin(t)."

Rodin(t) hung up and I fell backwards into the loft of several down pillows, stunned. The elusive artist Rodin(t) was Jeremy's half-sister. And now I was going to meet her. To save Jeremy from the scheming of the Cabal's First in Command and, it suddenly occurred to me, perhaps get the goods that would at last bring me and Jeremy face to face. I inhaled deeply and thought about what to wear.

In the end I went with your standard off-work fare. I think I wore a bustier, a sensible one with its own scaffolding. I wasn't going there to call attention to myself. I was going there because I had a duty—to the Bureau and to the American public. Possibly even to Jeremy, though the normal bonds that tie one-time intimates had been badly weakened by his Zed gambit.

I arrived at eight and marched to the back of the establishment, then pulled back the curtain hiding the private room. There was Rodin(t) stretched out on three floor pillows. It's true her hair was hard to ignore, but it wasn't her hair that got my attention. Because seated upright on the third pillow, underneath Rodin(t)'s upper body, was Director Jorg, playfully twirling Rodin(t)'s hair around a finger. She wore a clingy red dress and her hair was a gray-black cumulonimbus cloud. She looked smashing.

Rodin(t) sat upright and planted a hand on Director Jorg's knee.

"I didn't expect to see you here," I replied. For a moment I experienced a flare up around my cranium.

"You two talk your stuff I don't really give two hoots, OK?" Director Jorg took a hit off the hookah and Rodin(t) motioned for me to sit on a pillow facing them.

"We can speak freely. She knows everything."

"I'm a tomb, baby," Director Jorg interjected as she forced streams of smoke out her nose and extracted her Blackberry from her dress pocket.

I took a seat on a pillow across from Rodin(t). She had the same long green eyes and delicate jaw as Jeremy. But she was petite and furtive, I wanted to say mouselike.

"State your business."

"Sakhdvar's in danger."

"From V. if I understand our previous conversation. And I think I do which is not to say I believe it."

"V. is going to go public."

"That's been done. It seems the American people are unconcerned with the behaviors of consenting adults, no matter how exotic. Unless V. has something really far out there he's about to share."

"Please. I'm not here to waste time with the lumpenparaphiliatariat and their endless sexual judgmentalism." Director Jorg, who had been absently gazing at her Blackberry in between long drags of the hookah, leaned over and kissed Rodin(t) for what seemed like a long time.

"Don't let me intrude," I remarked, as they separated slowly, unwillingly, it seemed. "But you're wasting your time. Jeremy's Teflon."

"Things will go differently if they find out he's a collaborator."

"Holy shit he'll be fucked over poor guy." Director Jorg knocked back a shot of something. It appeared to be ouzo.

"Listen," Rodin(t) leaned in and looked at me with her seductive green eyes. I couldn't look away. "Sakhdvar and V. are supposedly fellow travelers committed to our cause, but we all know what Sakhdvar's in it for."

"The health and well-being of all Americans?"

"Guess again Betty."

"It's N—. Continue."

"Sakhdvar cares about two things: number one, the annihilation of our dad by waging a symbolic war against an actual deadly enemy that's infiltrating every aspect of our lives. Number two, his own advancement. Also, deviant non-penetrative sex. But that's a distant third."

"I'd have guessed you weren't a fan of that sort of judgment-laden observation based on your comment about the lumpenpara—"

"Deviant sex is the only thing that still ties me to him."

"Ha ha ha," Director Jorg interjected.

"Not actually the only thing. We have a common flesh and blood enemy. We differ as to tactics."

"Let's get back to Jeremy, V., and what you want from me, shall we?"

"Two things. First, neutralize V."

"I have no idea what you're suggesting but if it involves a hit or violence of any sort you can count me out."

"Not necessarily."

Rodin(t) and Director Jorg exchanged glances.

"This one comes to a Meet the Regulator forum and she reserved time in the open public comment part. She says to me 'You suck.' Not exactly but more like why do you let all this crappy biomedicaltechnology out there and then her five minutes were up so I said 'I'll tell you why later' and then she comes up to me at the open bar when I'm talking to some big shot who makes a sphincter product and she says 'OK its later it's so boring with all these fuckers here let's go to my room' and I said 'OK' the next thing you know she's my new girlfriend and in the morning she says to me 'what can we do about this guy V.' I said 'we'll make him pay' because anyway he was the guy talking trash about me and the former Bureau big boss guy but I didn't know what I was talking about when I said that because he seems like a dumb joke to me and anyway what do I know about making people pay? I'm a neurosurgeon."

"I never heeded rumors that you and Director Stan were—"

"Making the beast that's got two backs? Yeah we did that. This guy V. has a big mouth with reporters. Maybe you could get him to shut his mouth up. Without whacking him out."

"The idioms are taking him out or whacking him. Choose one."

"Why choose when you can have it all? Just mess him up but in the brain not physically, OK?"

"The point is, the director and I have given careful thought to what we mean by 'neutralize.' We've decided it's (a) a tactical matter and (b) your problem."

Rodin(t) squeezed Director Jorg's thigh and the director giggled. I was captivated. Yet a little annoyed.

"You lured me here suggesting the interests of a certain senator were in play. Not that I necessarily care but if your interests relate exclusively to the neutralizing of a well-known malcontent all I can say is take a number. Behind every single member of the biomedicaltechnology sector, that is."

"If we don't neutralize him he's going to bring down Sakhdvar. Sakhdvar and V. go way back. I should know, I introduced them. I knew them from two different underground networks, one of survivors of clergy abuse and their spawn, and the other of anti-tech radicals. Let's just say I had a finger in every pie. They were just a couple of New York fringe dwellers with aspirations for bigger things. Later they roomed together in DC, back when V. still went by NeVin."

"Impossible. Jeremy's roommate Ned was an upstanding fellow with a range of wholesome interests perfectly in keeping with his times—things like solidarity and legalized marijuana."

"So you met him?"

"I saw his walls." I remembered the poster of the naked woman with a video camera where her head should be. "And on that basis I can say with some confidence that Ned was no sexual ascetic. Which seems to undermine your thesis of a V.-Ned identity."

"You never slept with him. Holy-moly what a drag." Rodin(t) rolled her eyes around and around in an exaggerated display of exasperation. "Anyway, if you're talking about the *Seks, Kłamstwa i Kasety Video* poster broadcasting the playful eroticism of the cinephile while slyly winking at dehumanization, that was Jeremy's."

The revelation made sense. Yet I was stunned. V. and whatever dark principle he represented had always been there, lurking in Jeremy's shadow Jeremy. I couldn't let on, so I brushed aside the revelation with the first words that came into my head.

"No doubt he was reifying dehumanization qua sexual objectification to process the trauma of his conception, as a means of shielding himself from being retraumatized by the acknowledgement of the pain caused to women by male exploitation."

Rodin(t) looked at me, hard.

"I assumed you were an intelligent idiot. It's possible you're an idiotic savant."

"Her brain works OK but it has all the wrong stuff in it," Director Jorg murmured without looking up. "Like all you people."

Rodin(t)'s words rolled off of me but the director's stung.

"You people?"

"She means Americans."

"North Americans."

"So it's not personal."

"It's good to know where one stands."

Director Jorg still hadn't looked up.

"Back to NeVin." Rodin(t) snapped her fingers in front of my face. Which I found disrespectful. "He aka V. and I disagree about the N'Aut endgame. I say it's to unleash humanity from the artificial constraints imposed by our techno-capitalist patriarchal fascist regime so it's free to pursue its native state of community, creativity, pleasure, sensuality. And so on and so forth. V.'s goal is to set in motion a forever struggle against a perpetually mutating enemy, zeroing in on conflicts closer and closer to the home until you don't even know what separates you from your enemy, and the conflict lives insides of you in perpetuity ad nauseum et cetera. The conflict is the endgame."

"I thought we weren't to speak of motivation. At least not yours. If I'm not mistaken you have an alternative fashion boutique. I'd expect you of all people to appreciate that no one can ever be free when their choices are limited by well-meaning if fundamentally misguided perspectives of social weal."

"I have rent to pay."

"Her place in the Alphabet was on HGTV," Director Jorg offered.

"And excuse me for being passionate. I'll stop. Here's the deal: V. installed himself in his position so he could leak confidential information. He's not a whistleblower. He's a self-plant. And Jeremy's been more than happy to exploit the relationship to his advantage. The American people might not care where the senator hides his donkey, but last I checked they weren't down for governance by associates of the radical left anti-tech fringe."

She was indeed passionate. And not unattractive, in her angular, subversive, mouselike way. I was starting to feel a deep connection. But I couldn't let it cloud my judgment. Besides, there was something I needed to know. I remembered my encounter with V. on my first day at the Bureau, how even then he knew who I was.

"Interesting that Jeremy happened to focus his ire on a matter squarely within the purview of his former inamorata, don't you think?"

"He had no idea. V. didn't even know you guys used to—"

"Yeah I don't know what to call it either."

They smiled at each other. Gratuitously, if you ask me.

"When your story broke V. had a meltdown. He wanted to extend your anti-fraternization policy to past relationship with members of congress."

"That's a stretch," I said.

None of this was right. Jorg was the outsider, not me. And Rodin(t) was a dissident. Yet here they were, banding together, casting me out into the world of the solitary and the strange. I went on the offensive.

"Why me? You're Sakhdvar's half-sister. Maybe if you warn him of V.'s treachery—"

"The face of the global proto-anti-technology (and so forth) movement doesn't just call her senator's office when she needs constituent services such as neutralizing a contemporary rival for ideological hegemony in the dominant anti-capitalist counterculture, OK? He'd probably assume I was still pissed at V. for being a stingy, self-absorbed prig in the sack. Besides, we fell out."

"I wouldn't have guessed there could be tension between you two what with you both being such easygoing sorts."

"Like I said, Jeremy and I differ on tactics. He started chasing a 'work from the inside' strategy—suits, public office, the presentable wife."

"I never thought she was right for him."

"You know Leilani?"

At last, light was to be shed on the elegant woman who had come between Jeremy and me, if I played my hand right.

"I believe I know the type."

"Well-connected semiconductor lobbyists formerly live-in girlfriends of top DC lobbyists with deep ties to the donor class? Jeremy thought he was cultivating a benefactor but ended up with a wife."

I gulped inwardly without emitting a sound. Jeremy's elegant wife was the well-put together she-lobbyist, love interest of Fred or whatever his name was! Who'd launched my career in biomedicaltechnology by giving me a referral I ignored. The suggestion was fantastic. And yet, not unexpected.

"I'd heard they were married."

"The lobbyists? It was common law."

Director Jorg snorted happily.

"Her ex common law husband goes by Fred, I presume?"

"Friedrich."

"Impossible. His name was only somewhat German."

"Perhaps your recall of things isn't as reliable as you believe."

"That's preposterous. Let's get to the second thing."

"Unleash the Ə."

"I thought I just heard the secretive leader of the notorious if fictional anti-tech underworld direct me to release our era's most anticipated technology product unto the public. But I must have misheard."

"When those anticipations and hopes are dashed against the jagged rocks of technology's false promise, the people will throw off their silicon shackles and rise up to demand—"

"A four-day workweek and more pot, right my sister?" Dr. Jorg squeezed Rodin(t)'s thigh but Rodin(t) didn't respond. Her eyes were narrowed and a little glassy. They were focused somewhere on my face, just not on my eyes.

"We need the ə to ignite the revolution."

"That sounds oddly familiar." I took a drag of the hookah. It suddenly seemed critical that I signal complicity even
while my mind scrambled for purchase. "So let's say we neutralize V. and unleash the ə. What's to stop V. from taking
Jeremy out after his neutralization? (Now that we've cleared
the air, let's all assume I use all such expressions in a sense
that doesn't involve whacking anyone out, shall we?)"

Rodin(t) and Director Jorg looked at one another and
Director Jorg nodded, gesturing for Rodin(t) to answer.

"That's Jeremy's problem. The point is the neutralization.
This way even if Jeremy goes down V. doesn't get credit and
the ə gets out there, exposing him as ineffective. I mean
that's almost the definition of neutralization. Which it's up
to you to define but yeah."

I decided to turn the tables on them. I looked pointedly
to Director Jorg. "I can think of at least one person seated
at this table better positioned to stop V. and unleash the ə."

Director Jorg shrugged disinterestedly.

"I don't care about the ə. Maybe it's a Product maybe it's
a Non-Product. I'm more of a let the market decide kind of
girl. That's why I delegated the regulatory. To you."

Not long after I left the private room and made my way
out the door amidst a disorienting confluence of smoke and
low chatter. One might assume my head was spinning but
my head wasn't spinning. My thoughts organized themselves around a plan as I walked the several blocks to my
apartment. Once there, I pulled the door securely closed
behind me and made my first of two calls.

"How did you know I'd be at the office?"

Dr. Hrbek sounded irritated, as though he'd been interrupted while deep in a highly cerebral effort. No doubt he was.

"Because the American people needed you to be there. There's something I need."

"Yes?"

"Tell V. the canine data's come in and you need his sign off to finalize the decision."

"Are you mad? He'll leak it faster than—"

"Tell him it's 'highly supportive' of the Product's release. I suggest you use those words."

He paused again as he considered the request.

"I see the workings of the trap you've built but I'm afraid it's been constructed on a faulty foundation (if you'll pardon the mixed metaphors). Even if V. believes me, he's not going to go to the press with anything that supports the Ə."

"To the press, no. But perhaps to a co-conspirator."

"I'm not sure the ethics line up."

"While you decide that one maybe you can think about all the good times to be had exposing your one-time romantic rival. One other small thing."

"Proceed."

"Deploy the PPPDSP."

A silence ensued.

"I'll need the citation."

"It's in one of my speeches."

"I mean to the Code of Federal Regulations or United States Code."

"You won't find it there. The law is aspirational."

"No citation is just one problem. If the Provisional Producting Pending Data Supporting Producting existed as a regulatory tool, which it doesn't, it would be for producing something for which no data exists. Data exists for the Ə. Bad data."

"Canine data," I clarified. I found my purse and extracted

the report with the pink sticky note from Sorel Dern still affixed. My eyes raced across the Sorel's words.

"And 'if a controlled experiment on behind-sniffing produced hostile behavior in human subjects, you wouldn't conclude that dogs are averse to behind-sniffing, would you?'"

Dr. Hrbek paused again, as though carefully considering my words.

"I can't argue with that as a matter of science. As an ethical matter, deploying an untested product on—"

"It's already been deployed experimentally so that ethical bridge has been crossed. Besides, the Ə needs to be on the glidepath to the American consumer before V. figures out he's been had. How long will it take to pull off the PPPDSP?"

It seemed a full minute passed in silence.

"You'll sign off?"

"I always do."

"It's an expedited process. Give me forty-eight hours."

"That doesn't give me much time."

"For what?"

"Never mind."

I disconnected and immediately made a second call.

"Zed."

"N— here. I need to see the Senator."

"No can do—"

"I have something he'll want to hear about."

"If it's the whole fathered by a prominent member of the clergy/a man well-practiced in zymurgy/he debased his frock/impregnating his flock—"

"Kudos. Although frock/flock is a little obvious."

"Don't blame me his Chief of Staff wrote it."

"What's the last line?"

"I suggested 'to latex he had allergy' but apparently it's

anticlimactic. The point is no one gives a shit. As a concept paternity is a little quaint."

"If you say so. My business has nothing to do with his paternity and everything to do with the ə."

"I'll take a message."

"You can tell him N. called about an urgent matter. Tell him not to believe everything he hears. Concerning the canine data, that is. By the way, it is strongly in his interest to call in the next twenty-four hours."

With that I disconnected, entered Zed's number into my contacts, and climbed back into the warm embrace of down from which I'd been ousted a mere twelve hours earlier, a span so loaded with intrigue and consequence that it felt like an entire lifetime.

In contrast, the next day the hours dragged to their conclusion, as though bloated and weighted down with unrealized potential. I received no call from Jeremy, not even a call from one of his lackeys. Twenty-four hours hadn't passed, but I was impatient. I took matters into my own hands.

"You may have underestimated the urgency of the situation."

"Hi N—."

I was taken aback by Zed's familiarity. I got down to business.

"When can I meet the senator?"

"Midnight sounds good."

"He'll be there?"

"Where?"

"The Tidal Basin! I'll be there at midnight. If he has some other suggestion, he knows how to reach me."

"Don't be like that. He'll be there. Tidal Basin. Midnight. You have my word."

It had taken me twenty-four minutes to reach the Tidal Basin two nights earlier. So I left my apartment at 11:36. I like to be punctual, even when meeting with someone who had recently so cruelly dashed my expectations. As I was pulling into the parking lot, my phone rang, and Zed's name flashed on the screen. It was midnight, exactly. I didn't have to answer to know why he'd called. I disconnected, parked, and stepped out into the perfect summer evening, with the air warm but light and breezy and fragrant from a rangy vine. I walked towards the patch of grass where so many years before Jeremy and I had fallen to the ground, entwined in an invisible mesh woven of our wants and hopes. Only there were no down-on-their-luck spectators about now, and the sky was as clear as could be. I wasn't surprised that I'd been stood up, again. The strange thing was I wasn't particularly disappointed. I inhaled the strange, sweet smell blowing in on the breeze then exhaled slowly and returned to my car.

At noon the next day the PPPDSP dropped and the world changed.

From that moment forward, anyone who wanted to use the ə to improve sequelae of the human condition could buy a ə at the Glottal store or download the ə app online and wouldn't have to wait for Sorel's clinical team to produce data showing the sorts of things the Bureau usually expected to see before allowing such a claim, such as improvement, and which sequelae improved, and the level of significance of the improvement. The world would soon learn that the American consuming public cared not in the least that the approval was provisional as the American consuming public embraced the ə for the lifestyle enhancing innovation it was. In the months after announcement of the PPPDSP, the verb form "to schwa,"—conjugated just as one would expect—entered the vernacular, followed by the gerund "schwaing," soon shortened to the popular term "schwang," a term familiar enough in its common usage but with other obscure and coarse usages standard dictionaries have yet to include. Sorel's provocative statement about platform turned out to be prescient. The stealthy nano-based start-up Weensy announced a partnership with Glottal to develop a microscopic platform for the ə that could be implanted using a minimally invasive procedure. Soon, not only could one load one's ə onto one's laptop, smartwatch, or phone, but once could experience it subcutaneously. It was a matter of time before insertables came onto the market, allowing users a more intimate ə experience.

In short, life as it had always been lived on our planet was upended. Sorel Dern became a billionaire instantly. He texted me that evening to thank me not only for making him a billionaire but for putting the ə into the hands of humanity. I was moved. Who knows where he got my number.

In the end the PPPDSP was a win-win for everyone except Director Jorg, whose name was on the PPPDSP, naturally, as I'd signed it for her. She was removed. I doubt the nameless operatives responsible for her removal thought the PPPDSP was a bad idea. But, as became clear from a run of opinion pieces authored by the sort of people who spend all their time policing everyone else's ethics, a consensus view had emerged among the overseers, one that viewed the PPPDSP like the granting of the non-filing petition before it had been filed and the surveillance of the Cabal of Five before that. Each of those things, while eminently defensible on its own, in the views of the Bureau's critics and minders pointed to a complicated relationship with scientific integrity. Complication isn't necessarily a bad thing, but it takes explaining. And the person best equipped to explain such things was indisposed.

I wouldn't say I felt sad watching the video of Director Jorg leaving the Bureau campus for the last time, but I wouldn't say I was indifferent either. A resourceful videographer must have somehow gotten past the notoriously vigilant Bureau security, how else to explain the footage of Director Jorg, footage played over and over on the major networks, on cable, and streamed news online, taken in moments a less committed flack might have foregone filming to leave the Director with her private thoughts as she emerged from the austere entryway of Building 1. Director Jorg had her lab coat and a jacket thrown over her arm and wore only a sleeveless blouse and trousers as she walked stoically to her Volvo. Her posture was impeccable but her gait was a little loose, a devil may care trot that was neither slow nor hurried. She paused for a moment in front of the car and shifted her weight from foot to foot, causing a little bounce. Who knows what she meant by the bounce? She left the world dumbfounded.

It had been a while since she'd made my cranium itch but that doesn't mean I was surprised by the itching. What was strange was that for a moment, just after she stepped into her car, something loamy smelling seemed to waft from the screen. Of course, I knew there was nothing loamy smelling coming from my screen. One might surmise that the loamy smell coming from the screen was my way of processing difficult emotions, and I for one see nothing wrong in imagining a smell as a substitute for certain feelings one would rather avoid. Only my feelings weren't particularly difficult as feelings go. To be honest, watching the video of Director Jorg as she stepped into her car and exited the majestic arc of the main campus drive from the comfort of my chaise lounge was in some ways satisfying. Our relationship finally felt symmetrical.

I thought, perhaps the best way to think about all this is that she's finally been freed, she can now ride off into the sunset with her enigmatic artist lover, the two of them to negotiate the sweet middle ground between the director's faith in the invisible hand of the market and her lover's anarchic embrace of the human spirit, unfettered.

My phone rang and I answered, even as I realized the blower had brought me almost entirely intrigue and disappointment in recent days.

"Why didn't you tell us it was going to drop?"

"What was it that dropped? I'm not in on the lingo."

"The ə, obviously. We totally can't believe you producted it."

"PPPDSPed it if you care about precision. And I wouldn't say it was me."

"All it took was a few happy beagles and next thing you know. We better not find out Glottal's methods were inhumane."

"I could have told your boss about the methods if you'd had him meet me."

"That's not on me! He promised me he would be there. Then this quote unquote source called and he said he had a conflict. I tried to tell you but you didn't even pick up."

"They weren't the least bit happy by the way."

"They?"

"The canines."

"That fucking thing hurt the beagles?"

"I have the full report. But I don't want to take the senator away from further dalliances with his so-called source. So I can just—"

"Wait! I swear on anything, he'll be there. Name the time."

I hesitated.

"IlovebeaglesIlovebeaglesIlovebeagles."

The conversation was degenerating. I saw I had to bring it to a close.

"I'm free now. The Tidal Basin, I presume."

"The stable. He says you'll know what he means."

"I have no idea what he means."

"His wife owns a place that used to have a place to keep a horse."

So I'd been a kept woman in the horse's quarters of a property that belonged to my lover's future wife. Perhaps others would wallow in the sense of ignominy. It only increased my resolve.

"I think you mean the carriage house."

"I'm glad the horse got its own house. It would be bullshit if they made it live with them."

"I can assure you the horse had its own quarters."

I knew leaking the report of the canine data to Jeremy would be a violation of the public trust. And I'd never violated the public trust. But at last, the tables were turned. Jeremy was desperate to connect with me. On my terms. I detached Sorel Dern's note and placed the report on the passenger's seat of my car.

The sky was darkening as I drove past the rowhouse in front of the carriage house, the house the interior of which I'd fantasized about so many times but entered only once, after its occupants had gone, taking with them their enigmatic tchotchkes. The big bay window was brightly lit and I could see exposed brick, tall bookshelves and a chair with the back turned to the window. I drove past and turned onto the alleyway, where I saw a fine door with paned glass panels had replaced the shabby slab of wood through which I'd entered and exited so many times. Also, a wide, high window had been opened in the brick. I parked several houses down, beside a garage belonging to one of the homes on the main street.

As I walked from my vehicle I felt strangely calm, though I hadn't rehearsed a word I'd say. I remembered how, all those years ago, Jeremy had pronounced the couple in the house in front of my old home swingers. It seemed to me his words were a message, one the meaning of which would be known only when I recalled them years later. The moment I hung up on Zed, I decided I was going to swing it. I suppose the idiom is 'wing it' but it seemed close enough. In short, I had committed to responding on the fly, listening only to my heart. No matter what it told me.

I stared at the light coming from the window as I approached from my car. I was humming a song about food on a menu the lyrics to which were just a list of things both edible and inedible, the point of the song being, apparently, that one had to eat something if one were to persevere. It was thoughtless and distracting and kept me from thinking about what I would say, which I didn't want to think about. But I didn't know the words, I just knew the gist of the song—the interspersion of foodstuffs and other things inedible to increasingly nonsensical effect. I was trying to recall a rhyme, which I thought was perhaps between edible and dirigible, when I found myself in front of the window. With my face to the side I looked in. The appliances were stainless steel of a European make, if I had to guess, and black tile on the floor had been replaced with warm pine floorboards. But the French doors were uncovered and the space was unfurnished, save a foldable beach chair in the middle of the living area. The lonely chair, exposed to onlookers on both sides, filled me with unaccountable sadness. Perhaps I was thinking of the horse who'd lived there a century or longer ago, similarly alone and exposed to the mercy of the street-facing house dwellers. Then, from the stairs off to the side of the room, Jeremy appeared.

He looked at his watch. He raked his fingers through his hair in that gesture of his, though now there was no one to marvel at how nicely he'd retained his hair. And it seemed grayer than I recalled from the hearing. He paced to the end of the carriage house and back. Then he turned, suddenly, walked towards the door, opened it, and stuck his head out and there we were, looking at one another from a few feet apart.

"N—"

My name floated from his mouth with the pathos of the soul leaving the body. For a moment, we stared at one another like strangers. I broke the silence.

"Indeed."

"You look well."

"That's what I hear."

It seemed he didn't know what to say. Neither did I. We were silent.

"I have the canine data," I said, because nothing else came to me. "Follow me to my vehicle."

I could feel him hovering just a few paces behind me as we walked to my car. His presence felt desperate, controlling and not the least bit titillating. I opened the door, fell into the driver's seat, and placed my hand over the report as though about to hand it to him. That was when I knew what I would do. I slammed the door shut—on three long fingers with perfectly proportioned knuckles gripping the door opening, it turned out. A shriek of unbearable intensity pierced the air as I turned for a moment. There, not six inches from my face, was Jeremy, three fingers in his mouth, his features wrung in an agony of incomprehension and pain.

"I was right about Olf," I said, and his head bobbed and weaved, moving vertically as much as horizontally. It seemed entirely possible he was signalling a sort of dazed agreement.

I pulled the door shut, slammed my foot to the pedal and slipped out into the night. Which was balmy.

Z.

In life I'm often reminded of an experiment led by that cruel instructor from the boarding school I attended so many years ago. The victims in this case were pigeons. He instructed us to release grains of millet or whatever pigeons eat as the pigeons were going about their business in their lab cages. The pigeons would be doing what pigeons do, hopping on one foot, pecking the ground, cocking their heads, or engaging in other behavior one associates with pigeons, and out of the blue they'd get a grain of millet, if millet is even a grain and not a seed or whatever. The pigeons started to think that whatever they were doing before they got the millet was the cause of the millet, with an outcome that was completely predictable. You had pigeons hopping on one foot, pecking the ground, cocking their heads, even though they weren't getting any more millet. The hopping, the pecking, the cocking got out of hand, as though the pigeons were trying too hard. They became strivers. And to paraphrase the professor, expecting to be rewarded for being a striver is practically the definition of insanity. My point is that after what can only be described as the disappointing denouement of my decades-spanning affaire de coeur with Jeremy, I wasn't going to keep hopping on one foot, pecking the ground, and cocking my head, metaphorically speaking. I decided to take things in a different direction.

("Taking things in a different direction" had nothing to do with other developments in the Jeremy side of the Jeremy affaire de coeur. But I won't pretend I didn't follow

them. First there was the licensed Ayurvedic massage ther-
apist from the hotel in Newark where Jeremy led a delegation investigating unusual illnesses near the site of a phar-
ma-backed marmot research facility. Next it was that actress
from the cable TV political drama who shadowed Jeremy to
research her role as a staffer having an affair with a presidential candidate. Finally and most scandalously it was one of
Jeremy's former staffers. After that I stopped registering the
biographical details. The word "sordid" was thrown around
in the reporting, a word I never associated with Jeremy. But
I didn't question the motivations of these women, even if
"sordid" was a disconnect.

The sordid allegations weren't helpful to his candidacy,
but weren't all that harmful either, perhaps because the
American electorate understood that the presidency wasn't
for those with a weak stomach, and anyone who wasn't
down with a little sordidness was apt to balk when first confronted with sordidness in the role of the nation's chief executive. Some opined that Jeremy's candidacy couldn't survive
public reaction to his history of adultery, frotteurism, somnophilia, and supposed bobbing (though to be honest that's
where his accusers started to lose me, bobbing falling so far
outside Jeremy's intimate repertoire as I knew it). He hired
a new campaign staff (a good move, based on my experience
with Zed) including a new campaign manager known for her
incisive decision-making and her ruthlessness. ("He's screwing her," Nym opined without evidence apart from the cir-
cumstantial—namely that Jeremy appeared to disfavor non-
sexual arrangements with the women in his orbit). He held
a press conference, likely staged by the campaign manager,
with Jeremy and Leilani and their daughter and son standing
a few steps behind them. The daughter Antigone couldn't

have been more than fifteen but stood almost six feet tall. She had mauve hair cut at a sharp angle as though in defiance of her roundedness and her angelic features, her shoulders folded forward and her knees bent as though trying to compact herself into her navel. The son Ralph was nine or so and small for his age, bespectacled and squinting at who knows what. Only perhaps the campaign manager didn't anticipate Jeremy's elegant, enigmatic wife would appear at the conference not with her chignon intact but instead with her black hair down around her shoulders and red lipstick, bringing to mind no longer the restrained praise of a word like "elegant" but something more like "oxymoronically castrating yet eminently fuckable," as one of the more influential bloggers that catered to a male demographic put it. No one paid any attention to Jeremy's short statement because everyone was paying attention to Jeremy's wife, who didn't say anything but stared at Jeremy with a look that said *after this my plan is to remove your nutsack slowly with a dull-edged soupspoon then watch as I force you to eat it in a brown sauce and mirepoix,* at least according to the twitter account of Maddox Pinker, who occasionally allowed his rhetoric to get away from him. So it wasn't really surprising when Jeremy's wife announced through her spokesperson that she was divorcing him and that was when things started to look up, reflecting the basic kindness of American voters, who didn't want to feel like they were piling on when Jeremy was facing such a difficult situation on the home front.

Imagining Jeremy's victory instilled in me no small measure of pride as the one who, after all, lit the fuse to which his other accusers added their own gas, thus resulting in the sad but humanizing situation with his personal life, and stirring the American people to overlook whatever past indiscretions and errors in judgment may have occurred to rally around him. So no one was more disappointed than I by the change in fortunes after Jeremy's opponent announced Hieronymus Glick would take over as the campaign's new Director of Social Media Communications. Coordinated with the announcement was Hieronymus's inflammatory first official tweet: *Psyched to send Sakhdvar back to the Saladbar! #NautyNabob*. It seems I'd badly misjudged the character of this young man who I once considered a protégé and even a friend. Senator Saladbar trended on social media at the same time a fantastic fiction crept from the internet's darkest corners into the daylight, that Jeremy planned to confiscate every American's consumer devices to isolate and confuse the citizenry, leaving them defenseless against a N'Aut insurgency. One hates to validate the facile campaign post-mortems issued by every Tom, Dick, and so forth on cable TV. Yet the consensus view that emerged, that there is only so much exoticism that voters will put up with before they throw up their arms and cry "uncle," was hard to refute.

It was a little disappointing for me when Jeremy ended his candidacy and resigned from public office. He withdrew from public life, neglecting even to endorse the remaining primary candidate, the first female senator from her state and a former cabinet secretary whose campaign had never rebounded from Jeremy referring to her as his "dour opponent." But at least the turn of events freed him to return to his first love of litigating against products. In fact, his name appeared in an article alongside the name of my old client Cammo, the HomHunkulus™ founder, stirring an odd mix of excitement and pride. The article reported Jeremy's victory in persuading a court that the children of HomHunkulus™ users could bring a class action due to certain unfortunate effects observed in the offspring of HomHunkulus™ users, hypothesized to relate to deficits in nutrient absorption during critical stages of fetal development. Of course, I couldn't have been happier for Jeremy. At the same time, I felt a little sad for Cammo.

He didn't completely withdraw. Jeremy gave an immediate statement about a certain turn of events, which I must admit left me a little miffed, given Jeremy's history of delinquency statement-wise. This turn of events had to do with Olf, who'd moved on from injecting stuff from the buttocks intended for the glabella back into the buttocks to injecting a proprietary polymer intended for industrial uses into the buttocks. Things didn't go as well in court this time, and Maddox Pinker tracked Jeremy down for a comment on the historic verdict against Olf. Jeremy said, "We were right about Olf the first time."

Only it turned out his name wasn't Olf after all. It was Rolff. Not only was there nothing missing from the name. There was something extra added. The second f felt gratuitous. Like someone was rubbing my nose in something.

It gave me a feeling I couldn't put my finger on, a warmth climbing up the back of my head and a tingling in my nerve endings that reminded me of Director Jorg. I shook my head to get rid of it.

There was one other thing about Jeremy. A sighting reported in the gossip pages, accompanied by a candid shot of him looking leaner than when last I saw him and I daresay a little goofy, as though he'd grown back out of his looks. He was photographed outside an avant garde boutique on West Broadway, his arms hanging in a clumsy hug down the back of the fuchsia-haired proprietress, whose long eyes were half-open and looking somewhere outside the frame.

Rumors of an affair raged in the celebrity blogosphere at the same time speculation percolated in a N'Aut subreddit that the former senator and artist/activist were plotting a take-down of the technocapitalist world order.

The rumors continued even after Rodin(t) and Jeremy cosigned an Op Ed, announcing they'd brought togeth-er over twenty descendants of the cardinal and would be seeking reparations from the church. Jeremy announced he would be on the litigation team representing the plaintiff class, but didn't mention whether he was a member, per-haps because he felt he'd had enough of his private business disclosed. The Op Ed was a smash hit and for a short peri-od, Rodin(t) was everyone's favorite countercultural it-girl. I was a little jealous. I followed her press more closely than was seemly. So after the safe in the Rodin(t) boutique was looted and the lease went unpaid and Rodin(t) went missing from her Alphabet City apartment, I knew what was going on before anyone reported on what was going on. Well, per-haps Jeremy knew, but it should surprise no one that Jer-emy's only comment on his half-sister's whereabouts was "no comment." Obviously, she'd gone underground. Deep underground.

Rodin(t)'s disappearance complicated things, but overall I took the reforged bonds between Jeremy and Rodin(t) for a positive development. How better to face a difficult cir-cumstance than by allying oneself with someone simpatico, even consanguineous? Perhaps Jeremy was putting himself on a path of self-discovery. If so, good luck, I say. Even if that sort of thing has never worked for me.)

None of which has anything to do with my present cir-cumstances, which involve the different direction I headed in to avoid engaging in whatever the human version of hopping on one foot, et cetera, is. I relay it only for its appeal to human-interest.

My present circumstances entail personal business that often places me behind the wheel on that highway that for a stretch is a concrete bridge overlooking the surf and black rocks from stories above so it's hard not be aware of the pre-cariousness of the situation. Naturally I often think about my mother. I think, it's sad that my mother died driving when she didn't know how to drive, yet in one way some good has come from it. My mother's sad situation taught me to embrace and excel at difficult things so they wouldn't get the best of me. The difficult things I embraced and excelled might not have killed me if I hadn't embraced and excelled at them. But they might have stood in the way of fulfill-ment, its own sort of death. So when I contrast the thing that killed my mother—driving—with the things concern-ing which I've had such success—everything important that I've ever tried my hand at—I think how lucky I've been to have a mother who, metaphorically speaking, taught me to drive, even if it meant she wasn't around to provide moral instruction.

As often as not I'm schwang during these drives, and that may have something to do with the penetrating insights that come to me. To be clear, I don't notice any difference between drives when I schwang and drives when I'm not schwang, but that doesn't prove the schwang factor isn't in play. A journal of atmospheric science recently published a small study suggesting the widespread use of the ə may create a far-reaching herd effect for nonusers. Who's to say these deep thoughts are unrelated to ambient schwang?

(It's not the least bit surprising that the more conspira-cy-minded, a group that apparently resides even in the most elite scientific circles, has posited a connection between ambient schwang and the recent string of minor catastrophes in remote locales where ə has yet to penetrate the market—that unfortunate epidemic of self-immolation among arctic dwellers in Finland, Greenland, and Russia, the unexplained mass exodus of uncontacted peoples from the Amazon, the sad rash of cannibalism among Bangladeshi dogs. Sure, it's an odd coincidence that peoples separated by geography, climate, and culture—a Sami with 3rd degree burns over most of his body who was the sole survivor of the immolations and the few uncontacted people who didn't die within days of exposure to the civilized world—described their afflictions similarly in their native tongues as something like *the devil's unbearable shrieking.* Who knows what ailed the dogs! Glottal's clinical team has already announced plans to investigate, and their effort will no doubt show these sad events have nothing to do with the ə, are more likely tied in some little-understood way to other global phenomena that, while concerning, can hardly be blamed on Glottal. That is whenever Glottal finishes up that other study.)

Fortunately for me, not long after this personal business I mention arose career developments left me free to travel wherever I liked. A month or so into my sabbatical, I received a polite note from Bureau payroll referring me to the "Termination at Will of the Director" clause in the contract seconding me from the Firm, a provision that would have been triggered by Director Jorg's termination if the Firm's dissolution hadn't voided my secondment contract, making my employment status a little ambiguous. I received the letter a week after *The Washington Post* ran an article by Maddox Pinker making insinuations about my current romantic situation, but I'm not one to see conspiracy everywhere I look. Strangely, I felt no sadness at losing my connection to the place that had played so important a role in my life. I felt a lightness, a freedom I hadn't known in what seemed like forever. I've always understood that the end of one thing leads to the beginning of something new.

Sorel Dern's house is off that highway, by the way. I was lying in my bed after I returned from the carriage house with Jeremy's shriek still ringing in my ears when Sorel called again, this time to ask if he could send me a collector's edition Schwatch with a rose gold-plated titanium band. It sounded a little garish, so I said I had to check the terms of my secondment as far as gifts from regulated entities. But the conversation didn't end there and soon I was reminded of what it was like to connect to another person on a personal, intimate level, an experience I'd had to forego during my active tenure at the Bureau due to the pressing demands of public service.

"The alien contact stuff didn't quote/unquote happen," Sorel remarked out of the blue. I'd have never asked him about the alien contact stuff even though it was a matter of public record, the alien contact stuff being a little embarrassing. "I dreamed it. I don't mean 'dreamed' like something that happened to me while I was asleep. I mean 'dreamed' like when you imagine something impossible then you make it real. Like 'innovated.'"

"I've always been a fan of innovation," I said. The statement may have seemed like an obvious one, but I wanted to be clear where I stood.

"I knew that the minute I saw you."

He said he'd be in town the following weekend and I said, "Oh, super," casually but in a way that was not unencouraging and it doesn't take too much imagination to figure out what happened then. We couldn't very well go out in public, so he showed up at my apartment and suggested we stream this rom-com set on Uranus. I was having a hard time with the plot, which seemed a little far-fetched. So I was relieved when Sorel suggested we hit the pause button and have at it. I commandeered the remote and was ready for anything, except for what happened next.

"I'm planning a successor product to the Ə," he said, pausing from unbuttoning his shirt, which was polyester and printed with 1970's movie icons.

"Fabulous."

I was a little impatient, to be honest.

"It connects you with your authentic self and the cloud. Maybe I should call it the N—," Sorel intimated.

A charge spread across my nerve endings. But I played it cool.

"Oh. Not unlike a zeugma."

Sorel didn't ask what a zeugma was. He understood right away as it was the sort of thing one knows when one sees regardless of whether one can describe it. It was another way in which Sorel and I were more alike than different. We were guided by our hearts and content to leave those at the mercy of the organ between the ears to sweat the details. I realized what I must have known all along without ever knowing that I'd known it—that Sorel and I were different faces of the same Janus head. We were creators, inventors, my innovation in administering the edicts of the vast governmental apparatus overseeing biomedicaltechnology every bit as exciting and transformative as his in biomedicaltechnology itself.

I flew out to visit Sorel the next week and the week after that. We went public and that made everyone happy, and no one more so than the media. What could make better copy than a romance between the youthful, wavy-haired inventor of Products and the elite regulator whose calming grip on the regulatory gears had paved the way for the Producing of the inventor's invention? It was as though the snake and the tail sat down to dinner together instead of either one having to be eaten by the other one. In short, the media was highly supportive of my relationship with Sorel, except Maddox Pinker, who, just before my termination, wrote that poorly sourced piece questioning the ethics of the snake and its tail sitting down to dinner together as though the snake eating its tail were the God-ordained natural order of things. I knocked off a devastating reply, a letter to the editor written in my own words and by my own hand, pointing out that the Bureau's Best Practices Against Fraternization made perfectly clear that "fraternization" doesn't include regulator/regulated entity relationships. My letter ran the same day I received the termination letter. But I bore Maddox Pinker no ill will. It is often the case that the most prurient among us are themselves the most sexually conflicted, which may explain why Maddox Pinker couldn't put aside his journalistic angling for five minutes to share in my happiness.

Soon I was staying with Sorel for weeks at a time. He introduced me to a friend of his who was developing an app to track anomie and he put me on the start up's board. Everyone in the technosphere wanted to get into the biomedicaltechnology space and I was the one who could show them how. I could hardly wait to apply my savvy to the N—. I felt a connection with Sorel's new endeavor that went beyond the shared name, as though I had a special responsibility to ensure its unobstructed passage into the world.

"When do you expect the N— to launch?" I asked one

morning over a late breakfast of baguette and gruyere with pickled daikon radish. We'd been together at least a month, though we'd grown so familiar it felt like we'd been together for decades.

"The Zeugma will launch when it's time and not one nanosecond before," Sorel responded in that emphatic way of answering questions that would seem like a rebuke were one unfamiliar with the unofficial Glottal motto of "Be. Emphatically." So Sorel was just living his credo.

I didn't want to let him off so easily. I was about to ask him whether, strictly from a marketing standpoint, it was better to name his invention for a literary device no one had ever heard of or for his girlfriend, who was practically a household name. I stopped myself. Naming the ə successor for something Sorel wouldn't have heard of if it weren't for his relationship with me came from a place of emotional indebtedness. Still, I wanted more.

These little swells of tension were quickly flattened in the torrent of synergy between us. One of the best things about Sorel is that he didn't try to control me. Unlike the men one sometimes reads about in letters to advice columnists written by their cowed spouses, men who can't sit back and enjoy a situation of domestic harmony because they're too busy fretting over real and imagined rivals for their lovers' attention, Sorel has never stood in the way of my other interests and relationships. To the contrary. Nym flew out to retool my public image to sync with my new reality and Sorel generously had the guest accommodation readied for her.

"That's a lot of bungalow for one person," Nym commented the first time she saw her accommodations.

I kept Nym busy, but my work had become less stressful.

I didn't have the American people to worry about, so noto-riety became more of a plus than a minus. Unsurprisingly, my friendship with Nym also entered a new phase, one char-acterized by a mutual relaxing of the inhibitions that so often get in the way of connectedness. Sorel traveled frequently, so I started staying in the bungalow with Nym rather than stay alone in the main house. Besides a complete comple-ment of electronic entertainment devices from which Nym could blast her Irish-inflected indie folk-punk and beam cable news with the volume all the way down, Sorel also had board games and a wet bar. One night while Sorel was in Phuket for the launch of the new ə functionality in that part of the world (as Sorel likes to say, *it's not just our high-ly advanced culture that affects the human condition in ways that respond to improvement*), Nym and I helped ourselves to a few bottles of a vintage from a nearby vineyard, which we paired with a flatbread prepared in the pizza oven in the main house, her half with roasted cauliflower and a chia seed-based imitation cheese product, my half with fig and prosciutto. For the first time, I was beating her at a game of Scrabble, the irritant that caused her competitive streak to break out like a rash. She became reckless, challenging me when I built the word "echt" off "glyph" and "plinth" (her words, which gives you a sense of what it was like playing scrabble with Nym). Needless to say, her challenge failed.

"I always assumed it was a Teutophiliac appropriation," was all she had to say about echt. She slid the Scrabble board away and lay down on her back.

"That's something about Dr. Hrbek," she commented, pointedly changing the subject.

Of course, I already knew that Dr. Hrbek had been named Acting Bureau Director. The appointment of a new Bureau

Director, even if only on an acting basis, was a development with global repercussions. The biomedicaltechnology sector greeted news of Dr. Hrbek's appointment with trepidation, with many in the sector assuming Dr. Hrbek's reputation for logic could pose a greater threat to innovation than Director Jorg's reputation for unpredictability. But nothing could prepare me for the other personnel development that Nym shared with me.

"And about V.," Nym continued, airily.

"V.?"

I had hardly thought about V. since setting him up with the bad tip about the canine data. He'd been quiet after that, perhaps reasoning that with the ə released despite his efforts and Jeremy taking himself down, his best gambit was to avoid calling attention to himself. Calling attention to himself would only call attention to his ineffectualness, his unsuitedness for a leadership role of any sort, even over a bunch of malcontents.

"You know that he got whistleblower status," Nym said. "Meaning the Bureau can't retaliate."

"The Bureau doesn't tolerate retaliation," I reminded Nym. Occasionally I detected an undercurrent of her former dissidence and when I did I felt obligated to reorient her with a gentle but firm recitation of fact.

"They had to find a permanent position for him."

"I suppose they made him Special-Advisor-to-the-Director-of-the-Bureau-of-Biomedicaltechnology," I snorted. I am in full agreement with those who say sarcasm is the lowest form of humor. In rare instances, there is no other way to lay bare the absurdity of a counter-factual hypothetical.

"Uh-huh. On an acting basis. He's burrowing in."

"If that's what they're calling it these days."

"He'll never be one-tenth the advisor you were. I mean, everyone accepts you could get your job back at any time if you just asked Dr. Hrbek—"

I wasn't going to let myself be distracted by Nym's transparent attempt to deflect attention with flattery. The news that V. had assumed my former responsibilities prompted an onslaught of emotions and thoughts, foremost among the latter being concern for the American people, who relied upon the good judgment of Bureau leadership for the integrity of their biomedicaltechnology. Putting aside V.'s dissidence, a trait that almost by definition involved clouded judgment, V.'s history of romantic rivalry with the person he was entrusted to advise on the most pressing matters of national concern sent up my hackles. I took a moment to organize my thoughts to present them in a way that would preempt any suggestion that my objections came from a place of insecurity about my successor (the sort of over-reading of a situation that was not atypical from Nym, perhaps due to her academic background), holding up my right index finger to signify that though I wasn't speaking at the moment, I would be shortly.

"Itexthimsometimes." The words ran together out of Nym's mouth as if combining her words into a single word made her snubbing of my index finger less of a big deal than if the snub had involved multiple words. "I get lonely."

It wasn't the first time I was disarmed by Nym's candor. My mind shot unaccountably from V. to Zed. Any association between the two was difficult to fathom, other than that they both seemed like irritable fellows. But the instant the image of Zed entered my mind, it occurred to me that with the right accessory in those gaping earlobes and away from feature-blocking streetlamp, Zed could hold a subversive charm for someone of Nym's sympathies. It seemed to me that the meeting with Zed was serendipitous after all and presented an opportunity to repay Nym's friendship by arranging a meeting between the two. Maybe, also, he could pass along my condolences to Jeremy. About catching his fingers in my car door, I mean. Then maybe Jeremy and I could meet on different terms.

"Perhaps I could introduce you to a former member of Jeremy's campaign staff," I suggested.

"How do you think I got you your meeting in the first place?"

"Not to put too fine a point on it but you didn't get me a meeting with Jeremy."

"It was a honey pot trap set by *your* former grand maestro of sexual deviance, which I never would have fallen into if I hadn't been in a place of extreme emotional vulnerability. 'On the right hand, you have the future of the republic; on the left hand, you have fucking,'" here Nym dropped her voice several registers as she sat up and pulled a piece of hair from the back of her head upright, then she held her hands out to the side of her body at the same height on each side until she said "fucking," at which point she dropped her still extended right hand to the ground while lifting her also still extended left hand over her head. "'Which I'm not saying isn't super important but come on, a little perspective OK?'"

"I didn't know you two were intimates."

"Too bad I never got that detail to your staff," Nym sniffed, unexpectedly changing course. She'd made an issue out of her unsuccessful detail bid more than once. It was hard to know how I'd have put her unique combination of talents to work in my former role, which called for a level-headedness sometimes lacking in those who've spent so much of their

HOW THE ə GOT PRODUCED

lives immersed in fiction and similar pursuits. I let the comment pass in the interests of preserving the sense of repose between us.

"I could have done more with Director Jorg. We would have really hit it off. I hear she's at a think tank that promotes commodification, doing work on figments and other atypical capital. She got totally screwed by the fucking patriarchy."

"Excuse me?"

"Someone was going to out her personal business with a leader of the opposition unless they got rid of her."

"I think we all know who that would be."

"Speak for yourself."

"So you can't think of a single person who would leak damaging information about Bureau business for his own inscrutable reasons?"

"Of course V. leaked it. I mean who was she seeing?"

"Why don't you ask V.?"

"He claimed he didn't know but whoever it was ghosted her. Do you think he could he have been her—?"

"Sexually abstinent boytoy? It's the only explanation."

I'd grown protective over Nym and felt a responsibility to protect her from her own worst instincts. If planting false beliefs about V.'s subsequent romantic activities made her think twice about prospects for another go round, I'd done her a favor. Besides that, I admit I preferred that Nym remain misinformed about the director's personal life. The director's personal life was jumbled up in my mind with everything that followed my meeting with the director and Rodin(t)—the ə's release, the director's ousting, Jeremy's sad downfall, the sound of a high-pitched squeal escaping from a mouth twisted in pain. Nym was the sort to place blame for things that just happen. And I wasn't going to be held responsible for all that.

I said nothing further to Nym and shortly she fell asleep on the floor. I retired to the guest bungalow's second bedroom and slept fitfully. Eventually I started to dream. It was a bad dream, the sort one awakens from clammy and fearful, or so I've heard. I'd never before had a bad dream. I'm not sure I'd ever before had a dream.

I dreamed I was sitting in a white Volkswagen Rabbit, parked on the Tappan Zee Bridge. I was waiting for something when Jeremy's face appeared in the passenger's window, hanging upside down with snow falling upwards. He said, "You're a SO-CI-O-PATH," the four syllables of sociopath pronounced with a crescendoed emphasis, as if recorded then played back in slow motion, as he looked right at me until he pronounced "path." Then everything flipped so the car was upside down, the snow was falling downwards, and his head hung in the window right side up, but with the hair still hanging off of it. I sat upright in bed, breathing heavily. Then and there I decided I had nothing to apologize about to Jeremy, even if his fingers had looked rather bad. I thought to myself, with all I've accomplished, and all I have in my life, wanting anything more to do with Jeremy was worse than delusional. It was backward-looking. And if there's one thing that could be said for me, it is that I've always been on the side of progress.

My mind was focused with a piercing clarity. My thought was about the ə successor. If the new Product wouldn't be named for me at least it could be named by me. By me, for my mother. I don't mean my mother's name. The weight of all those associations would be too much to bear. I was thinking of the Tappan Zee Bridge.

I grabbed a laptop from the night table and found an online tool that could spit out every permutation of the letters in Tappan Zee, then cross-checked a half dozen against a baby name website that could tell you the gender, prevalence, famous forebears, numerological significance, ruling planet, et cetera for any name entered. Laptop in hand, I came for Nym and shook her from her sleep then put the screen with the list of baby names in front of her.

"What do you think of Nappaz?"

She straightened herself, rubbed her eyes and stared at the screen.

"I'm zero population."

"Not for a kid. For a Product." That seemed to perk her up. "Panzee?"

"You can't redeem the offensive history with a funky spelling. What about Ezpat?"

"I regret the global refugee crisis as much as the next person, but this is neither the time nor the place for a sly nod in solidarity to those unfairly denied a home due to climate conditions and rising nationalism."

We came to the obvious choice last. For the name Tappan we found the following:

GENDER: Unknown

PREVALENCE: Fewer than 500 since the advent of historical record.

FAMOUS PEOPLE NAMED TAPPAN: None.

NAME MEANING OF TAPPAN: We apologize, but we don't have a meaning for this name.

NUMEROLOGY INTERPRETATION: Unknown

POPULARITY: The name Tappan is ranked on the 87,198th position of the most used names.

At first, I had reservations about choosing a name not associated with even a minor celebrity, but as Nym pointed out, launching a Product unencumbered by the tendency of others to burden new things with the baggage carried over from past associations was a gift. Something surged in me, an irresistible urge to affirm with words the gush of connectedness that was rushing over me. But before I could say anything Nym got up and walked to her bedroom, muttering *Tappan Tappan Tappan* under her breath.

Sorel returned that evening and I was ready. I heated two bowls of SpaghettiOs with meatballs and Sorel was thrilled. We were alike in understanding that the things that give the greatest pleasure are often the simplest. I deployed the element of surprise to my advantage.

"If I were having a kid right now I'd name it Tappan," I said, quite out of the blue.

"I love kids! Let's do this!" Sorel started to unbutton his fly.

"It's too important to leave to human error."

"Of course! We'll build a zygote army in the lab from which we'll cull our line!"

"All in due time. At the moment, I have other commitments. I'm speaking of your new Product. Specifically, the name."

"What I like about Zeugma is it doesn't suggest a gender." He sounded a little defensive.

"Zeugma's perfect for a child. But for a Product ..."

"What's wrong with naming my Product the Zeugma?"

There was an edge to his voice. But I was ready for a fight, even if breaking the harmonious spell we'd lived under for the duration of our affair saddened me a little. So it threw me off when instead of putting up a fight, Sorel slackened his lower lip and a look of sadness and incomprehension fell over his face. For a moment, I felt uncertain, distressed. I was prepared for belligerence but not his petulance. Almost instantly I lit on a back-up plan, the sort of compromise that contradicts the very concept of "compromise" because everyone walks away feeling like they had gotten exactly what they wanted in the first place. The words tumbled out of my mouth before I could give them a second thought:

"What about 'Zee'?"

Sorel's lower lip retracted and a quirky smile cracked the side of his mouth with the happy realization that something he thought he'd have to work for he could have just like that. As his smile spread, a quiet thrill crept across my nerve endings because I knew I'd eked out a small win, hurled my little flag across the shifting loam of obsolescence not knowing where it would land, and watched as it planted upright, its insignia whipping with new life!

ABOUT THE AUTHOR

 N.K. von S. has been a government official and a private law partner, among a variety of other things. She grew up in New York City and has lived in Mexico and the Washington D.C. area, where she resides now with her family and her beasts.

CPSIA information can be obtained
at www.ICGtesting.com
Printed in the USA
BVHW031639180222
629427BV00002B/126

9 780578 769301